THE ISHI AFFAIR

By

STEVEN JAY GRIFFEL

Also By Steven Jay Griffel

FORTY YEARS LATER

THE DEADLINE

GRAND VIEW

GROSSMAN'S CASTLE

STAY THIRSTY PRESS
An Imprint of Stay Thirsty Publishing

A Division of
STAY THIRSTY MEDIA, INC.

staythirsty.com

Cover Design: Jason Mathews

ISBN 13: 978-0692878538
ISBN 10: 069287853X

AMAZON KINDLE ASIN: B00999041E

Steven Jay Griffel

THE ISHI AFFAIR

"When I learned there was a modern tribe of Stone Age Americans, I knew it would be the biggest story of the decade. I knew their destiny and mine were entwined. I knew we would make history together."

—Jill Black, screenwriter and filmmaker

Dedication

This book is dedicated to my friend and tennis partner, Stuart Green, a beautiful soul who left this world when he could no longer bear the pain.

Prologue

David's Dream of Ishi's Brain

A man walks down a long hallway, the kind you'd expect to find in a government office building. The hallway is wide and lined with identical doors to the left and right. On the ceiling, rows of florescent piping cast a cool, white light. The man walks quietly, not wanting to call attention to himself. At the end of the hallway he stops in front of an inconspicuous wooden door. Using a key he has been holding in his right hand, he unlocks the door and drops the key into his pants pocket. The door opens creakily, like the entrance to a crypt. After a moment's hesitation, the man enters the darkness. Slowly, carefully, he walks down an unlighted and winding staircase. There is no handrail. He keeps his right hand on the curved wall for support.... Down, down, down, a seemingly unending helix of stone steps.... Finally, the man touches bottom. To his right there is a familiar light-switch. With a simple upward flip he turns darkness to light. He now faces a circular room, approximately twenty feet in diameter. It looks like a combination root cellar and medieval surgery. In the center is a large examining table and a four-wheeled handcart. Encircling the room, like the tiers of a stadium, are three rows of evenly spaced shelves. Each shelf is tightly packed with large glass jars. Each jar is filled with a clear liquid and contains a human brain. Some are floating, but most have settled on the bottom like dead fish. The man takes a slip of paper from his left pants pocket, examines it, and returns it to his pocket. Then he moves slowly around the room, clockwise, randomly checking jar labels.... The man stoops to look at a particular jar on the bottom shelf. He takes his time reading the label, making sure it is the right one. Slowly and carefully, he lifts the jar off its shelf and places it on the four-wheeled handcart. Before pushing on, he stares at the glass container and its unusual cargo. The clear preservative is slightly aerated; a few tiny bubbles cling to the interior glass wall and float on the surface, just below the jar's paraffin cap. The brain itself looks like most of the others: pinkish-gray, convoluted, a deep vertical furrow dividing its cerebral hemispheres. Carefully, the man rotates the jar to take one last look at its label:

Yahi-Yana Indian

No. S2191952G

Born: circa 1860; Deer Creek Canyon, Northern California

Died: March 25, 1916

Cause of death: Tuberculosis

Brain removed intact

Weight: 1300 grams

Chapter 1

Towering Columns

It was a warm, late-summer evening. Dozens of family and friends were expected, but David Grossman insisted on arriving alone. An hour early, he stood awhile on the Fifth Avenue sidewalk, staring up at the towering columns and majestic archways of the Forty-Second Street Library. No religious pilgrim ever stood before a holy temple and offered more humble gratitude. David felt truly blessed. Nearly sixty years old, he had finally published a novel. So what if it was available only as an e-book. He had already made peace with that early disappointment.

Since the book's publication two months earlier, David had marketed his book like someone possessed. He contacted everyone in his family—even his most distant relations—to tell them about his joy and triumph. He e-mailed friends, and friends of friends. He worked every room like a politician. He chatted up strangers. He gave out his card with no more encouragement than fleeting eye contact, and sometimes not even that. He wrote to bloggers and reporters to explain why they should interview him. Eventually, his name became associated with Woodstock and the Digital Revolution, which led to more interviews, book clubs, and finally the golden ring: an invitation to speak at the world-famous Forty-Second Street Library, the American Beaux-Arts palace synonymous with books and knowledge.

David took a deep breath and hurried up the wide plaza steps, passing between a pair of marble lions whose stony indifference fed his insecurity. (The invitation had been unexpected. He knew it wasn't only his novel's literary merits that had earned him this special honor. He knew it was his personal story—the unemployed, never-say-die Baby Boomer; the rare book collector turned digital novelist—that most people had come to hear.)

He walked across the stage, the cover of his novel projected behind him on a wide silver screen. Nervous, he took his place behind a large lectern. His hands were shaking. On top of the lectern was a narrow ledge on which rested a glass of water, a gooseneck microphone, and a hooded brass lamp to illuminate his notes. He took a sip of water and adjusted the microphone. He then greeted the large audience and thanked them for coming. In the grid of faces he saw his family and friends. Everyone was smiling. His sister gave him a subtle fist pump. His wife's eyes brimmed with teary pride. An old fraternity brother gave him a thumb's up. Following that last bit of encouragement he took another sip of water and boldly declared: "I love books. *All* books!" Following that self-injection of confidence, he went on to tell how he had morphed from rare book collector to spokesman for the Digital Revolution. He spoke of his early literary yearnings; his rueful summer romance in the Catskills and of Woodstock lost and found. He spoke of his unfulfilling publishing career, missed opportunities, and other gnawing regrets. He spoke of his early failures to find a publisher for his novel, the serendipity of second chances, and the joy of redemption that came with persistence. He spoke of the power of narrative and the parade of technologies that had delivered the Word throughout history: the etched stone, the inked scroll, the bound book, and now, the e-book: a high-tech way of sharing his own personal story. When he concluded, nearly two hours later, people stood and cheered. His younger daughter hugged him, crying: "Daddy, I'm so proud of you!" His wife stood beside him, beaming. Strangers asked for his autograph. One woman, who had been seated in the back, walked hurriedly towards a rear exit. She looked familiar. Before he could place her, she was gone.

Unfinished Business

A few hours later David was home, alone with his wife Allison. It was late. He was tired but relieved in a way that champions often feel: exhausted by the effort, exhilarated by the results. It was a golden, gloating moment. As usual, he checked his e-mail on the computer before going to sleep. There was one new message from an unidentified sender. Subject line: *Great Performance.*

Still soaring from the praise recently lavished on him, he did not consider that the e-mail might be troublesome. Feeling emboldened and invulnerable, he double-clicked and read:

Oh David, David, David, so bittersweet to see you this evening. You were so close! If it weren't for the crowd and your family, I would have hugged and kissed you! But look how well I behaved! Not a peep! You see, I can be trusted. Past is not prologue here. I am all straightened out and itchin' for a comeback. I have some great ideas—one that will rock your world—one that will rock everyone's world! You'll see. Just hear me out and I know you'll join me. We'll make a great team. Just pick a time and place where we can talk.

Jill

P.S. I am very proud of you. After all, I was your muse, right? Without me, there would be no Forty Years Later. You'd have no readers … no library audience … no book clubs. I think you owe me.

Damn! David wanted to kick himself. He could have gone beddy-bye, visions of his admiring public dancing in his head—but no!—he had to feed his damn ego and read about his "Great Performance" … And now, there would be no sleep, at least not for hours. Instead, he would lie in bed, recollecting his history with Jill: watching the first Moon landing with her, pinky-swearing their teen devotion; breaking her heart by not taking her to Woodstock; slow-dancing with the middle-aged Jill under Woodstock's waning moon; seeing Jill in his rearview mirror, the prodigal husband returning to his loyal wife.

Allison

By noon the following day, David had received two dozen phone calls and e-mails. Friends, family, even his publisher had called to congratulate him on his stirring presentation at the library. Though David was thrilled with the praise, his satisfaction was tempered by a double dose of gnawing uncertainty.

First, Allison had not called him, as she usually did, during her mid-morning coffee break. (She had recently landed a six-month, on-site freelance job.) Though she'd been thrilled by his presentation the night before, her enthusiasm had switched off as soon as they had returned home. She left for work the next morning with a curt goodbye, leaving David alone to market his novel, write another one, play tennis, or anything else he damn well pleased.

Allison was bitter on the subject of her house husband. More than a year had passed since David had lost his job as Mr. Big Shot VP of a New York-based, Fortune 500 publishing company. Though David wasn't to blame for losing his job—shit happens when the economy is circling the drain—the past year had been a rough go. Initially supportive and loving, Allison had agreed to give her husband one year to recover, refresh, and reorient his compass. But without the big hunk of bacon David used to bring home every two weeks, they'd struggled to pay their bills. The year had also been marked by the slow death of David's mother and the even slower death of their best friends' café restaurant business, for which David felt responsible. On the plus side of life's ledger, the year ended with David finally getting his first novel published and inheriting two hundred and five thousand dollars from his mother. The inheritance gave David and Allison some financial breathing room, and David had used the boon to convince Allison to grant him another year's grace against having to go back to work. In return, he promised to market his novel, write another one, and to seek happiness—his mother's dying wish for him. At the time, David's proposal seemed reasonable to Allison. After all, it was his mother's money, and David's break from work was for only one more year. But very soon after they sealed their agreement with a kiss, her car was totaled (not her fault, no one was hurt), the boiler began sputtering feebly and needed to be replaced, and they both required expensive root canals and implants, "our crowning achievements," David joked—his only thwart against their mounting financial woes.

David heard his computer ping, signaling a newly arrived e-mail. He decided to ignore it for the time being. The morning was gone and it was time for tennis. He dry swallowed two anti-inflammatories, quickly stretched his back and hamstrings, grabbed his tennis bag, and drove to the park, where he played doubles, year round, weather permitting.

After the third game of the first set, David's cell phone rang. Because it was during the changeover, he was able to extract the phone from his cluttered bag before the call ended: *Unknown Caller*

"Hello? ... Hello?" he asked. He heard clattering, as of dishes crashing, and wildly sustained shrieks. He repeated, nervously: "Hello? ... Hello?"

"Hello, David. Can you hear me? ... I don't know if you got my e-mail. You didn't answer. So I thought I'd call. I need to see you. I have a problem."

Bellevue Hospital

As soon as Jill told David to meet her at Bellevue's psychiatric wing, an alarm sounded in David's brain as loud as the bells of Bedlam. As a native New Yorker, David knew the city was a magnet for mentally disturbed people and that many of the most desperate found their way to Bellevue. This is where jumpers, slashers, flashers, false prophets and true lunatics were restrained, evaluated, and oftentimes admitted.

Despite his high alert, David seemed surprised to find Jill in the interview room: "What happened? What are you doing here?"

Jill sat unrestrained at one end of a small conference table. She looked at him sadly. "That's how you greet me? No kiss hello?"

David looked at the white-coated doctor and the blue-coated police officer seated at the other end of the table.

"You okay?" he asked Jill.

"It's a simple misunderstanding."

The police officer flipped open a leather citation book and read: "Public nuisance, trespassing, possible hate crime." The doctor opened a manila folder and read from his notes: "Saw visions, spoke in tongues, banged a drum."

"What happened?" he asked Jill tenderly. As he said this, he touched her hand, and she began to cry.

"I'm not crazy. Perhaps I'm guilty of excessive, soulful passion. Give me a ticket and let me go."

"Not so fast," said the police officer. "You were trespassing. You climbed the pulpit at St. Patrick's Cathedral. You committed an act of audio desecration."

"Further," added the doctor, "you were seen talking to someone who wasn't there ... speaking in tongues ... banging a drum ... dancing wildly. You were a danger to yourself and the public."

"That's not what happened."

"Alright," said the doctor in a soothing tone. "Please tell me again what happened."

"I don't want to. You won't understand. I just want to go home. Mr. Grossman will vouch for me. Please release me into his recognizance. If there's a fine, he will pay it."

The police officer looked at David and asked him: "Who are you?"

"My name is David Grossman."

"What's your relationship with this woman?"

"She's my friend."

"He's my husband," Jill said.

"Your husband?"

"Well, my ex."

"Is that true, Mr. Grossman?"

"Actually—"

"We were a common-law couple," Jill asserted. "Perfectly legit."

The police officer snapped shut his citation book as if closing the case. "Look," he said, speaking to Jill, "what we have here is a couple misdemeanors. I checked California and New York and see no priors or warrants. Given the crowd of certifiable loonies waiting to be processed, I'll let you go with a warning. But I don't want you in St. Patrick's ever again. Understand?"

"Here's my card," said the doctor to Jill. "There's a Help Hotline number at the bottom. If you are visited by any more spirits or hear strange voices, please call. Our services are free and confidential."

East River Park

Together, David and Jill walked silently out of the noisy hospital and remained silent while they walked south on First Avenue, passing on their left the humming traffic on the FDR Drive and the briny tang of the East River. The river seemed to beckon them, and Jill suggested they go to East River Park, find a bench, and sit awhile.

Save for cyclists, the park was empty and they had their choice of vacant benches. Jill chose the last one before the park narrowed into nonexistence. She sat beside the left armrest and David sat beside her, but not too close: the better to watch her while she watched the passing waters, stirred to a modest chop by the river breeze. There they sat, without speaking.

[David had only a few crystallized memories of Jill from the summer of '69. But he had many strong memories of their more recent reunion, four years earlier, at a small Manhattan art gallery. It was still morning and they had the gallery to themselves. In one of the rear rooms they sat and talked. Having not seen her in forty years, he began the conversation by congratulating her for writing the screenplay for *The Knish Man*, the Hollywood hit about the Jewish Catskills and Woodstock. Jill got to her feet, turned away from him, unsnapped her jeans, pulled down the zipper, and began slowly rocking her hips and lowering her pants until he saw ... her crack ... and then, tattooed on her ass, one word on each cheek: *Woodstock Lives!* ... Remembering her tattooed ass, David immediately recalled their subsequent trip to Bethel Woods to attend Woodstock's forty-year anniversary; their pilgrimage to Max Yasgur's farm; their midnight traipse into the surrounding black woods. He recalled slow-dancing with Jill under the Aquarian moon ... and his unaccompanied drive back home to his wife, Allison.]

The river was like a silver-flowing anodyne, softening their regrets, encouraging silent reflection. But David could not relax. He still regarded Jill as dangerous. He worried about her statement "I think you owe me" and the lengths she might go to collect her debt.

Katz's Delicatessen

After another ten minutes of river-watching, David suggested they move on. The former teen sweethearts stood together and resumed their southward journey. This time Jill took his arm. David thought it was a lovely gesture, like a middle-aged pinky-swear, and for a moment he forgot his suspicions of murder and mania and was able to enjoy the enticement of her body.

"I'm hungry," Jill whispered. "Let's go someplace."

David led the way west through the streets of Alphabet City and then south again to the Lower East Side, where the names of the streets (Delancey, Rivington, Essex, Ludlow) reminded them both of their immigrant grandparents: old Jews, long gone. Moments later, on Houston Street, they stopped in front of Katz's Delicatessen, sharing a sense of fated arrival, as if they had been unconsciously guided there by an Unseen Hand.

The restaurant's misted door was like an entrance into Jewish Yesterday. Inside, savory fragrances triggered memories of childhood meals. In fact, everything about the place—the chipped Formica tables, the shpritzer seltzer bottles, the hanging salamis—suggested totems and traditions that reminded them both of their shared tribal culture.

"This place is exactly right," said Jill. "Let's eat."

Knowing from experience that the portions would be oversized, they decided to share a large matzo ball soup and a pastrami sandwich. The matzo ball was the size of a softball but feathery light, and the broth seasoned to perfection. The pastrami sandwich was huge, overflowing, each slice thick and roughly carved.

They both drank Dr. Brown's black cherry soda and took turns staring at each other. David thought she was still quite pretty, even at sixty. She looked like she was in good shape. Perhaps she jogged or did Pilates. Perhaps she was still on the lam, living in her car, skipping meals, drinking her calories.... Jill thought David looked good for his early sixties. Maybe a little soft in the middle: too much snacking ... not enough sex.

Jill was anxious to tell David of her revelations and discoveries. She wanted to enthrall him, ensnare him, so he would help her execute her plan. But she knew it was important to moderate her mood so as not to scare him away.

David had many burning questions but was loath to press them. First and foremost, he wanted to know if Jill had fulfilled her promise to whack the Hollywood suit, that weasel Elliot, who'd ruined her directorial debut. Knowing she was (or had been) an alcoholic, he wondered if she'd been able to bolster herself with enough liquid courage to poison the bastard or to use her twin knives, Cutter and Blade, to exact her retributive pound of flesh. David wanted to know the truth and wanted to hear it from Jill. But there was a part of him that didn't want a clear answer. Clear knowledge, especially if it revealed a crime, would require him to make a moral judgment and take some civic action. David wanted confession without confrontation—without his personal involvement. He decided on subtle humor as a way of kicking off discussion.

"So, climbing the pulpit at St. Patrick's was on your bucket list?"

He imagined her climbing the pulpit to be closer to God, to seek His forgiveness.

"The acoustics there are fabulous."

"The acoustics? You wanted to hear God's voice more clearly?"

"Not God's, silly. Ishi's."

Chapter 2

Chico

As a young boy, David read all the books he could find on ancient civilizations. He was particularly taken with the Egyptians and the Inca. He knew all about Howard Carter's discovery of King Tutankhamen's tomb and of Hiram Bingham's discovery of the Inca capital at Machu Picchu.

As a freshman at Queens College, David pursued his interest by taking a course in anthropology. One spring day his professor spoke of El Dorado, telling stories of the explorers who had set out in search of the fabled City of Gold.

Enrapt, David imagined himself hacking his way through the Amazonian jungle; hiking through the cordillera of the Andes; exploring ghostly cave dwellings in the American southwest....

Following the lecture (while David's mind was still ablaze), the professor made the following announcement: "The Queens College Department of Anthropology will co-sponsor a field school this summer at Chico State College in Chico, California." The professor then handed out fliers, the top of which read:

THE MYSTERY OF THE MAIDU
Discover the Stone Age Secrets of an Ancient Tribe!

David took one of the fliers. That night, alone in his room, under the light of a single, 40-watt bulb, which he fancied a sputtering candle, he read the flier over and over, his hands trembling, as though he were holding an ancient treasure map.

A month later, with his parents' blessing and backing, David enrolled in the summer program and began planning his trip to California.

13

Orientation (1)

The first day at Chico State College involved registration, dorm acclimation, and an evening presentation by the expedition's director and staff. The next day, Sunday, was unscheduled. The actual field school would commence with Monday's 4:30 a.m. wake-up call.

David ate his Sunday breakfast alone. There were other people in the cafeteria, including students, but they all seemed to be coupled or cliqued. At seventeen, David was the youngest member of the group and felt like an outsider. [He was reminded of his early days at Grand View, a summer bungalow colony in the Catskill Mountains, where he and his family had vacationed when he was thirteen years old. He'd spent that summer trying to fit in: fending off foes and forging allies. He recalled one lonely day when he went by himself into the woods with a copy of *Treasure Island*. The forest seemed Primeval; if there were paths, he couldn't see them. Eventually, the forest thinned and he found himself on the edge of a flat, scrubby field. Up ahead was an isolated mound that seemed out of place. Despite the tiny saplings and tufts of grass that grew out of its brown hump, the mound had a strangely regular shape, like a slightly oblated igloo. On the mound's far side David found a small portal. Suddenly (and surprisingly, for he was not known as spontaneous or bold), he was on all fours, crawling into the cavernous uncertainty like Alice entering the rabbit-hole. Inside, a beam of portal sunlight provided enough grainy illumination for David to see a circular floor of hard-stamped earth and a surrounding dirt wall. The room, or cave, whatever it was, was maybe 12 feet wide and nearly half that height. David got to his feet slowly, carefully (there was just enough headroom in the center to stand upright) and ran his hand along the curved wall. Wherever the packed dirt had eroded, he felt the architecture of flat stones pancaked together, confirming his suspicion that the place was a human construct, cool and slightly damp, like a root cellar. David looked about, hoping to find the remains of an ancient culture:

shards of pottery, projectile points, wampum, bones … but the place was empty. He assumed, ruefully, that whatever had been stored there—however utilitarian or glorious its purpose—had long ago been removed or pillaged. Still, it seemed to him a wonder—and a great privilege—to be standing in this place, upon which time (and his imagination) conferred a kind of holiness. He wanted to shout his discovery to the world. Though he had no illusions about its importance—it was, after all, no Machu Picchu or Rosetta Stone—he was certain it deserved the attention of the scientific community and fantasized about his place in history, imagining the text of an encyclopedia article that described his long and distinguished archaeological career.]

Digitally Remastered

"Climbing St. Patrick's pulpit … isn't that usually reserved for the Cardinal or the Pope?"

Jill looked at David with honest eyes. "I observed a great deal of tradition and reverence."

David recalled other cryptic conversations with Jill. Discovering Jill's truth was like unraveling the thread in a Gordian knot: cleaving the knot with a single slash of reasoning never seemed like a viable option.

"How were you planning to hear Ishi's voice?"

"That was the easy part."

"Easy? He died a hundred years ago."

"David, I'm disappointed in you!"

"I get that a lot."

Jill shook her head and smiled, the way an old friend might respond to an old joke. "Listen, Mr. E-book Pioneer, Mr. Digital Revolution. You know the connection between Edison and Ishi?"

"I know that after Ishi was discovered and put on display, his chants and songs were recorded on Edison's wax cylinders."

"Have you ever listened to them?"

"No, I never have. I guess they're archived somewhere."

"Well, I've listened to many of them—and they are amazing! Listening to them is like stepping back in time."

"How did you hear them?"

"Duh. Welcome to the Digital Age! All of Ishi's recordings have been duplicated and digitally remastered."

"Oh my god. That's incredible. "

"One of the great wonders of the modern world. Think of it: the actual voice of an ancient Indian from a Stone Age culture downloaded to your smartphone or streamed through your computer or—"

"Broadcast in St. Patrick's Cathedral?"

Jill smiled. "Yes. A wonderful venue. I considered Carnegie Hall, but it lacks the spiritual gravitas."

"But what made you choose St. Patrick's Cathedral?"

"I wanted to hear Ishi's voice in a holy, reverential place."

"There are plenty of those to choose from. Why New York City? Why St. Patrick's?"

Jill smiled. "Because I knew I would get arrested there. And I knew you would save me."

Orientation (2)

After his first breakfast at Chico State College, David went for a walk, intending to tour the modest campus, nearly deserted in the summer time. He strolled down sunny paths. He crossed quadrangles. He tried the doors of different buildings, but all were locked. Finally, seeing a young woman exit a large domed building, he hurried over, tried the door, and was able to enter.

Inside was a small rotunda, dark and cool, a relief from the sunny glare. The floor was a dark marble, the curved walls a dull white. Around the room, like the tier of a stadium, was a row of mural paintings, each signifying a landmark achievement in the field of Anthropology. On the far side of the rotunda, below the murals, was a sign for offices, classrooms, restrooms, telephones, and the Ishi Museum. David followed the arrow toward the museum, not knowing who or what Ishi was.

He walked down a wide corridor, passing offices and classrooms on either side. At the end of the corridor was a set of double doors spread wide open as if he or other visitors were expected, though no one else was in sight. Above the open doorway was a wood-paneled lintel supporting a sign that read *Ishi Museum*.

David entered the carpeted and softly lighted room. The center of the room was filled with glass cases displaying primitive native artifacts: furs, ropes, baskets, skins, bows and arrows. On the far right side of the room was a smallish and primitive tee-pee. On closer inspection, David learned that it was a replica of a Yana-style house built by someone named Ishi behind a museum in San Francisco. On the opposite wall of the room was a pictorial timeline divided into three labeled sections: *Through the Ages, Ishi's Life, Ishi's Legacy*.

Beginning at the far left and moving right, David studied the large black-and-white maps and pictures and read the explanatory notes that told Ishi's story.

David learned that Stone Age Indians had been living in Northern California for thousands of years before whites invaded the area during the 1849 Gold Rush. He learned that the whites brought infectious diseases that killed thousands of the natives. He also learned, with a growing sense of outrage, that the natives who weren't felled by disease were massacred, or killed one at a time, or enslaved, or forced onto reservations. Surviving members of one of the besieged tribes, the Yahi, part of a larger group called the Yana, retreated into the dense thickets and lava cliffs of Deer Canyon, southwest of Mount Lassen. As the persecution continued, the Yahi were forced to flee deeper into the Sierra Nevada. Eventually, as a result of continuing persecution and attrition, only one Yahi remained. In 1911 an emaciated and tattered Indian came stumbling out of the mountains into the town of Oroville. The Indian was jailed because no one knew what to do with him. Locals who knew the languages of the northern tribes could not communicate with this Indian. An anthropologist from San Francisco came to investigate. Before too long he was convinced that the Indian before him was a flesh-and-blood, honest-to-goodness Stone Age Indian. He took the Indian back to San Francisco by railroad.

Curious and well-meaning anthropologists installed the Indian as a living artifact in the University of California's anthropology museum. The Indian referred to himself as *Ishi,* his own language's word for "man." Though it was presumed he had a name, he never shared it.

Ishi built a tee-pee behind the museum and lived there for five years, teaching observers and tourists about his Stone Age culture. Most accounts describe Ishi as generally happy. But there were times, as when he sang his "Dancing Song of Dead People," that tears flowed from his eyes.

David left the museum, even more anxious to begin his field school research. By summer's end, he had earned twelve college credits, lost his virginity to a beefy sophomore, and learned more about the story of Ishi, which inspired his first novel, *Chico,* which he never completed and which haunted him with a low-grade gnawing until the day, forty-five years later, he was inspired to rewrite the novel as *The Ishi Affair.*

Chapter 3

Arc of Events

David couldn't tell if Jill were joking about wanting to hear Ishi's voice, so he nervously tried another tack:

"So, how long have you been in New York?"

"I arrived the day before yesterday. Everything worked out exactly as I saw it."

David paused. "Tell me exactly what happened."

"Where should I begin?"

"How about the beginning?"

Jill paused to review the arc of events. "No, that won't work. Too much backstory. I need to bring you up-to-date."

"Okay. Begin with your trip to New York."

Jill smiled and readjusted her posture, settling into story mode. "Well, about three weeks ago I left northern California by car, bound for New York."

"Where in northern California?"

"North of Chico."

"Chico? What were you doing there?"

"That's part of the backstory. Do you want to hear about my trip or not."

"Okay. Go on."

"Well, like I said, I was on the road about three weeks."

"It took you three weeks to drive to New York?"

"It wasn't a straight shot. I stopped in lots of places ... without planning ... sometimes all of a sudden."

"Why would you do that?"

"I wanted to make sure I wasn't being followed."

"By who?"

"Whom," Jill corrected.

"By whom?"

"That's more backstory. In any case, I finally made it to New York."

19

David decided to keep it simple: "Where are you staying?"

"I stayed at a friend's place the first night. But I don't think I want to go there again. Next day I went to St. Patrick's, then I went to Bellevue, and now I'm in Katz's Delicatessen—with you."

David smiled. "Tell me about St. Patrick's."

St. Patrick's Cathedral

Jill drew and expelled a deep breath as if knowing the telling would take some effort.

"I have some tough decisions to make. I thought I might get clarity if I were inspired by Ishi himself."

"What kinds of decisions?"

"We'll get to that—but not today. Anyway, I brought a CD player to St. Patrick's, loaded with my favorite Ishi recordings, including 'Dancing Song of Dead People,' which I chose for the occasion."

David didn't think he could handle anything more than the basic facts. "When did you get there?"

"About 2:15. I figured lunch hour would be over. There's no mass or confession between 2:00 and 4:00, so I figured the place would be as empty as it gets."

David offered no comment and Jill continued:

"I entered the main entrance on Fifth Avenue, where it was very sunny. When I pushed open the interior doors, I thought it would take a while for my eyes to adjust to the dark, but there was plenty light from the banks of flickering candles and all the glowing, stained glass windows."

"Sounds lovely. But how'd you know where to go? You case the joint?"

Jill smiled. "Actually, yes. I'd googled diagrams of the layout, so I basically knew what to expect. I knew the Pulpit was up front, on the right-hand side, so I walked quietly along the far right aisle, passing the Holy Water Font, some altars, and the

Stations of the Cross. When I got to the foot of the Pulpit, I stopped and looked behind me, checking the aisles and the pews, especially those in the shadows. I didn't see a single soul. I thought that was a good sign. I wanted to be alone with Ishi."

Jill drew and expelled another deep breath. "So, there I was, at one of life's crossroads. But I didn't doubt myself. I didn't hesitate. I carefully climbed the Pulpit steps and when I reached the top, I took the CD player from my bag and placed it on the lectern. I cued 'Dancing Song of Dead People,' maxed the volume, and hit *Play*. I knew I had about twelve seconds before Ishi's singing began, so I carefully walked down the Pulpit steps and took a pew seat about six or seven rows from the front. I sat down slowly, closed my eyes, and waited."

Jill closed her eyes. When she reopened them, her face seemed transfigured, as if lighted from within.

"Oh, David, it was wonderful! Ishi's voice is so resonant, so powerful! I heard his pain ... his living memories, and it was like they were mine!"

She closed her eyes again and was quiet for several seconds. When she reopened her eyes, they were filled with tears.

"I felt an exquisite sense of belonging ... of being in the right time and place ... my life in perfect balance. Oh, David! I hadn't felt that way since you and I danced at Woodstock."

David remembered the midnight moon, the black woods, the threat of knives, the music, their aroused bodies dancing.

"I had to dance again! I reached into my bag and grabbed a gourd filled with acorns. I rattled that gourd. I drummed it. I danced!"

"I bet that got someone's attention."

Jill laughed. "Yes. A priest approached me, smiling. He was very sweet and gentle. He thanked me for coming to St. Patrick's. He said he hoped I'd found what I was looking for. Before I could answer, I noticed the police officer behind him.... Next thing I know, I'm in Bellevue, telling a shrink all about you and Ishi.... And then I felt so tired. I remember closing my eyes ... and when I opened them, you were there—come to my rescue, just as I had imagined it."

Varick Street

Jill took a last sip of coffee and wiped her mouth with a napkin. "I've got to get going."

"Where you headed?"

"West side."

"Want some company?"

"No, I'm fine. We'll talk soon. I have a lot more to tell you. I'm onto something that's going to change my life—and yours."

"I'm all ears."

David was anxious to hear. Despite having his first novel published, he was unemployed and harried by financial pressures. Allying himself with Jill might be an act of desperate daring, but it also might prove profitable.

"All in good time," she said, laying five bucks on the table to cover the tip.

"By the way, how's Allison?"

David's heart clenched.

"Don't worry," Jill said, as if reading his mind. "I'll text you. And I won't show up at your doorstep ... unless invited," she added with a wink.

Outside the restaurant they said goodbye and embraced. Jill's kiss was light, but her embrace was intentionally strong: a more mature and binding version of their teen pinky-swear, stronger even than their pas de deux coupling under Woodstock's anniversary moon, making it less likely (she hoped) that David would forswear her yet again.

David watched her ass as she walked away, heading west on Houston Street. He'd intended to walk north towards Thirty-Fourth Street, making his way to Penn Station, but decided to follow her.

He tailed her cautiously, hugging storefronts and keeping his gaze low. Jill made a left on West Broadway, a right on Prince, and then walked several blocks to Varick Street, which she crossed when the light changed. On her right was a long blue awning advertising *Frenchie's Gourmet Food & Café*. Jill paused outside, deliberating whether to enter. Deciding against it, she walked to a building entrance to the left of Frenchie's. Again she paused outside. When she finally moved towards the entrance, the door suddenly pushed open from within; a tall thin man with a deathly white complexion and blood-spattered shirt loomed over her, smiling. Jill looked down and let him pass. The man walked straight ahead towards a waiting cab. Jill backed away from the building and hurried into Frenchie's. David saw it all, including the pale woman in the second–floor window with the giant beehive hairdo, who had been jealously watching the tall man in the bloodied shirt.

David made a beeline north. At that moment, all he wanted was to get back to his Long Island home and to Allison, his wife of many years.

Oneness

O Allison! My Allison! You are my prop and staff, my stalwart support and guiding light. You are my counselor and creditor, my challenge and goad …"

David liked thinking in such rhetorical and overblown terms. They would never do for his writing, but they were great mood-setters when he wanted to take stock of his marriage, assess whether he should be bullish or bearish; whether it was worth his continued emotional investment.

Earlier in his marriage he'd been able to bury disturbing worries, but entering what was likely the penultimate phase in his life (retirement, Social Security), he found it strangely comforting to apply a conscious calculus to help him determine how he wanted to spend his golden years. *Risk-reward,* a phrase used repeatedly by his financial planner, was a strategy he now used to help decide the probability of his future personal happiness.

David thought about his early years with Allison. Even as a young couple they considered themselves a pair of Miniver Cheeveys: both believing they were born out of time ... into the wrong century ... old souls struggling in a new age. Allison was born an artist. She especially loved painting women and their apparel: rendering the folds of satin gowns, the curlicue details of lace, the shadows on feminine necks and hair. For many years she prided herself in being able to manufacture her own eco-friendly paints. For her pigments she used natural products de-rived from plants, insects, iron oxides, and minerals. For her binders she used flour, casein, and linseed oil. To create texture and add bulk she used talc, limestone, and silica. Even her sol-vents were natural: only citrus thinners and natural turpentine would do. When she drew, she especially loved the tactile thrill of pastels, using her fingertips to massage perfect blends of depth and subtlety. Inspired by the Moulin Rouge posters and Vogue covers of yesteryear, she developed an arty style that ap-pealed to many advertisers and art directors. Her illustrations sold well and life was good ... until Madison Avenue demanded that digital photography replace paints and pastels. As a result, Allison's freelance business dwindled. Wisely, she used her in-creasing free time to connect with her deepest self—and with the larger Oneness outside her body. Her explorations began with a few books and a yoga class. Then there were lectures here and there. She met new friends at the local Buddhist temple. Soon, she preferred spending long weekends with her friends at holistic healing centers and New Age retreats like Peace World in upstate New York. She knew David would eventually run out of excuses and agree to go with her again for a weekend of spiri-tual exploration, to see if they might regain their loving togeth-erness.

Chapter 4

Vegas, Baby!

Having spent the previous day at Bellevue Hospital, East River Park, Katz's Deli, and Varick Street, David was anxious to get back to his normal routine, which included a morning of writing and an afternoon of tennis. Once again, his cell phone rang in the early afternoon, just after the first set. Once again the screen showed: *Unknown Caller.* Assuming it was Jill, David wavered a few seconds before answering.

"Hello?"

"Davey-boy, it's me!"

David did not recognize the gravelly, goodfella voice.

"Hi. Who is this?"

"For Christ's sake, your sister dumps me and you forget me? That's cold."

David's brother-in-law, Bill Manes, was oddly charismatic: rough around the edges of his blue collar but intelligent in his way. Always on the make, he hustled as naturally as other people breathe and go to work.

For years Bill spent his lazy afternoons at an Off Track Betting parlor on upper Broadway, handicapping the horses with a clique of skanky lowlifes. To cover his losses he sometimes went bar-to-bar looking for loans. "Amortizing his debt" was how he put it. Occasionally, Bill was into local bookies for steep tabs and his wife Sandy, a retired corporate exec, had to bail him out. But Sandy's love and patience were not boundless. One day, a pair of low-level goombah mobsters, guys with calloused knuckles and nice suits, waited for her outside her apartment building. The one with two-tone shoes said they had some business to discuss with her husband. Sandy said she had no idea where he was. She had thrown him out. When they left, Sandy called Bill on his cell phone and told him not to come home. He begged for one more chance. "Get a job, clean up your act, call me in a year" were her final words on the subject.

Bill wasn't sure what to do next. He was broke. His wallet was empty, save for his MetroCard and a pawn ticket for one of Sandy's gold bracelets, which he figured she'd never miss. He had no place to stay the night.... Two years earlier, when the local OTB had closed its doors, the neighborhood had witnessed a diaspora of undesirables, *aka* Bill's closest associates. Bill knew a few of them well enough to have their first names listed in his cell phone contacts. He called each one and left a message, but no one returned his call.... Bill recalled the night Sal Esposito lost his last twenty on a sure-shot pony in a stakes race at Belmont. Sal was broke and asked Bill if he could spend the night at his place. Bill put his arm around Sal and led him to a homeless shelter in Washington Heights, a squalid place that stank of human effluvia and wet tobacco. At the entrance, Bill patted Sal's shoulder and left him to his fate.... With Sandy's banishment still ringing in his ears, Bill thought of that homeless center, knowing he'd rather hang himself than call that place home, even for a single night. And then he remembered *Atlantic City*—and his prospects brightened. He had friends there, and not all of them were losers. A few actually had jobs: card dealers, cooks, valets, security. Bill knew the place like the back of his scarred hands. He knew which hotels offered free buffet meals to draw gamblers to their casinos. He knew where there were unlocked conference rooms, where a guy could grab some shut-eye. With most of the hotels open 24/7, he knew he could scratch by until he scored something better. Only then would he call Sandy and try to convince her to take him back. A year wasn't such a long time, he thought. Many of his friends had been sent away for longer stretches and did not seem worse for the wear and tear when they showed up, years later, at the racetrack or at the poker games behind Pelham Manor.

Bill now had a plan: *Atlantic City here I come!* ... Only, he had no way of getting there. Trains and cars cost money. And then Bill remembered *the bus;* the poor man's limousine: big tinted windows and someone else doing the driving. Subsidized by the casinos, dozens of free busses made the New York-Atlantic City run every morning. Having made the trip just a couple months earlier, Bill knew that a bus left at 10:40 a.m. from Van Cortlandt Park and 242nd Street. He knew the trip was approximately three hours and thirty minutes and would bring him to the Atlantic City Bus Terminal, which was right behind Bally's Atlantic, which was on the Boardwalk, along with most of the other major hotels. *Sweet,* thought Bill.... Except, with only the clothes on his back he felt like a goddamn hobo. He called Sandy. Expecting his call, she told him that she'd left a suitcase with his essential belongings in the lobby with the doorman. Bill went there posthaste. When he arrived (at what had been *their* Riverdale hi-rise, but was now *her* Riverdale hi-rise), he considered going upstairs to beg Sandy's forgiveness. Instead, he retrieved his suitcase and left quietly. He knew it was time to face the music.

As it turned out, Atlantic City wasn't the boon Bill expected. Recession blues, high unemployment, soaring gas prices, and a glut of new hotels competing for dwindling business were driving the city from boon to bust. After only three months, Bill had to use a chunk of his meager savings for a one-way flight to Las Vegas, where he hoped he'd find better times. When Sandy heard this news from a friend, she said: "I don't care what happens in Vegas, I just hope he stays there."

But Vegas had its own problems. To reverse its reversals, the Chamber of Commerce had decided to remake the city's core image, replacing *Sin City* with *Family Fun.* Somehow, the Chamber had lost sight of the fact that the bread of Las Vegas was buttered by gamblers, and serious gamblers rarely travel with their families in tow. The families that arrived in Vegas for sun and fun rarely entered the casinos. Business went from bad to worse and was unlikely to improve until Vegas returned to its sinful roots. Meanwhile, Bill lost his job and needed to move on.

27

A friend told him of a job that was right for him. It started in a week. Bill used the time for a quick trip back to New York. His son, Bill Jr., was getting married for the third time and Bill wanted to give him a wedding present, which is why he contacted David.

"My son likes you, always did. I thought we'd go into it together—give a present from the two of us."

[David remembered once meeting Bill in the smoky OTB parlor on upper Broadway. "Just the man I wanted to see!" said Bill, sailing towards him like a ghost ship across a foggy sea. As he hove to, Bill threw a grappling arm around David's shoulder, lowered his head, and whispered, "Davey-boy, can you spot me a twenty? I forgot my wallet. If I have to run home I'll miss the next race at Pimlico." David gave him the twenty, tugging on it as it exchanged hands to suggest he was not an easy touch— that Bill should remember where it came from.]

"So, how much would you like to give?" Bill asked.

"You do know that I'm unemployed?" asked David.

"Of course, brother. But I also know you have a published novel that's a big hit."

"Who told you that?"

"Jill."

"Jill?"

"Yeah, that Jill."

Triangulations

"Jill Black?"

"Yeah. Your Jill."

That stopped David cold.

"She's not my Jill," said David.

"Sure she is. You were teen sweethearts. You wrote about her in your book. You even had a little fling with her at the Woodstock anniversary."

David felt shamefully exposed. "That's not exactly true."

"Whatever, bro. We're adults here."

David needed time to sort things out.

"How do you know her?"

"I met her at Sandy's retirement party."

David was flummoxed. Worlds were colliding. Nothing made sense.

"She wasn't there," said David. "I saw her for the first time in forty years just a few weeks before the party."

"She was there," said Bill.

"She wasn't invited. I didn't see her."

"And yet she was there."

"How?"

"I suppose she walked in like everyone else. How hard could it be? It wasn't a club with a bouncer. It was some kind of art gallery that was rented for the party, right?"

"Yeah," said David. "It was a Korean art gallery." David wondered if Jill had been there to spy on him and his wife Allison, whom she'd never met. He recalled the crowded main lobby and the crowded smaller rooms of the gallery.

"Interesting place," said Bill. "I remember staring at a big bronze shrine, like a giant gong, and this nice-looking lady came up to me and made conversation. She said she was a business associate of yours, so I chatted her up and we exchanged business cards."

"You have a business card?"

"Well, more like a calling card, I guess. It just says *Consultant* and has my name and phone number. Anyway, the lights started flickering to announce the big toast to Sandy in the main room and I lost the lady in the crowd. I never heard from her again—until about a week ago."

"She called you?"

"Yeah. She asked if I was still doing *consulting* work. We both laughed about that. I guess she saw through me a little bit. She said she knew I'd been working at the MGM Grand in Vegas and that I'd been let go. She asked if I wanted another job. I said it depends."

"Didn't you wonder how she knew these things about you?"

"I figured you told her."

"Well, I didn't. Until two days ago I hadn't heard from her in years."

The conversation seemed to stall.

"So, how much you kicking in for the wedding present?" Bill asked.

David gave Bill a hundred bucks.

"Thanks. I can use it when I fly back out to California."

"Why California?"

"That's where my new job is."

"What kind of work?" asked David, miffed that he'd just been taken for a hundred bucks.

"Similar to what I've been doing. Except it's a small, Indian-owned and operated casino."

"Where?"

"Don't recall. Someplace just north of Chico. Not far from the Cascade Range and Mt. Lassen."

"Indian country," said David.

Bill nodded. "That's what Jill said."

Jill Black

Of course I went to Sandy's retirement party to spy. Not like Mata Hari-spying—I wasn't looking to subvert or murder—but I did want to see Allison. I wanted to see the woman David married. Sure, I was jealous. David was my first love.... I remember the summer we met and the night we watched the first Moon landing on TV. Under the cover of darkness I took David's shy hand and whispered: "How far would you go with me?" I could tell I shocked him. "How far? You mean like in miles? Like to the Moon?" "Yes," I said. "Would you take me to the Moon?" I remember he drew a sharp breath. "Yes," he whispered hotly. "I would take you to the Moon—and beyond." "Promise?" I asked. "Promise," he said. "Pinky swear," I said. I lifted my pinky and he lifted his and then I hooked our pinkies together and kissed them, looking up into his eyes. I wanted him to kiss our hooked pinkies to show his love. But something distracted him. He tightened his pinky grip and let my hand fall. Our pinkies separated, unkissed by his lips. He had failed to seal the deal. When he went back to his own bungalow, I cried all night.... Weeks later, I gave him another chance. We'd been hearing news about a giant rock concert to be held just miles away. Fat Rubie, the truck driver who delivered our newspapers, gave David the scoop. He said a giant stage was being built and it would have amplifiers the size of refrigerators and a helicopter pad for flying in all the rock stars. I was so excited. I had to go. I knew it would change my life. On the first morning of the concert I sat outside the colony on this big rock beside the road. We never had traffic, but that morning the stalled traffic stretched forever. Some people had pulled their cars to the side of the road and just left them. I waved to the people walking by. It was like a parade. No, a pilgrimage, a hippie pilgrimage! The hippie pilgrims wore T-shirts covered with peace signs, butterflies, and doves. They wore lots of buttons, beads, and sandals ... and every sort of blue jean denim: patched, bleached, and bell-bottom. There was music playing: guitars, tambourines, piping flutes! ... I heard someone approach me from behind. I knew it was David and I turned to him. "I want to go. I belong with them," I said. When he didn't answer, I said: "Take me! Tonight! Let's go—you drive. Get your father's car. Take me! We'll be together! All the music! All the people! Let's do it!"... But he never came for me. He lacked something. Nerve? Heart? Conviction? Whatever, he failed me ... and I despised him. We did not speak for forty years.

David

I wanted to go. I wanted to take her. I wanted to be a part of the great event. But I was just sixteen and afraid. I was afraid I wouldn't know how to get there or how to get back. I was afraid I couldn't protect her from the bullies. I was afraid she'd abandon me when we got there—and I'd spend all my time frantically searching for her among the drugged-out crazies. I was afraid I'd be forced to swallow pills that would cause my brain to pinwheel forever in mind-numbing colors. I was afraid of the night, and the rain, and the cold. All in all, it just didn't feel right.

Allison

I met David when were both eighteen. He was so cute. And skinny! We were both at Queens College. I was a freshman planning to study Art but he was already a junior and a Creative Writing major. He always knew what he wanted to do. So, it's not like he's chasing a silly dream ... he's channeling his Chi, directing his fate. I get that. But here's the thing: regular life still goes on—we have bills to pay and I'm the one who writes the checks. I know what things cost and I know we can't survive without more money coming in. I certainly don't blame David for losing his job ... but facts are facts: his occasional freelance jobs and book royalties aren't enough. We need more. It's that simple. It's not easy to talk to him about it. That's why I want him to come to Peace World with me. Next month they're having a special four-day couple's workshop on sharing and communication skills. We need it.

David and Sandy

David knew he must tell Sandy that he'd spoken with Bill. Even though she had kicked Bill out, she still missed the big lug and occasionally asked David if he'd heard from him.

"As a matter of fact, I heard from him yesterday."

"What's that bad boy up to?"

"Headed to California to seek fame and fortune. A one-man Gold Rush."

"I think you mean bum's rush."

David didn't mention that Bill had lost his job in Vegas. And he avoided mentioning the Jill connection, which would have embroiled the situation way beyond necessary. He also avoided the fact that Bill was in the city for his son's third wedding; the less Sandy knew about Bill's gold-digging children the better she felt.

"Why's he going to California?" she asked.

"I think he has a special opportunity in a new casino. It's owned and operated by Indians."

"Oy. I have my reservations."

They both chuckled.

"You know anything else?" she asked.

"No, he was a little light on details."

"I think the word is *sketchy*," said Sandy.

"Perhaps, but he seemed in a good mood."

"I find that particularly disturbing."

"You never know. He may come back a changed man." David said this with a chuckle, suggesting the unlikelihood of Bill ever changing.

"I need to keep an eye on him. You busy these days?"

"I have my work."

"I know, but you haven't started writing a new novel, right? And Allison says you don't have a freelance job. So, I'm just thinking, perhaps you can visit Bill after he settles into his life in Indian country. See what he's up to—and report back."

Sandy's interest in Bill's business affairs went way beyond simple curiosity. Knowing what Bill had up his sleeve, she'd sometimes been able to thwart his worst-laid plans. She had no qualms about this. As a former corporate manager and mentor, she had a dozen mantras that spoke to the virtue of Preparedness. Now semi-retired, she still did occasional consulting work for international banks and corporations. Inasmuch as her reputation was a large part of her business, her husband's *indiscretions* were a potential liability that must be managed. It was well worth the investment of sending her unemployed brother to California to watchdog Bill.

"I'll pay for your trip and living expenses. I just want to know what scheme he's hatching this time."

"How do you know he's scheming?"

"He's breathing."

Chapter 5

Takes One to Know One

David recognized that he also could be a schemer, clever as a coyote, sneaky as a shape-shifter. Because David believed his schemer-self was manageable, he rarely was concerned about its ethics-bending character, and thus the two occasionally worked together to blur the fine line between flirtation and infidelity.

If asked, David would say that his marriage was a wonderful, loving arrangement. Make no mistake, he adored Allison. And Allison adored him. But it should be pointed out that Allison had tested the elasticity of her marriage bonds with a swarthy carpenter, a heavy tool belt slung low on his hip like a holstered weapon. And David knew ... because Allison confessed. Because her bonds had not snapped back so easily, Allison had decided that stretching them casually was hardly worth the effort. David, however, seemed better able to stretch his marriage bonds without fear that they would snap under pressure. People might judge as they please, but David and Allison knew they had a real love—even if one or the other occasionally felt the need to test its resiliency.

Peace World

When Allison thought David wasn't listening to what she had to say about their money troubles, a shrewish voice, sharp as winged razors, flew from her mouth. She couldn't help it. David's apparent unconcern drove her crazy. He didn't seem to see that their financial straits were dire. He didn't see how it was affecting their marriage. But she was the one who balanced the books, who wrote the checks, who truly understood the sorry state of their financial affairs. David seemed to ignore the warning signs, even when she screamed them to his face.... Eventually, she decided on another tack. She realized she couldn't change him. Only he could change himself. But, she thought, she might be able to guide him towards enlightenment. Understanding this, she strongly suggested that he choose one of these couple's workshops offered by Peace World:

- Calling from the Heart: The Dreamgiver
- Realization of the Self As Part of a Couple
- Choose, Change, and Become Your Karma
- The Positivity of Love and Forgiveness
- Raja Yoga: Inner Peace, Supreme Power

Unfortunately, Allison made her suggestion in her cutting, shrewish voice, which sounded to David like an ultimatum. He felt cornered. Once before he had experienced a four-day spiritual workshop with Allison and was not keen on going there again. But what choice did he have? If only he had some freelance work.... If only he were busy, writing another novel, Allison might call off her dogs. David sighed. He wondered how Jill was doing.

Chapter 6

Museum of Jewish Heritage

Jill hadn't slept well in two days (not surprising, given her frightening accommodations in a horror house). By night three she'd managed to fill her California prescription for sleeping pills. Though she knew a double dose would guarantee a deep sleep, she feared what might happen to her body (and even her soul) if her sanctum were invaded during the night. But her need for sleep was so great she threw caution to the winds and swallowed the pills. The sleep aid proved effective. When she awoke the next morning in a coffin ... inside a windowless crypt ... decorated in a flying bat motif ... she had several moments of doubt and pain before realizing she was not dead and consigned to Hell.

Down a corridor there was a public bathroom where she was able to pee, brush her teeth, and give herself a quick whore's bath. Ten minutes later, she was seated at Frenchie's, ordering a cheese and onion omelet, well-done home fries, and coffee. Thirty minutes later she called David.

"You free today?" she asked.

"I have some work."

"Well, I need to see you. It's important. It's time to discuss our plans."

"Our plans?"

"Oh yeah. Meet me at the Museum of Jewish Heritage in Battery Park."

"I'll meet you in the lobby at noon," said David.

"No, the lobby's too conspicuous. Meet me at the entrance to the Catskills exhibit."

"What floor?"

"Just follow the sign to *The Other Promised Land.*"

A Question of Murder

David had been to the Museum of Jewish Heritage only once before, about four years earlier. On that occasion a large crowd was gathered to celebrate the opening of the new exhibit on the Jewish Catskills. Jill Black, screenwriter, was one of the principal speakers. Her debut film *The Knish Man* (a combo Catskills and Woodstock homage) had featured some big stars early in their careers and had become something of a cult classic, at least among Jews with a Catskills connection. The film had been the high point of Jill's career. Based on its modest success, she'd headlined several Hollywood screenwriting projects and had even done some television work. But over the years the offers had dried up and Jill had slipped into second-class status. Fortunately, she'd been thrown a lifeline by a sympathetic Jewish studio exec: the opportunity to write and direct her own film. The opportunity was a godsend and Jill had devoted herself to developing a screenplay treatment based on her own life:

Sophia Levy is turning fifty. She's a Professor of Archaeology, famously gay, and a former advocate of gender separatism. Over the years she has altered her outlook and tempered her rhetoric. Now, approaching middle age, she feels the need for even more dramatic changes. To celebrate her fiftieth birthday she has invited four close friends (two married, one divorced, one never married—like Sophia) on a GIRLS ONLY vacation: five days of heart-to-heart talking, drinking, laughing, crying in Mulegé, Mexico. Mulegé is Sophia's Eden, Haj, Fortress of Solitude, all rolled into one. Every few years—or whenever she feels compelled to think straight, regenerate, find herself—she makes the trip to Mulegé—which is why she has chosen this place to celebrate with her friends. On the second night, the day of her actual fiftieth birthday, Sophia announces that she is coming out of the closet. Going straight. No more gay. Her friends are stunned silent. Slowly, they begin to ask hesitant questions, meant lovingly. But the questions become increasingly sharp, even cutting: Are you sure? Maybe you're just Bi, you know? You think it's just a phase? When did this happen? Why didn't you say anything until now? How could you keep it from us? … Each of the women defines herself by the questions she asks and how she responds to the others. Everyone on the trip grows, everyone changes. In a sense, it's a coming out party for all of them.... It's a niche film—relatively small budget, targeting mostly gays and women; a tear-jerker, feel-good, and adult coming-of-age all in one.

Unfortunately for Jill, the Hollywood suit given the job of shepherding the film had been perfectly unsuited for the task. After reading the script, he said to Jill: "I like it, I really do. It's great. Very deep. Important. But I think it can be improved. Just a bit. Tweaked, you know. First thing we do: Lose the lesbian. Why does Sophia have to be gay? Can't she be something else? Have some other problem? And why only women? Where are the guys? The love interest? Five drunken, middle-aged women talking about gay stuff? That's a movie?"

A few months later, when it appeared that the film would be scrapped, Jill had told David of her plans to murder Elliot, the little Hollywood twerp who'd killed her film and ruined her life. With impressive composure she'd debated the pros and cons of poison, gunshot, and sharp knives, eventually declaring that her personal pair of butcher knives, Cutter and Blade, would most likely deliver her retribution. Soon after, David had lost touch with her. Some months later, when Jill reappeared in his life, he did not know whether or not she had committed murder. Even when they danced together at the fortieth anniversary celebration of Woodstock (finally making good on his forty-year failure), he did not know if she had blood on her hands. Soon after their midnight dance, they fell out of touch yet again. Years passed. The next time he saw Jill, she was in Bellevue Psychiatric Hospital, talking about Ishi.

The New Eden

Having arrived at the museum and found his way to *The Other Promised Land* exhibit, he saw Jill, standing alone, looking haggard and unkempt.

"You look like hell," he said, aiming at funny and affectionate.

"Spent the night there. I don't recommend it."

Without another word, Jill led the way through the exhibit, taking her time to view all the descriptions and artifacts. David was tempted to take her hand, but there was something in her focused attention that dissuaded him. After a while, he stopped staring at Jill and paid more attention to the exhibit, a timeline of Jewish-American experience that focused on the Jewish Catskills: The New Eden.

David was beginning to wonder why Jill had asked to meet at this place. Remembering her fear that she was being followed, he looked about but saw no one suspicious. Just then Jill spoke:

"The New Eden.... You ever wonder what this country looked like just a couple hundred years ago?"

"Yeah. I suppose."

"Well, I think about it a lot.... The thing that gets me is how beautiful it must have been. So natural and unspoiled.... So many different native peoples living off the land.... So few are left."

David shrugged. "People die. Cultures die. That's part of evolution."

Jill shook her head.

"I understand evolution and natural selection. And I can handle extinction by cataclysmic event. But I can't handle genocide. There is nothing natural about genocide."

David nodded. "I understand. But the Jews didn't perish. We still exist. We thrive. We even have our own nation."

"I know," said Jill, "but not everyone was so lucky. Look at Ishi."

"Last of the Stone Age Indians."

"That was the prevailing wisdom."

"Was?" David asked

"Was," said Jill.

River Walk

Jill seemed suddenly restrained by the boxy indoors. "I need some fresh air. Let's find the river."

David followed Jill out the building. Together they walked a few short blocks west and south, where they found a great view of the Hudson River and the bay waters that fed the Atlantic. The wide and seemingly limitless vista encouraged a historical perspective.

"I remember my history," said David. "Chingachgook was the last of the Mohicans, and Ishi was the last of the Yahi."

"Chingachgook was a fictional character," said Jill. "He was the last of his tribe—according to Cooper's story."

"But Ishi was real."

"Yes, but fictional too," said Jill.

"What do you mean?" asked David.

Jill turned from the waters to face him. "Most of what we know about Ishi was written by the men who knew him when he was in their custody—and by a woman, years later, who never even met him."

"Theodora Kroeber."

"Yes, the head anthropologist's second wife. Good woman, good writer. It was her books—based on Alfred Kroeber's research and writings—that made Ishi famous in the 1960s. The good news is that she helped create a modern Native American hero. The bad news is she romanticized him."

"How'd she do that?"

"I don't want to get into that now. But I'll give you a really good book that describes Kroeber's spotty scholarship and romantic outlook. Suffice to say, Ishi was not quite the Noble Savage she described."

"He wasn't a pimp or a drug lord, was he?"

"No," said Jill, laughing and shaking her head. "It seems he was a wise man, remarkably generous and kind, given what had happened to him. But he wasn't a Happy Hiawatha either.

He had his demons. And there were things he never told Alfred Kroeber and his team."

"I don't think he ever revealed his name," said David. "*Ishi* is the Yahi word for 'man.'"

"Tip of the iceberg," said Jill. "Ishi played lots of things close to the vest."

"Quite the poker player that Ishi."

"He must have had a good poker face. He never let on that he was not the last of the Yahi."

That stopped David in his tracks. "Not the last? Really? Tell me."

Jill stood to her full height. This was her pitch, her oracle: "Ishi sacrificed himself so that the few others, left behind, might survive and endure. The living Yahi regard Ishi as a god. He's their Jesus."

David was stupefied. "How do you know all this?"

"I have friends who know things."

"Are you sure? Like, verifiably sure?"

"One hundred percent."

"Wow," said David.... "All the books and films will have to be changed: *Ishi, NOT the Last of the Yahi.*"

Jill smiled.

"There will be new books and films," she said. "That's where we come in."

Chapter 7

Nurse's Aid

A few years earlier, Jill stood on the bedroom terrace of her Santa Monica condo, staring at the famed marina and lighthouse. In the waters directly below, small boats with spindly masts reminded her of the tiny paper umbrellas that floated in those sissy cocktails Elliot liked to drink. She was thinking: *I'm gonna kill that bastard. I'm gonna cut him to pieces and watch him bleed out....* She'd been drinking hard for several days. At first, she'd practiced her ladylike habit of pouring gin neatly into a crystal glass—but after two days she began pouring the dulling pleasure straight from the bottle into her mouth.... Poor Jill. Without her film she had nothing do. With her latest lover gone and David back with his wife, she had no one to love. Without booze she had no way to dull the pain.

A week later, drinking less but still woozy, she received a text message from the hospital reminding her that she had a routine colonoscopy scheduled for that Friday. She saw this as a fortuitous sign. Knowing the drill, she figured she could use the cleansing prep as a first step to detox her demons. The procedure went well ("Clean as a whistle," said the doctor, referring to her large intestine and rectum), but the anesthesia had left her nauseated and dehydrated and she was a long time in recovery. Among the attending staff was Patricia Escobar, RN, who recognized Jill from Circle of Support, an LGBT chapter of Alcoholics Anonymous that met at the Lincoln Park Recreation Center on Wilshire Boulevard. The two had once been close but had lost touch in recent years.

Nurse Escobar patted her hand.

"How you feeling, honey?"

Jill recognized her.

"Patty," Jill said, smiling weakly.

[Patty remembered the rough outline of Jill's history. She knew Jill had survived an awkward adolescence in Brooklyn ("circle peg, square hole"). She knew Jill had moved to Midwest corn country, where she soon tired of life as a schoolteacher. She knew Jill had driven to Los Angeles on her thirtieth birthday, moved in with Alysha Marx (a black political activist), and had helped raise Alysha's biological son. Patty recalled that while Jill was living with Alysha in East L.A., she'd enrolled in an MFA screenwriting program at UCLA. Patty remembered that Jill's senior thesis had won the Goldwyn Award for best screenplay and was produced by Miramax as *The Knish Man*. Patty knew the film had won critical praise and a cult following, but she also knew the sad truth that Jill had never been able to repeat her success and had lived on the exhaust fumes of her early fame for many years. Patty knew Jill during the time of her great depression (which began the day after Alysha and her son vamoosed L.A. for Pittsburgh), but the last Patty had heard, Jill was in New York, reconnecting with an old friend she hadn't seen in forty years.]

Juice, crackers, and an extra hour of rest helped restore Jill's body. When Jill's head had cleared, she told Patty about a great Hollywood offer she'd had to write and direct her own film—and how it been ruined by a pissant assistant producer who hates women.

"Honey, I'm so sorry. You'll have more chances. You're a great writer."

Hearing words of support, Jill cried softly.

Patty gave Jill a tissue to dry her eyes and then changed the subject. She said she was moving east to work as a nurse in New York and to help her brother, who had just launched a new business after a long career in theater set design, special effects, and lighting.

"It's crazy. It's like a horror house thing. He makes good money, but he needs some help. He never married—like me—so we would be good for each other. Nice to have someone, you know, for companionship."

Jill nodded and again her eyes filled with tears.

Patty continued: "You remember Kenneth and Gloria?"

Jill had met them both at a Screen Actors Guild party in Burbank. She had slept with Kenneth twice, Gloria once, and the three had spent a crazy-ass weekend together at Carmel-By-the Sea.

"They still together, sort of. They schedule their trips to New York when my brother's horror house is open—Halloween, Valentine's Day, special events. They make good money working as actors and he lets them sleep there too. That reminds me: Give me a call if you ever need a place to crash in New York."

Chapter 8

Cost of Doing Business

Jill hadn't been returning Bill's calls. Finally, he got through.

"Hi, it's Bill. You forget about me?"

"Hell, I was just thinking of you."

It was true. When her phone rang, she had been walking around the horror house, imagining Bill beside her as a wide-shouldered, stiff-walking Frankenstein: her loyal servant and protector.

When she'd first arrived, Patty said she could crash wherever she liked. "Most of the comfy spots are taken. I think Kenneth and Gloria have the two best, but you should be able to find something that isn't too horrible." Patty was speaking literally, which Jill saw for herself when she walked around the place after business hours. Most of the rooms or niches that contained anything like a bed or cot showed signs of being occupied. Jill reviewed the remaining options, passing on the unclaimed bed of nails and the rubber, snake-filled sarcophagus. But she simply couldn't pass on Count Dracula's empty, silk-tufted coffin. By comparison, it was a deluxe accommodation.

"So, what's next?" Bill asked Jill.

"Before next Friday, I want you to fly to Sacramento. I'll meet you at the airport. From there we'll drive to the casino."

"You sending me a ticket?"

"Travel is on your dime. Cost of doing business."

Bill paused. "I may need a little advance."

"You want to borrow money already?"

"This is all on very short notice. I need time to access my revenue streams."

"Right. All those off-shore accounts and Swiss banks."

Bill laughed. "I see you have thoroughly vetted me."

Jill smiled. The guy was a scoundrel. A handsome, capable scoundrel.

"I'll loan you five hundred bucks. But you owe me. Big time."

"Deal," said Bill. "See you in Sacramento."

Chapter 9

A Holy Calling

David used to enjoy staring at the plaques and mementos in his big corner office. His favorite, by far, had been a brass copy of Frederic Remington's "Bronco Buster." For David, the hat-waving, "Ride 'em high!" cowboy symbolized his hard-charging success as a maverick editor.

He never saw the arrow that knocked him off his high horse. Perhaps he should have seen it coming and been pre-pared. As it was, he'd had no exit strategy. He arrived home that day, shocked and depressed at his sudden transformation from Editorial Director to unemployed husband. His wife, however, was a wonder of support, at least initially. "Are you okay?" she asked. "You can tell me anything. We'll get through this. It's just a bump in the road."

Practically speaking, Allison understood the loss of David's income—that big hunk of bacon he'd brought home twice a month. But she yearned to also understand the situation in spiritual terms and was anxious to practice the relationship skills she and David had learned a few years earlier at Peace World's Renew Your Marriage Vows workshop. But David had not enjoyed that experience (despite having been moved several times to tears, disproving his wife's long-held belief that he was lachrymose intolerant) and was not a cooperative partner. He balked at the touchy-feely communication strategies she insisted they use to help them better understand each other. After a few weeks of ineffectual job-searching, Allison demanded to know when he was going back to work. David hemmed about the tight market. He hawed about his unattractive middle age. Finally, he broke down, tearily confessing that he didn't want to go back to work; that he would rather die than return to that torturous salt mine.

"What do you want? Tell me," Allison asked.

He told her the truth. He spoke from the heart. He said he wanted a different life. Allison's hand flew to her mouth—she thought he was leaving her. David saw her terror and softened his tone. He said he loved her … but that after forty years of office work he needed a change. He said he yearned to be a novelist. "I want to give myself to my art." He said *art* to make it sound like a holy calling.

Allison responded swiftly: "We have bills to pay. We need your salary. We can't live without it."

Husband and wife began an honest and fair negotiation. This was a good thing, a sharing thing, an exercise in communication and compromise…. At last, husband and wife reached a deal. Allison granted him a one-year reprieve: twelve months of grace to write a novel. When the deadline arrived, he would have to find a new job.

Persistence Rewarded

David's career as a full-time novelist did not begin well. Every morning, eight to noon, he sat in Café Amazon: a hip place with lots of cool-looking people, comfy chairs, and little round tables for one's latte and laptop. But he wrote nothing, not even a title. He finally had the time to write but could think of nothing to say.

Empty days passed. Finally, Fate rewarded David's persistence by bringing back into his life a former teen sweetheart he had not seen or spoken with in forty years—not since the summer he'd disappointed her by failing to take her to Woodstock. David's teenage crisis of conscience, his failure to act, had haunted his adult years, but his renewed relationship with Jill—culminating in their midnight dance in the woods behind Yasgur's Woodstock farm—resulted in his first novel, *Forty Years Later*. And then Jill was gone. Hours after they'd danced together under the Aquarian moon, he was in his car, flying south on the Thruway, back home to his wife Allison. Jill headed somewhere west, alone.

THE ISHI AFFAIR

David didn't hear from her for nearly four years. During that time his novel *Forty Years Later* was published as an e-book by a savvy indie publisher. Though he would have much preferred to hold a paperbound book in his hands, David was thrilled to be a published novelist and marketed his book fiercely, relying on social media and his own frenetic flesh-pressing to acquire new readers, one at a time. But now he faced a new quandary: His publisher was anxious for his next book. According to his publisher, it was important for David to extend his brand as soon as possible. Once again, David agonized over what to write about. And once again (could it possibly be coincidental?) Jill reappeared in his life—this time with her story about Ishi.

Jill's Pitch

Jill sent David a text message:

Change of plans. Flying to Sacramento tonight. Heading to Chico. Things falling into place. Here's the deal: Ishi's surviving Yahi are alive and well. Secret and isolated. Still living according to Stone Age. I'm going to film them. You're going to write about them. We're going to work together. Details to follow. This is going to rock the world. We're going to make history.

Jill's message had the impact of a shocking telegram. It made everything seem real and pressing. David guessed that Jill's pitch to his brother-in-law Bill was related to this Ishi plan ... but there were a whole lot of dots that remained unconnected. Where would he live out there? What kind of relationship would he have with Jill? How would that affect his relationship with Allison? How did Bill fit in?

David was trying to make sense of it all when he received another text message from Jill:

Fly to San Francisco in ten days. Just tell me when. I'll meet you at airport. I promise to make everything clear. Love.

David's mind went round and round, but his heart had decided.

Stars Align

Allison needed David's love and support to keep their shared hearts and household strong.

Sandy needed to protect her business reputation and was willing to pay David to go to California to watchdog her ne'er-do-well husband.

Bill needed a regular paycheck and a place to go where the mob wasn't looking for him.

Jill needed Bill as her inside man, her muscle, and as another hook into David. Jill needed David because she needed love, a connection to her happier past, and because she knew he could write a great novel about Ishi that would help pave the way for her film's success.

David needed to keep peace with Allison; to pay his bills; to help his sister; to reconnect with Jill; and to revisit with Ishi, the subject of his first novel, which he never completed and which he hoped would become the subject of the new novel his publisher craved.

It was a win-win-win-win for all concerned. What could possibly go wrong?

Chapter 10

Westward Ho!

David suggested to Allison that they meet at Saffron, her favorite eatery after an afternoon of Buddhist prayer. He knew his wife would be beaming with karmic energy and impressed with his willingness to forsake his carnivorous appetite and join her in a vegan repast.

"Hello, sweetness," he said, greeting her with a hug and kiss. "How was the lecture and prayers?"

"Wonderful!"

As they took their seats the waitress approached.

"Namaste," said David, posing his hands vertically in front of his heart.

The waitress returned the traditional Hindu greeting. "Namaste. What can I get you?"

David scoured the extensive menu, a testament to everything tofu. "Hmmmm," he said, mentally passing on the meatless burger and fishless fillet. "I think I'll have the coconut-cardamom oat muffin and carob coffee. What are you having?" Allison chose the grilled eggplant Caprese, with a side of artichoke and spinach dip.

During their meal, husband and wife talked about their daughters, Lydia and Louise; their friends; and what needed to be fixed around the house. David mentioned that he'd heard from Bill.

"What's he up to?"

"He has a job offer."

"That's wonderful," Allison said with enthusiasm. "He should be working."

David detected a jab at his own unemployed status.

"The job's in California. An Indian-owned casino somewhere in the sticks."

"A job is a job. I'm sure he has bills to pay."

51

David sipped his carob coffee.

"Sandy thinks it sounds fishy," he said. "And get this: she offered to pay me to go out there to keep an eye on him and report back."

"What would she pay you?"

"All my expenses and a thousand a week."

Allison weighed the facts, as presented.

"We could use the money. How do you feel about it?"

"It's the middle of nowhere. I might go stir crazy. But it's near Chico. I guess I could visit there—maybe get inspired to revise my first novel. Worth a shot."

Allison had a look of focused calculation. "Sandy could wire the money directly into our account."

"I'm sure she could."

"How long do you think you'd be there?"

"Don't know. A month. Maybe two."

"That's a lot of money."

"Yes, but there's something else."

"What's that?"

David looked away, as if staring into the limitless ether. "Hard to describe. It's vague. I keep thinking about the past. How it's not really past if I keep reliving it in my mind. I want to revisit Chico—the setting for the unfinished book I wrote when I was young. The trip seems like a mission to me. Like a spiritual calling."

Allison was beaming. "I think you should go ... if you want to. It's up to you."

"I guess I should. It appears Fate is beckoning."

Allison touched his hand. "My *beshert*."

David smiled. *Beshert*. The Hebrew phrase for soulmate.

"One question," said Allison. "What are you going to say to Bill? You just can't show up in the middle of nowhere. He'll know Sandy sent you to spy on him."

"You're right. That's exactly what he'll think."

"Don't you think he'll mind?"

"Nah. He'll welcome me. He'll see that Sandy still cares about him. He'll see me as his chance to get back in her good graces."

Allison took a few seconds to take it all in.

"So, you going to do it?"

"I think so."

The Great Divide

David had told Allison everything—except the part about being with Jill for the next month or so. The omission gnawed at him. Allison deserved better.

David was fast-reviewing his ethics-bending excuses when the pilot's voice announced: "Folks, if you look out your windows on the right side of the cabin, you can see the Continental Divide."

Despite the macro distance, David easily imagined a thousand streams and rivers behind him—every raindrop, every snowflake, every fallen tear—flowing towards the great Atlantic.

As he continued flying westward, it occurred to him that when he returned home (on a plane just like the one he was sitting in, but headed in the opposite direction), all the waters behind him—fed by raindrops and fallen tears—would be emptying into the great Pacific.

53

Chapter 11

San Francisco

Jill stood by the arrival gate, shaking her acorn-filled gourd to catch David's attention. David heard her, saw her, went to her. When he closed within an arm's reach, Jill bopped his head with the gourd.

"Ow!"

"You're late."

"Traffic," he said, rubbing his noggin. "Snow-geese over Saginaw."

Jill laughed. "You see, that's why I love you."

David carried his old college rucksack and a small suitcase to Jill's car, a red convertible coupe.

"What's this spiffy little thing?"

"Mazda Miata. You like? It's my hot crossover."

"Crossover?"

"Yeah, it's tops with the bi-crowd."

"Buy now, pay later."

"You're such a goofball," she said, popping open the trunk.

David wedged in his luggage, closed the trunk with a firm hand, opened the passenger door, sat down, and buckled himself in.

"Okay. Let's see what this baby can do."

"Hold on, cowboy," said Jill. "Before we head north, I've got to take you somewhere."

"Fine. Where we going?"

Jill pressed a button and the ignition roared.

"City of the dead."

Colma, California

Colma is a modern necropolis. The town's motto is "It's great to be alive in Colma!" but there are as many marble obe-

lisks and tombstones as there are trees. And for every living resident, there are a thousand buried below.

Jill drove to 1601 Hillside Boulevard, passing countless
graves along the way.

"This town is one giant cemetery," said David.

"Close. Three-quarters of the town is burial ground and
memorial park."

"Why? Who built this place?"

"Years ago, San Francisco needed a place to bury its
dead. Death and burial is the town's leading industry."

David shook his head. "But why are we here?"

Jill parked the car and they both got out.

"You need to be here."

"Only one problem," said David. "I'm not dead."

"I don't mean you. We're here to pay our respects to
someone else."

Suddenly, David understood.

"Alas, poor Ishi! I knew him, Jill: a fellow of infinite jest,
of most excellent fancy."

"Save the eulogy. He can't hear you."

"Jill, the dead can hear."

"I'm sure Ishi could—if he were here—but he isn't."

"Then what are we doing here?"

Jill stopped walking. "He was here, but he was moved.
But his spirit is still here. I can feel it. I want you to feel it too."

"Why was he moved?"

"He needed to be reunited."

"With his people?"

"With his brain."

With that, Jill turned around and resumed walking.
David followed her across the flat grounds of Olivet Memorial
Park, passing a stone wall that looked like a Roman aqueduct
with the name O-L-I-V-E-T spelled out, one letter per archway.
Beyond the wall and to the left were large sections of graves set

apart by palm trees, stone fountains, and rock gardens. Jill led the way to an office building.

"Normally, we would announce ourselves, but I know where I'm going. First time I was here I filled out a Location Request Form. I fantasized about finding Ishi's ashes in a sealed Pueblo pot under the wide blue sky—but I was directed to the Columbarium, Room F. It's a chapel sort of place—just what you'd expect: carpeted, quiet, air-conditioned. The walls are filled with small, glassed-in niches with a visible urn in each. I checked every wall, but there was no niche labeled 'Ishi.'"

"That surprise you?"

"No. I knew his remains had been removed in 2000. I came here because his ashes had been here for many years. Anyway, I just wanted to point out the place—we don't have to go inside. Actually, I find it depressing.... But when I walk around these gardens and stare at the hills in the distance, I can still feel Ishi's presence—and it's easy for me to remember that he was once here."

David looked about, moved by the serene beauty. "His ashes and brain were reunited? Tell me about that."

"I will, when the time's right. Right now I just want to walk around here with you, thinking about Ishi."

David took her hand.

"One last question," he said. "Where are the ashes and brain buried?"

Jill looked him in the eye. "I tried to find out."

"What happened?"

"Some nasty son of a bitch threatened to kill me."

Chapter 12

The Upper World

Ishi spent his last five years in a museum that was part of the University of California, Berkeley. Mostly, he busied himself as a janitor and Stone Age Indian in residence, sharing his Yahi-Yana life skills, language, and mythos with the university anthropologists, most notably Alfred Kroeber and Thomas Waterman. When Ishi wasn't sweeping floors, flint-knapping, or chanting his tribal songs, stories, and prayers, he often walked about the university hospital, visiting the sick and injured, dispensing looks of gentleness and sympathy that spoke more than words. According to an unsubstantiated story, Ishi one day wandered into a surgical theater or morgue and saw doctors dissecting cadavers on marble slabs. He witnessed a half-dozen naked humans, each gutted like a deer carcass, disembodied organs lying about, festooned with bloody viscera. He was shaken, horrified. He knew white men could be maniacally murderous, but this? This was unconscionable. This was filthy desecration. He imagined his dying ancestors shinnying up a rope that reached through the sky to the Upper World. Ishi begged his white friends Kroeber and Waterman, and his best friend Saxton Pope (surgeon, and head of the medical college) to protect his deceased body against any such degrading sacrilege that would prevent his spirit from climbing through the sky to join his ancestors.

Illness, Death

It has been speculated that many more Native American Indians died as a result of exposure to communicable Western disease than from violent persecution. Even if Ishi had been young, virile, and in peak health, he might not have lived many years among the whites. As it happened, he was around fifty, hungry and dehydrated, when he stumbled into the town of Oroville, California, on August 29, 1911. By the time he was first brought to San Francisco (October 4, 1911), he suffered from chills and fever. Though he recovered and regained some of his lost weight, his installation into his new museum home put him in contact with thousands of potential, germ-carrying visitors. His many visits to the University Hospital (where there was a particularly high risk of infection) likely sealed his fate.

In November, Ishi was hospitalized for a respiratory infection and tested for tuberculosis. The tests were negative. In December, Ishi was hospitalized for bronchopneumonia. Photos and casts were taken of his feet, the beginning of a comprehensive anatomical accounting (*qua* racial profiling, which appears to have begun with his lower extremities and would end five years later with the making of his deathmask and the removal of his brain).

For the first nine months of 1912, Ishi enjoyed solid health, fulfilling his janitorial duties and continuing to demonstrate his arrow-making and fire-building skills to the public. In September, Ishi was hospitalized with abdominal pain and treated by Dr. Saxton Pope, who would soon become his close friend and primary medical chronicler, preserving for posterity all medical and anatomical information relevant to the "last wild Indian in North America."

Other than a bout of back pain in May 1913, Ishi's health remained uneventful for another year. In fact, in May 1914, Pope conducted a complete clinical history of Ishi, noting "No premonition of Illness." That summer Ishi was well enough to guide Pope, Kroeber, and Waterman to Deer Creek, Ishi's former home territory, about 20 miles due north of Chico. In December 1914, Ishi was hospitalized for 62 days. In early 1915 came the first diagnosis of tuberculosis. Pope noted Ishi's cough, painful abdomen, and his inability to tolerate food and water. Ishi's medical team was sensitive and caring, but it was the beginning of the end for Ishi. In March 1916, Ishi was hospitalized for the last time. Not long after, he suffered a large pulmonary hemorrhage. Pope administered a large dose of morphine to ease Ishi's pain. On March 25, 1916, Ishi died.

Chapter 13

Old Friends

Jill drove instinctively, without the aid of a GPS device. For someone who sometimes seemed lost in life, she knew exactly where she was going when she was behind the wheel.

"I have a question," David said, about a half hour after leaving Colma.

"You don't have to go to the bathroom, do you?"

"No, I peed in the cemetery."

"Okay. What's your question?"

Actually, David had two questions. First: *Why'd you tell the police I was your common-law husband?* He thought it might have been a clever ruse to get her out of Bellevue. He also thought her response might open a can of worms. He kept that question to himself.

"We headed straight to Chico?"

Jill smiled. She knew David was roiled with issues he found hard to discuss. She liked that.

"We're going to meet some friends of mine, pick up some goodies at a farmer's market, and then we're back on the road."

"When do we reach Chico?"

"Tomorrow."

"Tomorrow?"

"That's the day after today."

David didn't want his next question to betray too much emotion.

"Where we staying tonight?"

"It's a surprise. Don't be such a scaredy-cat."

David hoped his silence would be interpreted as cool, not sulky.

Jill looked confidently focused. Her left elbow rested on the armrest, her right wrist on top of the wheel. Her red Miata was ripping eighty, windows down, warm air rushing through her hair. She put on the radio…. An hour later, she exited Route 80. Pulling off the highway, David saw a large sign: University of California, Davis.

"This where we going?"

"Yup. I taught a screenwriting course here. My name was fading in Hollywood, but I was still a draw for college writing workshops, panel discussions, stuff like that. A friend of mine runs the film department. I got him the job. Two other friends work here too, as adjuncts."

"You are well connected."

"Used to be. Consider this my comeback tour."

"Who's the friend who runs the film department?"

"Glad you asked," she said, shutting off the radio. "Remember the bastard Elliot who ruined my film and destroyed my life?"

David wasn't sure what tone to take. "Yeah, I remember."

"How much did I tell you about him?"

David rubbed his chin, a caricature of contemplation. "Hmm. Let's see…. Last I heard, you were deliberating whether to carve out his guts with a pair of knives you bought on eBay, slip him an arsenic mickey, or push a slow-release, radioactive plutonium pill up his ass."

"You've got a good memory."

"I'm a sucker for subtle detail."

"Well, I went with the arsenic."

David recoiled—until he remembered that Elliot was alive and well at the University of California, Davis.

"What happened?" he asked, hesitant but curious.

"We were in Venice … California, maybe eight blocks from the beach, a seedy part of town. I took him to an everything-goes bar called Pirate's Booty to discuss what had happened to the film. He was probably thinking I wanted to clear the air and let bygones-be-bygones, but as soon as he turned his head to get the waiter's attention, I slipped the arsenic into whatever sissy cocktail he was drinking. For about a minute we continued our small talk—I actually had the feeling the bastard was coming on to me—and then I saw the first signs of his ... discomfort. I threw twenty bucks on the table and led him out of the bar to a nearby vacant lot where I'd planned to watch him die."

"Geez."

"Anyway, inside the lot, behind this giant rusted container, he drops to his knees and starts convulsing. I was okay with that. I mean, that was the whole point, to watch him writhe like a poisoned dog—but then he looks up, stares at me, and starts crying."

"Oh god."

"Yeah, well, I didn't expect that. I thought the bastard would just die like a man, choking on his curses."

"What happened?"

Jill drew a deep breath.

"I couldn't take the crying. It brought up all kinds of emotions. I have a big heart."

"You're a regular Mother Theresa."

"Not quite—but thanks."

"So, what happened?"

"I had parked nearby. You know—quick getaway thing. So I ran to the car and drove it back to the lot—got out, managed to drag him to the car and shove him in the back seat, then drove like hell to the hospital in Marina Del Rey. As soon as I pulled up, I saw some orderlies out front and told them my friend had just collapsed. They immediately took him from me and asked me to go inside to fill out some paperwork. As soon as they turned their heads, I took off."

Jill drove slowly, skirting the campus, headed for the downtown area. She made a left turn on Second Street and parked right in front of the Varsity Theater.

"We're here."

It sounded to David like she had finished her story.

"Uh, hold on. You got some 'splaining to do."

Jill sat very still, staring through the windshield.

"When I left the hospital I drove home and went straight to my bedroom. I closed the blinds, lay down on top of the covers, and just stared at the ceiling. I knew the police were on their way. I just lay there, waiting for the banging on the door. My life was over. I wanted to die."

David pictured her alone in a darkened room and wanted to hug her.

"I guess I fell asleep. When I woke up, the room was still dark, but I could see sunlight outlining my blinds. I didn't move. I just lay there, staring at the ceiling until I really had to pee. When my bladder was about to burst I hobbled to the bathroom and collapsed on the toilet. I just sat there, peeing, my head down, my face buried in my hands. I didn't want to see anything. I didn't want anyone to see me. Eventually, I stood up, flushed the toilet, brushed my teeth without looking in the mirror, and went into the kitchen. The thought of eating made me queasy, so I went back to bed. I lay there for hours. I watched the bright outline around my closed blinds grow dark. More hours passed and I started thinking that I had escaped, like all was forgiven or forgotten, or had somehow passed unnoticed. And then the phone rang. I didn't answer. I let it ring and ring but it was driving me crazy so I finally answered. *Hello?* ... It was Elliot."

At this point Jill was crying freely. Without bothering to wipe her tears, she turned to face David.

"He was home. He was okay. But he was crying. 'Thank you. Thank you. Thank you,' he kept saying. I didn't know what he meant. I didn't know which end was up, so I just said, 'You're welcome.' And then I could hear him crying really hard, like blubbering. 'I'm so sorry,' he repeated, over and over. And then he said: 'You saved my life.'"

David's jaw dropped.

Jill continued: "I know you have questions, but I can only tell you what I know—or what I guess, because he never really explained much. He knows he ruined my film. He knows it was his fault and he's really truly sorry. I'm unclear about the poison part. I mean, I don't know if he knows what I did. I don't know if the doctors told him what made him sick. Maybe they told him about the arsenic. Maybe they didn't. If they knew, I think they would have notified the police. Maybe the doctors told him but maybe he said it was an accident. Maybe he said he'd been suicidal, but now he's fine. I don't know what he said. In my heart, I think he knows what I did. And he knows he was a minute from death—and that I saved his life. I think he thinks we're even—better than even—like we're special friends forever.... No one else knows about this—except you."

This last bit made David uncomfortable. He could feel another of Jill's hooks pierce his hide and tug him closer.

Jill continued: "Because of all that had happened, he was a wreck. He lost his job at the studio and was unemployed for a year. He was such a sad case. I felt like I owed him. So I made a few phone calls and got him a job as an instructor in the film department here at Davis. And he's done really well. I think he's like head of the department or something. Anyway, I think he's happy."

"So, we stopping by for a friendly visit because he's on the way?"

"Not exactly. You need to meet him. He's our producer."

"Producer?"

"That's the guy who works with the screenwriter, hires the director, supervises casting, oversees production—"

"I know what a producer does."

"Well, he's ours. The three of us are partners."

David drew a deep breath. "I need a drink."

"You don't drink."

"Then please get me a coffee—strong."

Jill got out of the tiny Miata and stretched. David did the same, then walked around the car and stood next to Jill. Jill touched his hand and spoke:

"I think you'll like Elliot. He's not a stupid misogynist like I first thought. He's actually quite bright and sensitive. I think he was acting the part of the tough-talking Hollywood exec when we first met. It was his first job as an assistant producer. I think he was nervous and over his head."

"Okay," said David, nodding his head. "I'm following all this. But how did he go from film teacher to being your producer?"

"Our producer."

"Our producer."

Jill smiled, but it quickly faded.

"After you and I were done with our Woodstock thing, you went back to your wife, and I went back to California. I was really lonely. My girlfriend Alysha was long gone and I really missed her and her son, who I'd helped raise since he was a baby." Jill's eyes flooded with tears. "Every day was empty. I wasn't getting any script offers. I wasn't teaching. I had nothing. I just wanted *something*—and when that didn't happen, I just wanted to get away. I'd read about this small Indian-owned casino up north, near Chico, and decided to go there. I figured I'd gamble and drink myself shit-faced and no one would know or care. So that's what I did.... So, one day I'm drinking house gin and pumping dollar coins into this bullshit Indian-themed slot machine when this beefy guy holding a big plastic tub filled with coins takes the seat next to me. I'm the only person in that section and he sits next to me. And I'm thinking *Oh, Jesus—just screw off.* I could tell he was an Indian, not from his clothes—they were more cowboy than Indian—but he had a face like the guy on the old buffalo nickel. I just prayed he wouldn't speak to me. Anyway, as he's settling in to gamble, he puts a book on the floor next to his stool, and I see it's *Nobody's Fool* by Richard Russo, a favorite of mine, and suddenly it's like I want this guy to talk to me because he suddenly seemed interesting and there was no one else on the planet for me to talk to. But he doesn't say a word to me. He completely ignores me. Just starts pumping coins into the machine—and then, bingo! He hits a jackpot. Just like that, his machine starts flashing lights and ringing bells and these two casino goons come over and tell him he's won a thousand dollars. They give him this special souvenir coin and a receipt to collect his money when he's ready. I look at him and say 'Congrats.' And he just says, 'Thanks' and bends down to pick up the book. And I say, 'How do you like the book?' And he says, 'I love it. You read it?' And I say, 'Yeah. I loved it too.' And then he looks at his watch and says, 'Join me for lunch? I'm buying.' And that's how I met Simon. He's the one who first told me about Ishi. He knows a lot about him. He says he's part Maidu and part Wintu and part related to Ishi. He's really proud of his heritage. One night when we were both really drunk, he told me about the living Yahi. I could tell he was serious. But I think he regrets telling me."

"Why? What did he say?"

"He said if I ever told anyone I'd be killed."

"What'd you say?"

"I said, 'What's the big deal? Who cares?' He said, 'It's a very big deal, and I care.'"

David looked at her tenderly. "Do you think he would hurt you?"

"I think he likes me a lot. So yeah, he would hurt me."

David drew a deep breath and thought of his next question.

"Did you tell anyone?"

"You mean other than you?"

David's heart jumped. He realized he'd been ensnared in yet another situation that involved Jill—one that could prove very dangerous.

"Yeah, besides me."

"Duh, I told Elliot, of course. That's why we're here."

His mind on overload, David begged Jill to spell everything out.

"It's simple," Jill said. "When Simon told me the story about Ishi, I was fascinated. When he told me about the removal of Ishi's brain, I hung on his every word. When he told me how the brain had been lost, rediscovered, and then reunited with his body in a secret ceremony, I was enrapt. But when he was drunk and told me about the living Yahi—about a surviving Stone Age tribe living secretly just twenty miles from Highway 99, I knew I had to make the movie. I knew this was my chance—possibly my last—to make a statement film that would get me back on Hollywood's A-list. But I knew I couldn't do it alone. And that's when I went to see Elliot."

"But he was out of Hollywood. At that point he was just a college film instructor."

"Yeah, we'd both been kicked to the curb. But we have complementary skills and viable contacts—enough, at the very least, to create a small-budget film that a studio might be willing to distribute or, possibly, redevelop into a big-budget feature. Either way, we're back in the game, which is what we both want."

"You have the funding to make even a small, indie film?" David asked.

Jill smiled brightly. "Here's the secret sauce: Elliot runs the university's annual film festival. That why we're here today—because he's busy preparing for this year's premiere. The festival shows all kinds of short, student-produced films. Elliot works closely with the departments of Theatre and Dance, Art Studio, Design, Cinema, and Digital Media. That's a lot of resources—equipment and human labor—that can be donated or volunteered to help develop our project."

David was impressed with the apparent reasonableness of Jill's plan.

"But why do you need me?"

Jill smiled. "Two reasons. One: It will take a couple years to get the film made. If you start writing now, or at least start taking notes and sketching ideas, you can probably finish the book within a year. Once it's published, Elliot and I will use our contacts to put a spotlight on you and your book so we can create a buzz. Then we start leaking the news about the film to come. And we build on that."

David nodded. "It's a plan. What's your second reason?"

"I need you in my life. You complete me."

David took a step back. Jill's declaration frightened him. He looked at Jill. She looked much younger than her sixty years. Her pixie hairdo was hip; her jeans were tight and stylish. Hiking and Pilates had kept her slender and toned. She was a sexy, smart, impressive lady. But she wasn't Allison, another smart, impressive lady, who happened to be his wife and mother of his children.

"Don't worry," Jill said, as if reading his thoughts. "I'm not going to ruin your happy hacienda. I'd just like to borrow you from time to time."

David felt relieved, and slightly excited.

"Also," Jill added, "I give as good as I get."

David look perplexed. "Not sure I understand."

"I mean, you're good for me, but I'm also good for you. You need me—whether you know it or not."

David's expression was noncommittal, so Jill explained:

"I remember your story of the Potato Cave, the Indian mound you discovered in the woods when you were a boy. I know how that experience motivated you to go on that archaeological dig in Chico. I know how you first learned about Ishi and tried to write about him. You see, I understand you. Perhaps even better than your wife because I'm not lost in your routines and trivia. I know you need this adventure as much as I do. We both have good reasons for doing what we do—and for doing it together."

Just then the theater doors opened and Elliot appeared.

"Hi—saw you through the lobby window!"

Elliot Pence had the neat, stylish clothing and careful grooming that suggested to David that he might be gay. He approached Jill with open arms, embraced her, and kissed her cheek. Then he left her and moved towards David. "You must be David," he said, moving inside David's proffered handshake for a warm hug. "Nice to meet you, partner."

"Aww, group hug!" said Jill, throwing an affectionate arm around each man's shoulders. David was flattered by the attention but uncomfortable with the public scrum.

Elliot looked at Jill and then David. "I know I promised to join you two for dinner, but I just can't get away. So much stress!"

"Don't worry, honey," Jill consoled, rubbing his back. "Where are your helpers?"

As if on cue, the theater doors opened again and an attractive, fortysomething couple emerged. They were both theatrically tall and attired in scarves and boots.

Jill took the lead: "Kenneth Voorhorst and Gloria Messing, this is David Grossman."

"Hi, David, so nice to meet you," they both said, taking turns shaking David's hand.

"Congratulations on your novel," said Kenneth.

"We know about the Ishi film," said Gloria. "Count on our help!"

They both looked familiar but David couldn't quite place them.

"I hate to do this," said Elliot, "but we really have to get back inside. The festival opens next week and we have so much to do. We'll all get together soon!"

Hugs and kisses and promises of fellowship and great success.

David and Jill watched their three friends return inside the theater.

"Perfect," said Jill as soon as the doors closed and they were alone. "I just wanted you to meet them. Now we can have dinner by ourselves and just relax."

David followed Jill back to the car. As they walked, his eyes on her swishing ass, he remembered following her west on Houston Street, all the way to Varick Street, where she approached a nondescript building whose door was suddenly pushed open from within by a tall thin man wearing a deathly white complexion and blood-spattered shirt. The man loomed over her, smiled slyly, then walked straight into a waiting cab. David remembered noticing a movement in a second–floor window, looking up, and seeing there a tall woman wearing a white gown and giant beehive hairdo, who looked like she'd been jealously watching the tall man in the bloodied shirt. David remembered rushing away towards Penn Station to return as quickly as he could to his Long Island home.

Chapter 14

Mr. and Mrs. David Gross

Jill and David continued their journey to Oroville. That was Jill's surprise. She knew David would be fascinated to see the town where Ishi had surrendered himself into white custody.

When they arrived, they both were tired and hungry and agreed it would be best to find a local motel and a quiet restaurant and leave the exploration of the town for the next day. Jill volunteered to pay for the room. David paid for dinner. Both paid in cash, minimizing their paper trails and digital footprints. (David was married and didn't want the world to know his itinerary. Jill had begun asking questions about Ishi's brain and reburial, which she knew had not gone unnoticed. Moving forward, she knew she must be more tactful and inconspicuous.)

When they returned to the motel after dinner, they stopped by the office so Jill could ask about the local farmer's market, which they intended to visit the next morning. While she and the night manager chatted, David happened to see the names Jill had registered in the Guest Book: "Mr. and Mrs. David Gross." David's response was conflicted: half smile, half grimace.

When Jill's conversation ended, David accompanied her back to their room. While they walked, Jill's phone rang and she answered it immediately.

"Hi. I'm fine.... Busy day.... I know you're bored. Just hang in there.... I don't know when, but soon.... Sure, he's right here." She handed her phone to David. "It's Bill, your brother-in-law."

David took the phone reluctantly, as if he'd been caught in *flagrante delicto,* which is how he felt. "Everything's great.... Yeah, small world.... See you tomorrow," he said, ending the conversation quickly and handing the phone back to Jill.

Jill blithely dropped the phone into her shoulder bag and took David's arm.

Oroville

The next morning, following their very satisfying continental breakfast, Jill and David happily greeted the new day.

"What's first?" asked David, sliding into the passenger seat.

"The Devil's Dip."

"What's that?"

"The ride of your life."

"I thought that was last night."

Jill patted his left thigh and smiled. "You'll see."

The morning was bright and sunny. About a mile from the motel Jill turned onto a hilly backroad that reminded David of his boyhood summers in the Catskills. Jill drove for about ten minutes. Approaching the crest of the highest hill, she pulled over to the right but kept the engine running. She turned her head to speak to David.

"When boys in this town get their driver's license they take a girlfriend to this spot. It's a rite of passage."

"What do they do?"

"They spit in the Devil's face. Ready?"

David nodded.

Jill floored the accelerator. The red Miata took off like a rocket, its sudden propulsion lifting the car above the crest. For a split-second of airborne thrill, David saw the tops of the hillside trees and the blue sky above—and then felt the car land with a jarring, heavy thump. Jill pulled off the road, near a small grove of spindly trees and bushes.

They both sat still, staring at each other as if in post-coital wonder.

"That was a leap of faith," said Jill. "Thank you."

David remained still, waiting for his revved heart to slow down.

For a while they both were silent.

"If only ..." said Jill, her sentence hanging in the air.

"If only what?"

"If only you had taken me to Woodstock."

David was surprised. He thought this old argument had been settled long ago.

"Yes," he said, "that would have been wonderful."

"I might have married you if you had taken me."

This was a new and unnerving twist.

"Married me? We were kids. We were barely boyfriend and girlfriend."

Jill looked at him intently. "I knew you were special. When you failed me, I lost faith in you."

David chose his words carefully.

"I was just a boy."

"You were entering college."

"I was sixteen. I didn't know anything."

"Still ..."

David paused to order his thoughts.

"I'm sorry I disappointed you. I really am. But we were kids. The summer was over. You lived in Brooklyn. I lived in the Bronx. We went our separate ways. Life is like that."

"I know."

Jill sat very still, staring through the windshield. "I brought you here for a reason," she said, barely above a whisper.

"You mean right here, this spot?"

"Yes."

She got out of the car and stretched. David did the same.

The landscape was semi-arid, a palette of yellow-green. All was quiet. The wind, the crickets, the birds, all stifled by the heat.

Jill walked over to a cement slab, a subtle blemish among the tall, wispy grasses.

"This is all that's left of the killing floor."

"The killing floor?"

"From the slaughterhouse. Ishi was discovered over there, where the corral used to be." She pointed to an empty stretch of wild grasses. "August 29, 1911."

David stared at the cement slab. "*Slaughterhouse* seems painfully ironic, given the attempted annihilation of the Yahi."

Jill stood by his side, looking down at the killing floor. "Switch *annihilation* to *holocaust* and you double-down on the horror."

David's mind flashed scenes of barbed wire camps, cattle cars, and mounds of naked, skeletal bodies.

"Who discovered him?" he asked, still staring at the cement slab.

Jill had a faraway look, as if searching through mental archives for the beginning of the story. When she was ready, she turned to him. "There was a boy who used to hang around the slaughterhouse and do odd jobs. He was walking to the corral to get two horses on a halter for the meat wagon. When he got close, he heard the four cattle dogs barking and saw a man hunkered down by the corral fence. He thought it was a Mexican. He ran back to get one of the butchers: 'Ad! Ad!' There's a man here! By the corral!' The butcher, a guy named Adolph Kessler, ran outside in his long johns and cowboy boots. As he approached the corral, he picked up what they call a hog gambrel—an oak two-by-four used to lift a dead pig by its feet."

"Oh no."

"Meanwhile, the dogs attacked Ishi."

"No!"

"Ishi got away, but the dogs treed him up a big black oak." Jill looked about. "That black oak might still be around."

David looked about—but he couldn't tell one tree from another. "What happened?"

"A couple more men came from the slaughterhouse and shooed the dogs away. When the dogs were no longer a threat, Ishi slid down the tree and collapsed on the ground. Kessler, the man with the gambrel, was about to strike him—"

"Stop! I can't take it."

"It's okay. He didn't hit him. He saw that Ishi was an old man and he took pity."

"Oh lord. What happened next?"

"The butchers discussed what to do. Figuring the old man was a Mexican, they started speaking Spanish to him."

"How'd that go?"

"Apparently, Ishi didn't know enough Spanish to carry on polite conversation."

"Did he answer?"

"I don't think so. But when the men approached for a closer look, they saw that Ishi had a small piece of wood through his septum."

"What kind of wood?"

"What do you care?"

"It's a good detail."

"I think it was yellow pine. But it might have been bay or juniper."

"Nice touch. Go on."

"The men also saw that in each of Ishi's earlobes was an ornamental, knotted piece of buckskin, so they figured he wasn't Mexican."

"What'd they say?"

"They said: 'I think we got us a wild Indian.'"

"Those boys were sharp."

"In any case, they did the right thing. They phoned the sheriff, who locked Ishi in jail for his own good."

"Protective custody?"

"I guess. I'm sure there were some yahoos around who might have hurt Ishi. It wasn't so many years since the government paid big bounties for Indian scalps and heads."

David remained silent for several long seconds. "I can't imagine what Ishi was thinking. He's emaciated, he's exhausted, and they put him in a cage. He must have been scared out of his mind."

"Not exactly. I mean, I'm sure he was exhausted, and he was probably hungry and dehydrated. But he wasn't exactly starved. That's what the history books want us to believe. It makes it easier to forgive the whites if we see them as saving and nurturing Ishi."

"Still, locked in a cage, he must have been frightened."

"Not the way you're thinking. Ishi had been on the run his entire life. He'd seen his people—*his own family*—murdered and slowly starved. He knew he couldn't help them anymore. The only thing he could do was to protect their future. And the only way to do that was to sacrifice himself."

"But how did that save the Yahi?"

"Because he lied. His story about being the last Yahi was a lie. He knew if he told the world there were no more Yahi to hunt and kill, or even to study, the whites would call off their dogs. He convinced the world he was the last Yahi."

"But he wasn't."

"No. There weren't many left.... And some were unhealthy, crippled ... probably suffering from a lack of nutrition .... I don't know.... They weren't the strong Yahi of yesteryear."

"But they could survive."

"Yes. A few were young enough and healthy enough to procreate. That was the basis of Ishi's plan. He sacrificed himself to take the target off his people."

"But how would his people survive? How would they remain a secret?"

"Ishi believed the Yahi could survive by hiding in caves, fishing and foraging at night; even then, only under a weak moon, minimizing the possibility of being seen. Over time, his people would grow strong enough, numerous enough, to be a viable tribe once more. That was Ishi's vision. He thought it would take one hundred summers for his tribe to regenerate its strength and numbers."

"One hundred years," mulled David. "When did Ishi die?"

"1916."

"It's 2016. Almost one hundred years."

"Precisely. That's why we're here. The time has come for the Yahi to rise!"

Jill reached into her shoulder bag and took out her old CD player. With the push of a single button, Ishi's chanting voice carried over the grasses where the corral and slaughterhouse once stood. Jill reached into her bag again, this time withdrawing two acorn-filled gourds. Handing one to David, she bent forward and began a kind of buffalo shuffle, waving her shoulders, neighing her head, and stomping her feet to an acorn-rattled rhythm. David shook his own gourd but didn't move—other than turn his head to see if people were watching. But Jill's dancing fervor was infectious and he soon joined her spirited tribute to the Yahi dead—and to all the living Yahi who mourned them.

Farmer's Market

David and Jill left the Devil's Dip, driving across town to Oroville's outdoor farmer's market. The market was like many others David had visited, and he had little interest in this one. In his view, street vendors and their wares tended to be much alike, despite variations in local influences. But shopping with a woman who wasn't his wife was something new and profoundly titillating and made the expedition unique.

For her part, Jill seemed completely at ease walking about the market with David. She bought dried apricots and plums, walnuts and almonds, and several Clingstone peaches. When David pointed to a sign that read "Brooklyn Bridge Bagels," they both squealed like children.

In one corner of the market ethnic foods were available as hot meals.

"Do you like Indian food?" Jill asked.

"Do you mean Indian food or Indian food?" asked David.

"What do you think I mean?"

"I don't know. That's why I asked."

"I mean Indian food. Like naan bread and dal."

"I like Indian food, but I don't care for the other Indian food."

Jill shook her head. "What planet are you from?"

"Uranus."

Jill shook her head and giggled. "How old are you?"

"Sixty-three."

"You act eleven."

"Part of my boyish charm."

Jill hooked her arm with his and they continued walking together through the outdoor market.

Chapter 15

Bait and Switch

The prospect of visiting Chico filled David with pointed nostalgia. His father, dead twenty years, had worked one hundred extra hours of factory overtime to send him to Chico State College for a summer of archaeology. In one of the college's dormitories David had lost his virginity. In another building he'd discovered the story of Ishi. When the summer program ended, but while still in California, David had begun describing his youthful adventures in a novel he'd titled *Chico,* hand-writing his florid sentences on the blue-ruled pages of a schoolboy's spiral notebook. But he'd never been able to finish it, lacking the sophistication to develop a compelling narrative arc. The notebook was preserved in a box on a high closet shelf of his home bedroom, along with dozens of other nostalgic keepsakes.

Driving north on Highway 99, David saw a large sign that said "CHICO Welcomes You." He sat up in his seat, excited about revisiting his past.

"We going straight to the hotel?" he asked.

Jill kept her eyes on the road. "I've been meaning to tell you about that."

"What's that?"

"I think you should manage your expectations."

"How so? It's a hotel and casino—but modest, right?"

"Let's just say it's not the kind of place you'd find Frank Sinatra."

"Because he's dead?"

"Smart ass. I mean it's not exactly a destination for high rollers."

"What's it like?"

"Okay. Imagine a palatial casino with glitzy gaming rooms, cabaret lounges, four-star restaurants, fitness room, spa—and you're thinking Vegas."

"What should I be thinking?"

"Think Motel 6 with a roulette wheel, poker room, and some video slot machines."

"That's it?"

"Well, there's bingo. Indians love their bingo. And there's a bar—at least five stools—and you can eat there. Constant, the cook, will whip something up if you ask her nicely. And there's a pool—not great, but there's water in it."

"Oy."

"Hey, don't go glum on me. I never promised you Caesar's Palace. I said this would be an adventure—and that you would have material for your next book—and that it would make you famous. So, just sit back and enjoy the ride."

David shrugged. "Okay. Got it. But my question stands: We going straight to the hotel?"

"Actually it's just north of Chico."

"How far north?"

"About thirty miles."

"Thirty miles! Is that still called Chico?"

"Not exactly. The town is Los Molinos."

"I thought we were staying in Chico."

"I don't think I ever said that. I said we are going to Chico—and we are. Actually, we're almost there. But we're staying in Los Molinos."

"Why?"

"Quit whining. Los Molinos is only a half hour from Chico. And it's closer to the Ishi Wilderness—and that's where the Yahi are living."

David was silent for several seconds.

"Anything in Los Molinos worth seeing?"

"There's a weigh station."

"*Away* from civilization."

"Don't be snarky."

David felt like he was being played.

"This is a classic bait and switch. How the hell did you sell Bill on this? I'm surprised he didn't shoot you."

"He wanted to. But I drew first."

Jill reached into her shoulder bag and pulled out a gun.

"Meet Walther."

"Walter?"

"No, Walther. Pocket 9mm. Small but packs a wallop."

Dicey Situation

David recoiled. He'd never seen an unholstered gun so close to his face.

"What's that for?"

"Safety."

"Better safe than sorry?"

"Better safe than dead," Jill said, returning the gun to her shoulder bag.

For a while David remained silent. Finally: "What are we doing that's so dangerous? What are you preparing for?"

"I'm preparing for all contingencies ... and for the unexpected: someone lurking in the shadows."

"That's comforting."

"Look, I'm not going to lie to you. The situation is dicey. There are people who want to keep the Yahi story a secret. There are people who want to tell the world. People on both sides have passionate opinions."

"How passionate? Would they die for their beliefs?"

"They would kill for their beliefs."

Chapter 16

Chico Redux

Jill and David agreed that they didn't need to tour Chico. It would suffice to visit the campus area and then have a late lunch before pushing on to Los Molinos.

They left the car in the parking lot of University Inn, right off Esplanade. From there they crossed Sol-Wil-Le-No Avenue and followed the Big Chico Creek into the college.

"I don't remember the creek," said David.

"How could you not remember? It runs through the middle of the campus."

"I don't remember it."

"That would be like living in Manhattan and not remembering Fifth Avenue."

"Sue me. I don't remember."

They followed the creek to the college and wended their way throughout the campus. Each time they passed a building, Jill called out its name and David shrugged, indicating he had no recollection of it. *Shasta Hall, Bidwell Hall,* and *Butte Hall* sounded vaguely familiar to him, but he wasn't sure.

"I didn't go to this school."

"You lied?" Jill asked.

"No. This just isn't the same place. Everything is new and different."

"It's been a long time."

"Forty-five years. I was here 45 years ago. I was 17."

"That's the summer after you and I met. Do you remember that summer?"

"I do."

"Do you remember watching the Moon landing on my porch and pinky-swearing with me?"

"I do."

"Do you remember lying on my backyard grass while we watched the clouds and listened to the entire *Tommy* opera?"

"I do."

"Do you remember the first morning of Woodstock, when those hippie pilgrims marched right past our colony?"

"I do."

For thirty seconds they continued walking, both lost in nostalgic reverie.

"Kendall Hall," said Jill.

The scene brought David to a halt. Before him was a large, two-story brick building with decorative columns, three arches, and a Spanish tile roof. Above the central arch was an impressive dome. David gasped. He remembered walking through the central arch on a hot summer day and entering a large rotunda.

"Is there an Ishi Museum here ... or at least an Ishi exhibit?"

"I don't know," said Jill. "Let's go inside and see."

David took a few hesitant steps forward. Chiseled above the central arch was the school's motto: "Today Decides Tomorrow." David stopped suddenly. "I don't want to go inside."

"Why?"

Into his mind flashed a scene from the summer dig of 1970: Pointing to an excavated landscape and mounds of piled earth, Professor Muller was discussing the essential conundrum of his profession: "Archaeology is the only science that destroys itself."

David stood still, shaking his head.

"What's wrong?" Jill asked.

"I don't want to go inside," David repeated. "I want to remember what I remember, just as I remember it."

Jill gave him a quizzical look. "What if your memory isn't accurate?"

"Then I'd rather not know."

Wiley Calhoun

"I'm getting hungry," David said, turning away from Kendall Hall.

"Me too," said Jill. "I know a great place. My friend Wiley owns it. I want you to meet him."

On Ivy Street, just a few blocks from the campus, David saw the sign: *Chaps & Scraps.*

"Most inclusive place I know," said Jill, pushing open the saloon-style door.

"Inclusive?" asked David. "What's that mean? They welcome every weirdo in northern California?"

"You know," said Jill, "beneath your snarky exterior is some serious fear and loathing."

David was about to respond when Jill pointed across the room. "There's Wiley."

David was surprised to see a black man. A very, very large black man.

"Big guy."

"Looks like he's put on some weight. I bet he weighs 400 pounds."

"Whoa! How does he move about?"

"Best soft-shoe dancer in the West."

"You're kidding."

"No, for real. Wiley is amazingly light on his feet—considering."

"Considering his tonnage."

"Don't be cruel. I love Wiley. And you will too. And you will be impressed. He has a big heart, quick wit, and even quicker feet. I bet he could beat you in a race."

"I doubt it. I still play tennis. I'm still pretty quick."

"Well, I bet he could beat you in a forty-foot race."

"I think you mean forty yards. That's the standard."

"No, I'm pretty sure he couldn't run that far. But forty feet—like if he saw a bus about to pull away and was less than forty feet away—he'd be banging on the door before the driver turned the wheel."

"Impressive."

"You have no idea. Wiley is a force of nature."

As if to prove her point, Wiley suddenly stood before them, as if he hadn't bothered to sashay across the room. "Jill! May the Schwartz be with you!" he said, lifting her up as if she were a light bouquet. "Who's your friend?" he added, still holding her aloft.

Jill waited for her feet to touch the ground before responding: "Wiley Calhoun, this is David Grossman."

Wiley glared at David. "The one who left you standing at Woodstock's altar?"

Suddenly, David feared for his life.

"We've gotten past that, Wiley. I love him and want you to love him too."

Wiley moved forward and enveloped David in a prolonged embrace.

"I hope you two are staying to eat," said Wiley.

"Yes—we're both famished," said Jill.

"Great. Let me get you a table."

When Wiley was gone, David asked: "May the *Schwartz* be with you?"

"Wiley used to be an actor. Mostly commercials and voice-overs. We met in L.A. and became best buds."

"Don't tell me he's Jewish."

"No," Jill said, smiling. "But he's like family to me and he knows my story."

"I guess he knows you were Jill Schwartz before you became Jill Black."

"Oh yeah, but that's just name, rank, and serial stuff. He really knows my story: why I came to California, how I met Alysha, how *The Knish Man* put me on the map."

"And the really personal stuff?"

Jill paused. "He knows about the drinking. He knows about Elliot. And he knows all about you."

David felt spotlighted, compromised. "Why do you tell people about me? That's not right. It's indiscreet."

"I'm sorry. But sometimes I'm very lonely and angry. I need someone to talk to. I'm not married."

At that moment, Wiley returned with a pair of menus. "Please follow me!" he said with great flair.

After they were seated, had given their lunch order, and were alone once more, David said: "I'm sorry."

"Me too."

Jill fiddled with her knife and fork. "One more thing," she said. "Wiley knows about our Ishi plan."

David took a long drink of water, put down the glass, and then slowly wiped his mouth with a napkin. "Why did you tell him? Why are you telling so many people?"

"Because it's dangerous ... and sometimes I'm afraid. That's why I involved Bill. And that's why I told Wiley."

David knew he wouldn't be much good at protecting her and was secretly glad that Bill and Wiley were on their team.

"Can you really count on Wiley?"

"Honey, I'm counting on all of you. And Wiley's case is special."

"Because he's so imposing?"

"Because he's only a half hour away and has a big force behind him."

"That butt is pretty formidable."

"Stop it. I'm serious. Wiley is the president of the GBBB."

"I'm afraid to ask."

"The Gay Black Bikers Brigade. It's a motorcycle club. They meet here once a month."

David stared at her in a comic show of open-mouthed horror.

"Gay. Black. Bikers. Brigade…. That's a Jewish boy's worst nightmare. It's like the third, fourth, and fifth circles of hell rolled into one."

"Don't be petty. Oh look, here's our food."

Leather-Vested Heart

When they had finished eating, Jill waved Wiley to their table.

"That was wonderful, honey, what do we owe you?"

Wiley pressed his hand over Jill's, which was holding her wallet.

"Nothing, my love. If I live to be a hundred, I'll never be able to repay your many kindnesses."

"Oh, Wiley!"

"My love!" he said, pressing his huge splayed hand over his leather-vested heart.

David thought he saw Wiley's eyes well with feelings.

Wiley bowed his head so he could nearly whisper to Jill: "Call me if you need anything. I mean it. If you can't reach me, try this number." He jotted a number on a napkin. "His name is Ralph."

"Ooooh! Someone new. Good luck."

"Luck has nothing to do with it," Wiley said, as he verily danced away to another table.

David considered several comments, none of them charitable—so he bit his tongue.

Chapter 17

The Great Central Valley

With Chico in her rearview mirror, Jill continued north on Highway 99, passing farms, fruit and nut orchards, and even a few rice fields.

"This is Main Street," she said.

To David it looked like a freeway.

"Main Street?"

"That's what they call Highway 99. California's Main Street."

David was silent.

"Want to know why?"

David shrugged. "Why?"

"A lot of the country's fruits and vegetables are grown here and moved to market on this road."

"Duly noted," said David.

Jill smiled. She knew David was annoyed. She knew he hated having his expectations continually manipulated.

For several minutes they rode in silence, passing miles of planted fields and green pastures.

"They call this the Great Central Valley," she said.

David remained silent.

"Want to know why?"

"Why?"

"It runs north-south for more than 400 miles. It was once a great inland sea. The sediment remains make it the largest, most fertile valley on the planet."

David remained sullen. But Jill smiled again. She knew he loved such details and would probably use them in his book about Ishi.

Sierra Spa and Casino Hotel

"We're almost at Los Molinos," said Jill.

"How big a town is it?"

"Don't know. Not very big. It has a post office, a few doctors ... some painters and potters."

"Does it have a used and rare bookshop?" asked David.

"I don't think so."

"A Kosher deli?"

"Highly doubt it."

"Tennis courts?"

"There might be some by the high school."

"How many people all together?"

"Couple thousand."

"I have that many Facebook friends."

Jill didn't respond. She was learning how to handle David.

After a couple minutes, David asked: "We're staying at the Sierra Spa and Casino Hotel?"

"Yes."

"Does the place actually have a spa?"

Jill paused. "I think it's closed. But there's an old bunk bed that Morgan turned into two massage tables. I don't know how comfortable they are."

"That's the spa?"

"I hear Morgan gives a vigorous massage. For an extra fee Morgan will exfoliate your face, rub your legs with oils, or lay hot soothing stones on your back."

"Morgan sounds very talented and accommodating."

"He or she will do whatever you like," said Jill.

"He or she? You never met Morgan?"

"I've met Morgan many times."

"And you don't know if he's a he or she?"

"It's hard to tell ... from my limited experience."

David chewed that cud for a couple minutes.

"We have rooms at the casino?" he asked.

"Yes. We have separate rooms. Of course, your brother-in-law lives there too. So does Constant, Morgan, Simon—the Indian who reads Richard Russo—and my friend Ezra."

"What does Ezra do?"

"He's an amazing guy: surveyor, spelunker, survivalist."

"Wow. And that's just the *s*'s."

Jill laughed. "You won't like him at first. He's not talkative and he's not funny. But he's a rock. And he's the reason we're here."

"Explain."

Just then they passed a sign that read "Welcome to Los Molinos."

"What does *Los Molinos* mean?" asked David.

Jill took a few seconds. "I think it means 'the grinders.'"

David shook his head. "Please, not another word."

Living on the Edge

The highway exit for Los Molinos is roughly equidistant between the Sacramento River to the west and the foothills of the Sierra Nevada to the east. Highway 99 essentially serves as the town's western boundary. On the opposite side of town, Tehama Vina Road serves as the eastern boundary, the last road before the rolling foothills of the Sierra Nevada. At the point where Tehama Vina begins its northwest dogleg, the two-story Sierra Spa and Casino Hotel squats in the afternoon sun. Behind the hotel there is an unnamed and restricted road that leads about a mile and a half west before becoming the Lassen Trail. An old pioneer trail, largely forgotten and rarely traveled, the Lassen Trail stretches twenty miles into the Ishi Wilderness.

Trickle Down

Jill parked in the almost empty hotel parking lot.

"Business is booming," said David.

"Morning is a down time."

"It's afternoon."

"Even worse," said Jill.

David got out and walked towards the trunk.

"Leave your stuff," said Jill. "I want your unencumbered first impressions."

David followed Jill back to the street, where they stood facing the Sierra Spa and Casino Hotel.

"I don't like the look," said David.

"Neither do I," said Jill.

The building was classic adobe but with gleaming steel pilasters and sconces—an odd fusion of Indigenous and Industrial styles. Elderberry and honeysuckle bushes had been planted around the perimeter to soften the stark façade.

"Honestly, anything adobe would seem like a cliché," said David.

"Hard to say *Indian* without saying *Indian*," said Jill.

"Which brings me to my next point," said David. "You said this is an Indian-owned casino, right?"

"That's right."

"Well, I thought most Indians—most *Native Americans*—are relatively poor. How do they get casinos?"

"Individuals do not own casinos," said Jill. "Not even groups of Indians. Only federally recognized Indian tribes can apply for a casino license. It's a question of tribal sovereignty, of government. In fact, no other entity other than a tribe can possess any stake in a casino's ownership."

David paused to gather his thoughts. "If that's the case, where does the money come from? It must cost a fortune to capitalize these casinos, especially the big ones."

"I don't know the financial subtleties," said Jill. "But I know there are layers of lenders."

"Layers?"

"Layers, loopholes, laws … and the rich get richer. It's a billion-dollar business."

"How many billions?" asked David. "Two, three?"

"More like twenty-five to thirty."

"That's big money."

"Yes, but many of the investments don't pay off," said Jill. "Some of the big ones, like Foxwoods, needed a massive restructuring of debt to survive."

"But some casinos are successful, even very successful?"

"Yes, I suppose."

Jill paused to gather her thoughts. "But it's not like a lot of Indians are getting rich. By law, Indian tribes must use their casino profits to promote their tribe's economic development and provide for the general welfare of their members."

"So, some of the profits must trickle down to the hoi polloi."

"Not usually. Most tribes don't distribute per capita gaming revenue to their members. Typically, tribal leaders don't want to hand out cash to their members."

"Oy," said David. "Better to keep wealth and power in the hands of the one percent."

"I'm sure that's what they think. But what they say is that large cash payments would undermine the work ethic of their tribe members."

"Can I say *oy* again?"

"Go for it."

"Oy again."

Countless Manzanitas

Jill smiled and shook her head. "Silly boy. Let's go around to the back."

David followed Jill down the street and around to the rear. With the hotel behind them, out of sight, they had clear views of the Cascade Range to the north and the Sierra Nevada to the east. In every direction, shrubs of evergreen and evergray stretched to the mountain horizon, along with stands of blue oak and box elder, and countless manzanita bushes of variously colored barks and flowers.

Jill seemed particularly moved by the scenery, but her vision was unfocused, aimed at the unseen.

"Somewhere out there Ishi is buried," she said. "Body and brain finally reunited."

David was moved by the scenery and by Jill's passion for Ishi's story.

"Remind me," he said. "Why was Ishi's brain removed in the first place?"

Chapter 18

Ishi's Brain Removed

Alfred Kroeber, head of the Museum of Anthropology at the University of California, Berkeley, was on sabbatical in New York City when he was informed by letter from Edward Gifford, his young associate and acting director of the museum, that Ishi was now certainly dying of advanced pulmonary tuberculosis. Though not unexpected, the news hit Kroeber hard. Not only had he grown personally fond of Ishi, but American anthropological science faced the loss of its greatest living historical resource. Further, the news undoubtedly brought to Kroeber's mind the recent death of his young first wife, Henriette, also ravaged by tuberculosis.

On March 24, 1916, Kroeber wrote to Gifford with instructions regarding the disposition of Ishi's body and estate. He made it clear that Ishi should have a Christian burial like any other friend. He also reiterated his unequivocal opposition to any autopsy, as it would be a gross violation of Ishi's stated wishes and an unnecessary investigation of racial comparative science, a field already fiercely debated. "We propose to stand by our friends," Kroeber famously wrote. "If there is any talk of the interests of science, then say for me that science can go to hell." The letter arrived too late. The autopsy had been performed, the brain removed and preserved in formalin. When Kroeber returned to his museum office, he found on his desk a glass jar containing Ishi's floating brain.

Ishi's Estate

Ishi's body was cremated, along with these of his possessions:

- One of his bows
- Five, steel-pointed arrows
- A basket of corn meal

- Ten pieces of dentalium (tooth-shaped shells)
- A box full of shell bead money (which Ishi had saved)
- A purse full of tobacco
- Three rings
- Some obsidian flakes

Ishi's ashes were placed in a black Pueblo Indian pot, plugged with a smooth plaster. These words were inscribed across the pot's belly: "Ishi, the last Yahi Indian, 1916." The urn was brought to Olivet Memorial Park in Colma, California, and stored in a niche in the Columbarium.

Ishi died leaving $369.52, which went to the Public Administrator, who disbursed the money as follows:

- Floral piece at museum: $7.50
- Funeral and cremation: $150.00
- Niche in columbarium: $40.00
- County tax: $1.00
- Hospital bill: $171.00

Chapter 19

Subtle Motifs

David and Jill crossed the sere ground behind the hotel, returning to the parking lot. There were still only four vehicles in the lot, including a battered pickup truck and the spiffy red Miata. As they approached the car, Jill remotely popped open the trunk. While David gathered his luggage, Jill retrieved the bag of parcels they'd bought at the farmer's market. She then closed the trunk with her free hand. "Let's get you checked into your room," she said, leading the way back to the hotel's main entrance.

Entering the lobby, David was struck by its tasteful decor: a subtle combination of western and Indian motifs. Among the decorative elements were paintings and pottery from local artists and an array of local Indian baskets, strategically placed on plinths and niches all about the room. One wall, painted in the yellows and greens of the Sierra summer, showed a dozen framed photographs of Ishi, all in native loincloth, none in western garb.

Jill led David to the check-in desk. "This should go smoothly," she said.

She was right. Within five minutes, David had his key and was walking to his room, guided by Jill.

They stopped in front of his door, number 219. David was unsure what would happen next.

"Give me the key," said Jill. "Door's a little tricky." He gave her the key and with a practiced twist and push she easily opened the door. Inside, past the ample bathroom to the left and the commodious closet to the right, was a single bed. On the far wall, the curtains were sashed and the blinds raised. Three large windows, like a Renaissance triptych, looked out on the sunny Sierra.

"I need to lie down," said Jill.

David's heart skipped ... but Jill was already backing out of the room. "I'm two doors down, number 221. Knock or call if you need anything."

The door was closing when David asked, "When are we eating?"

David heard Jill's trailing voice. "As soon as you're settled, go to the lobby. Ask where the Cantina is. I'll meet you there in an hour."

Ellie

In the lobby, David asked the hefty young blonde behind the counter how to get to the restaurant. The woman's name was Ellie and she was about eleven years older than her college freshman looks. Smiling warmly, she told David that the hotel's restaurant was "closed for the season" but the bar—La Cantina—was open, and she pointed the way. Because Ellie had smiled so warmly, and because she seemed so happy to answer his question, and because it wasn't yet time to meet with Jill, David decided to dawdle awhile, making small talk. He asked Ellie if she hailed from the area. Ellie replied that she was part Wintu and had been born and raised in Los Molinos but had traveled as far as San Francisco, which was where her sister worked for a marketing company, which was nice because that's what she'd studied at Chico State College, which is also what Ellie had studied, but only for one semester, because it wasn't for her, she said.

David glanced at his watch. "Well, it's been nice talking to you."

"Stop by anytime. It gets a little lonely here."

"Not a lot of business?"

"Not too much. But there's talk of expansion."

David nodded.

"But I get a lot of reading done," Ellie said, lifting an electronic tablet from her desk to prove her point. David perked up. He wanted to tell her about himself and his book—but he decided to play it cool and hold back until their next conversation.

"So, La Cantina. Down the corridor and to the right?" he asked.

"That's it. You'll see the sign. It's really just a bar, but for now it's our restaurant too. There's a limited menu—but Constant is a pretty good cook."

"Many thanks," said David. "See you soon."

"Hope so. We're pretty much the only ones here."

David smiled and waved goodbye.

Wax On, Wax Off

La Cantina was a cheesy homage to the Old West: faux rough-hewn timbers, stretched animal skins, Wanted posters, and crisscrossed Colt 45s on the walls.

The bar table was a long walnut box with a zinc counter top. Behind, on the back wall, were two sections of shelved bottles divided by a surprisingly ornate mirror, the word "SALOON" arced across the middle in classic western type.

Bill was sitting alone on the middle of the bar's five stools, facing the mirror.

David was two tentative steps inside the room when Bill spun around. He looked lean and sun weathered, like the Marlboro man. He stood slowly, hands holster high, fingers twitching. And then he opened his arms for a big hug. "Mishpucha! How are ya?"

David was surprised. He knew Bill liked talking Frenchy, but Yiddish was something new.

Bill tapped the stool next to his, indicating that David should sit, which he did.

"So, who is it?" Bill asked, as soon as they had worked out the logistics of their four long legs.

"Who is what?"

"Who's responsible for you being here? It has to be Jill or Sandy."

David gave Bill his best steely look. "Could be both."

That surprised Bill. He hadn't considered the possibility that the two women had colluded. "Unlikely," Bill said, "but I suppose it's possible." He turned from David to face the counter. "Constant," he called. "How about a beer for my brother."

Constant appeared from the left, through a passage David hadn't noticed. She looked like a foot-soldier for some angry god: baggy camo pants, military canvas belt, sleeveless black tee, tight and braless. She looked wiry tough, like she enjoyed body boot camp when she wasn't kickboxing. Her hair was roughly shorn. Across her right shoulder was a startling tattoo: a savage swipe of a tiger's claw: four black marks outlined in blood-red, suggesting that the wound was fresh—or not completely healed. Surprisingly, instead of jackboots she wore scuffed and dirty ballet shoes, the satin frayed and the square toes dented.

She didn't make eye contact with either man. She didn't ask David what he wanted to drink. She grabbed a large glass, yanked the tap, and filled the glass with beer. With the side of her bare hand she sliced away the excess foam, banged the glass on the bar top, and exited without saying a word.

There followed several seconds of stunned silence.

"Great lady," said Bill. "I think she liked you."

When David reached for his glass, Bill clinked it with his. "To the great ladies in our lives," he said. "God bless them all."

David sipped the beer, wiped his mouth, and put his glass on a coaster. "So, whatcha been doin'?" he asked.

Bill smiled. "Cut to the chase. That's good." He took a long swig of his own beer. "Been preparing."

"For what?"

"Good question," Bill said, studying the amber bubbles in his beer. "When I arrived, a couple weeks ago, I wasn't sure what to expect. I thought I'd been hired to work as a pit boss, maybe a dealer, a bouncer … but we've had maybe two dozen customers since I arrived." He smiled ruefully.

"After the first week, I thought I'd get fired because, really—what the hell was I doing here? What was my professional raison d'être?"

David smiled at the butchered pronunciation.

"Truth is, I was worried," said Bill. "I have no place else to go."

"I'm sorry," said David.

Bill shrugged. "It's all my doing—or my undoing. In any case, I'm feeling better about myself lately—even if I have no idea what's going on."

"What has Jill told you?"

"Not much. But when we do chat, she doesn't talk down to me. She respects me. She knows I can handle myself—knows what I'm capable of. She knows she can rely on me in moments of *extreme duress*—that's how she put it."

David let that sink in. "What about the preparations?"

"Jill's cagey. It seems like she's bringing me along real slow. I feel like the boy in *The Karate Kid*: wax on, wax off … without understanding why."

"What has she told you?"

"At first, she told me to spend my time scouting the area—ten blocks in every direction until I knew every door, every alley. Then she widened my scope to a mile, and then two. She said she wanted me to know my surroundings like the back of my hands."

"Didn't you wonder what this had to do with casino work?"

"Of course. But from the very beginning she was the one who paid my salary: Cash. Every Monday morning. Never late. In my line of work, you learn not to ask too many questions."

David hesitated but decided to keep it simple: "So then what?"

"She's the boss. I did what I was told. And I liked those scouting missions, so long as I stayed in town. But then she wanted me to get familiar with the desert and hills and mountains, and I told her: 'I'm from the Bronx, for Christ's sake.'"

"What did she say?"

"She said it was time for me to meet Ezra."

"Hadn't you met him before? I thought he lives here."

"He does, but he's rarely here. He's a naturalist and survivalist. He makes his living taking people into the wilderness for training lessons, sometimes for weeks at a time. He's a local legend. If you want to explore Lassen National Park or the Ishi Wilderness, he's your man. He's One with the Great Outdoors.... He's like a guru Grizzly Adams."

"Have you been out on the trail with him?"

"I don't think he spends much time on trails. He's more of an off-the-beaten-path kind of guy. But no, we haven't been out together. Mostly, I've been scouting and reading."

Another surprise for David. He'd never known his brother-in-law to read anything but the Daily Racing Form.

"What have you been reading?"

"You know, how to use a compass, follow the North Star, find water, apply first-aid. Nothing fancy, just some basics."

"Survival 101."

"Yeah. And I've been training—physical training—to keep myself sharp and strong. And I've been learning how to shoot. I'm pretty damn good, if I say so myself."

"Ezra's been teaching you how to shoot?"

"Ezra gave me and Jill a lesson, and Jill and I have practiced a couple times."

With that, Jill entered La Cantina.

"My guys! Glad you're both here. Let's eat."

With that, Constant reappeared, smiling at Jill. "What can I get you?"

Scorpions, Snakes … Oh My!

Constant would not reveal how she had seasoned the meatloaf, but everyone agreed it was delicious. They also agreed that the home fries were crisped exactly right and the onions caramelized to perfection.

"Magnifique!" said Bill, standing up and rubbing his stomach as if to encourage digestion. "But it's back to work for me. Back to the salt mine. Isn't that what you used to call it, brother?"

Constant looked back and forth between David and Bill. "Are you two really brothers?"

Jill, Bill, and David exchanged quick glances. No one, it seemed, was in the mood to discuss wives and families.

"Yes!" declared Bill. "Till death do us part!" He then picked up a napkin and patted his mouth with feigned delicacy. "Adieu!" he said, turning towards the door and walking away quickly, as if late for an appointment.

Constant cleared the dishes, which left Jill and David alone.

"Is he actually going to work?" David asked.

"He's checking to see if there are any customers. If there are, they're probably playing the slots. In which case, he'll just hang back and watch. He likes talking to the people who come in, but not everyone is sociable. But if anyone wants to play real blackjack or poker, he'll get the cards and deal."

David yawned.

"It's too early to fade," said Jill. "Come, I'll show you the casino. You'll see what passes for action around here."

David yawned again. "Excuse me…. Jet lag…. How about you show me the casino tomorrow, after breakfast? I need some serious shuteye."

"Fine, sleepyhead. See you in the morning. I'll meet you here around seven-thirty."

"Excellent."

"You know how to get back to your room?"

"I think I can manage that much."

"Okay, sweetie. Good night. Don't let the bed bugs bite."

David stared. "There aren't bed bugs, are there?"

"No," said Jill. "The place is quite clean. But never, ever, walk barefoot."

"Why?"

"There are snakes and scorpions."

David blanched. "In the room?"

"Rare. But it happens."

David paused. "What's worse, a snake or scorpion?"

Jill paused. "Snakes are more common. Gopher, coach-whip, sharp-tailed ... they're all over the place."

David shivered.

"Don't worry. They're not poisonous."

"You sure?"

"Positive. But we have six kinds of rattlesnakes—and they can all kill you."

"Oh god."

"The scorpions aren't as bad ... except for the big ones."

"How big?" asked David.

"Big enough to hold a snake with its pincers and eat it alive."

David's eyes flashed terror. "Oh god. Nightmares for sure."

"Honey, don't worry. I'll take care of you," Jill said, rubbing his back in tender circles. "When you get to your room, look on your wall, over your bed. You'll see a dreamcatcher. A gift from me."

"What is it?"

"Protection against evil spirits."

"Like a mezuzah?"

"Yes, a mezuzah, Indian style. But instead of a parchment prayer, it's a loosely netted wooden hoop, decorated with feathers. Evil spirits are caught in the netting. Only good spirits will enter your dreams."

"Sounds nice."

"It works," Jill whispered tenderly. "But wear your slippers."

Chapter 20

Last of the High Rollers

Next morning, after breakfasting in La Cantina, David and Jill walked through the corridor towards the casino.

"Did you know Ishi was a gambling man?" Jill asked.

"I don't think I knew that. What was his game?"

"He didn't play casino games."

"What about friendly card games?" David asked.

"I don't think so."

"Not even Go Fish?"

"Maybe that one, but I doubt it. I know he played a kind of a guess-which-hand game."

"What would he hide?" David asked.

"A piece of bird bone."

"Hmmm. What were the stakes?"

"Colored sticks."

"Ishi, Last of the High Rollers!"

Jill laughed. "The stakes must have mattered to Ishi. He recorded like ten different gambling songs."

"Do you happen to know any?" asked David.

"I do."

"Are you taking requests?"

"Are you asking nicely?"

David cleared his throat. "Jill Black, screenwriter extraordinaire and now songstress, would you please honor us by singing one of Ishi's classic gambling songs?"

Jill whispered in his ear: "It's really more of a chant."

David cleared his throat again. "Jill Black, would you please honor us by performing one of Ishi's classic gambling *chants*?"

Jill took a step forward and curtseyed before an imagined packed house. Without further ado, she began a long chant, all the while shimmying and stomping, much like her buffalo-shuffle. The chant lasted about two minutes.

"I'm speechless."

"Do you know what I said?" she asked, breathless.

"I caught the mood precisely—but perhaps not every word."

"That's okay. Your ears are untrained. I said: 'ha aimino ina ha aimino.'"

"That's what I thought you said. But it sounded much longer."

"I repeated it seven times. It's like a chorus."

"Why does it mean?"

"I have no idea."

Faux Grand

Jill had exaggerated the shortcomings of the casino. In fact, the main room was large and contained enough faux gilding to impress gamblers who had never been to Vegas or even Reno. While not exactly grand, the casino offered all the standard games: roulette, craps, blackjack, poker, a variety of slot machines, and—in a small, separate room—a modest bingo parlor. Still, upon entering the main room, David had a sense of something missing. Aside from the fact that there were no customers, it took a while before he realized that there was no loud music, no cacophony of voices, no cascade of metal coins spilling into tinny trays—nothing that reflected busy casino life.

"I see why Bill worries about his job security," said David.

"Bill's job is safe, for now," said Jill.

David thought he detected a tiny, sly smile.

"Bill isn't working for the casino. He's working for you."

Jill smiled. "That's why you get the big bucks," she said. "You've got the brains. Bill's got the brawn. And I've got the management skills. It's a good team."

For several seconds David was busy connecting the dots.

"Why the ruse about the casino work?" he asked.

"Actually, it wasn't entirely a ruse. The casino really did need another hand for the occasional small crowd. Morgan lives here and works part-time. Same for Simon, but he's not very reliable. The hotel owners were here one day and we got to talking, and they happened to mention they were understaffed. By that time I was already developing my plans about the surviving Yahi and knew I'd need someone like Bill to protect my back. So I worked out a deal with the casino on his behalf. For his part-time work he gets free room and board—and I pay him a modest salary, which, I believe, he's been banking every week."

David nodded. "Thanks for explaining. But how did you know I would come too?"

Jill smiled and shrugged. "I didn't. But after I learned about Bill and his relationship with your sister, I figured she might want to keep tabs on him. You were unemployed. You needed a job. The pieces seemed to fit."

"Still, you couldn't have been sure."

"Even without your sister's backing, I thought you'd join me here."

"Why? I can't resist your siren's call?"

Jill shook her head. "I can't make you do anything you don't want to do."

"But you know my weak points."

"I know your strengths … and your ambitions. Look, I think you've always been a dreamer. But you chose a quiet, constrained, burgher's life. No, no—don't interrupt. I'm not being critical, just descriptive…. The bottom line is, I know you're getting older—as I am—and, recognizing this, understanding this, I thought you might be more motivated—more willing—more daring—to do whatever you could to finally fulfill your dreams. I'm not reading tea leaves. I'm reading you—and myself. I think we share some basic traits. We both need to express ourselves. We both need to be heard. We both need to be successful. And we both feel an increasing pressure to shape our legacy. Look, we're not getting younger. The time is now. I think we both understand that. No, no—let me finish. Bottom line: I know about your passion for explorers and the book about Ishi you began as a boy. I know you need to write and publish another book. And I know that the situation I stumbled into here is the perfect opportunity for you—and me."

David was impressed by her reasoning. "Anything else?"

"I know you need some time away from your wife.... I saw all that.... I considered all that."

David struggled over one final point. "But what if it hadn't happened? What if I hadn't come?"

"If you hadn't come ... if you weren't here with me now ... I'd still be doing what I'm doing. I'd still be pursuing the story of the surviving Yahi. I'd still be planning to make a movie about it. But it's better with you here. It's easier. It's more fun.... Maybe I won't have you with me for the rest of my life, but I have you now, and I'm going to make the most of it."

"You really think I can help?"

"I know it. You're going to write that book about Ishi you were always meant to write. And it will be terrific. It will sell. It will help bring attention to my film."

"Our film," said David.

"Yes, our film," Jill said, smiling.

The two friends walked about the casino. They did not hold hands. Still, when they were sure no one was looking, they took turns goosing each other's butt.

"It all started in this room," said Jill.

"What do you mean?"

"This is where I first met Simon. I told you: He had a copy of *Nobody's Fool* and he hit a slots jackpot and he asked me to lunch."

"He's the one who first told you about Ishi?"

"Yup."

"And he's the one who got drunk one night and mentioned the surviving Yahi."

"Yup."

"And he's the one who threatened to kill you if you ever mentioned it."

"Yup. You're a good listener."

"Where were you sitting when you first met him?"

Jill led the way to the far right, towards an emergency door marked Exit. As they approached, a subtle furriness in the air grew increasingly strong until the scent bordered on toxic.

"Simon calls this section the Reservation," said Jill. "He says it brings him luck."

David mimicked a violent hacking cough. "I bet he smokes while he gambles."

"So does Morgan. They often sit side-by-side, puffing away."

"I guess this is the smoking section."

"Actually, smoking is allowed everywhere in the casino."

"I'm surprised."

"Don't be. Remember, the tribe that owns this hotel is recognized as a sovereign nation. It can make its own rules—to a point."

"I guess they made a point about allowing smoking."

"Yes—but most people who come here don't smoke. The Indians are usually the smokers and they tend to sit in this section."

"Why here?"

"Look around, Sherlock. Tell me what you see."

From where he stood, David could see all the casino slot machines in their section and most of the machines in the other rows. At first glance, he thought all the machines looked pretty much alike. All were decorated with colorful themed images and gambling icons. But in the casino's "Reservation" section, images of tomahawks and peace pipes replaced the red cherries and yellow bananas on the rolling reels, and Pan-Indian themes like Coyote Moon, Big Chief, and Buffalo Thunder replaced standard gringo themes like Empire Stakes and Vegas Nights.

"I don't get it," said David. "Why do Indians like this section? Aren't these images offensive clichés?"

"Some Indians see it that way," said Jill. "But many see these images as a celebration of their basic 'Indianness.'"

David chewed on that. "Okay, I can see that."

"Identity is a complicated issue," said Jill. "Let me ask you: What are you first, a Jew or an American?"

"Don't ask me that."

"Why not?"

"Because I'd run around in circles trying to answer."

Jill nodded. "Remember that thought when we discuss where Ishi is buried."

"You know where he's buried?"

"Like I said, hold that thought."

Jill rose from her stool and stretched. "Let's get out of here. I feel like we're trespassing."

"You want to take a break?"

"Good idea. I have some phone calls and e-mails to get to."

"Me too," said David.

"How about I knock on your door around five?" asked Jill. "We'll go to dinner. There's a place in Los Molinos I want to take you."

"Bill too?"

"No," said Jill. "Tonight is just the two of us."

Chapter 21

David's E-mail to Sandy

Hey Sis. All quiet on the western front. Been here just a couple days and nothing much to report. The Sierra Spa and Casino Hotel sounds a lot more glitzy than it is. I think it's fallen a little on hard times—perhaps the recession put a dent in its business. As for Handsome Bill, he seems to be staying out of trouble. He does general casino work—pit boss, dealer, bouncer stuff—you know the drill. I've got my eye on him. Hope you're feeling well. Love ya.

Sandy's E-mail to David

Spend more time with Bill. Watch him closely. Find out who he's drinking with. I'm working on a couple big consulting projects and I don't want any shenanigans or fallout from him. Biggest thing: if he has a sudden windfall and gets the idea that a quick visit to New York might be fun—let me know IMMEDIATELY. I don't want him showing up unannounced. Keep up the good work. Love, Sis.

David's E-mail to Allison

Hi Honey! Sorry for not writing or calling sooner but have been on the road and Wi-Fi is unreliable in these parts. I thought I'd be staying in Chico but the casino where Bill works—the Sierra Spa and Casino Hotel—not nearly as grand as it sounds—is actually a little north of Chico in a little burg called Los Molinos. It's a quiet place, not much to do. I'm keeping an eye on Bill, but he seems to be working hard and minding his business. I made a trip to Chico—where I'd first learned about Ishi—and the stirred memories have given me some early ideas for a new novel. Not sure where it's going—but I think the historical Ishi might be at the heart of it.... The desert, the foothills, the mountains are very beautiful, and I think they will help bring me to the right frame of mind to tell this tale. Hope your job is still going well. Give my love to the girls—I will write to each of them very soon. I love you very much.
    Shalom. Namaste.

Allison's E-mail to David

Hi Honey—so glad to hear from you. I was starting to get a little worried. I know you're busy but write whenever you can. Things are well here—a little more rainy than usual—but you know how I love the rain!

My job is going well. I like the illustration and design parts but the production work is boring and stressful. But I have a job—so I'm grateful. Unfortunately, we have some unexpected bills—which always seem to come up. The brakes in the Corolla need fixing and I lost my sunglasses—the good ones—the ones with the prescription lenses—sorry! And it looks like I will need yet another crown—that back tooth I was telling you about.

But there is good news too. The girls are well. Lydia still likes her job and says things are going well with Jonathan. And ... Louise got a job! Her first job as a fashion designer—fulltime—with benefits. She's excited and she'll tell you all about it. I think she's seeing someone but she's mum on the subject. Give it a few more weeks and we'll see.

I had lunch today with Sylvie at Saffron. She sends her love. Next time I go, I'll buy a few coconut-cardamom muffins and send them to you.

I miss you. I looked up Mount Lassen National Park on the Internet. It's so beautiful! I printed out some photos of the mountains and valleys to help me imagine that I'm right there, with you.

I love you, my beshert.

Jill's E-mail to Wiley

It was great to see you, dear Wiley. You look fabulous! So happy the restaurant is doing well—Chaps & Scraps—what a great name! And the food is great too!

I'm glad you finally met David. I am introducing him slowly to my plans. Soon he'll meet with Ezra to give him a better idea of what we're dealing with and what's at stake.

I am very grateful and comforted by your love and support.

Jill

P.S. Good luck with Ralph. I bet he's hunky. Send me a photo of the two of you!

Wiley's E-mail to Jill

Hi darlin'! So thrilled you stopped by—you said you'd surprise me one day soon—and you did. You are a woman of your word.

By the way—do you really think I look fabulous? I put on a few pounds—don't pretend you didn't notice! Ralph doesn't mind—but he worries it might not be good for my heart. We go dancing every week—sometimes twice—so I think the exercise will do me good. Next week I'm doing some riding with my GBBB group. After that I should have some free time. Perhaps you and David would like to come dancing with us one evening. He's cute!

Love you. And remember, if you need me, just call. I can be there in a flash if I ride my bike.

Jill's E-mail to Elliot

How's the film festival shaping up? I'd love to go but won't be back in Davis any time soon. Meanwhile, keep cementing those relationships with your star students and faculty. As you know, we won't have any budget to create scenes in a studio—we're going to have to shoot where the story takes us. Also, way before we're ready to film, we're going to need some practice runs. This will be a huge challenge. Not only will we have to transport equipment without an experienced gaffer and key grip, we'll have to do it in rough country—sometimes at night—sometimes in complete silence. I am exploring some possible practice sites—including caves and caverns, riverbanks, even high in the Sierra where the footing is treacherous. Just remember: When the going gets tough, the tough get going! We can do it!

By the way, David liked you, but when I mentioned Kenneth and Gloria, he gave me a strange look. Don't know why. I don't think they ever met.

Speak soon. Good luck with the festival—break a leg!

Elliot's E-mail to Jill

I'm a wreck. I have a million things to do and I have no idea how they are going to get done but I know they will because they always do. It helps that I've done it before. That's why your plan for filming practice makes sense. We won't work out all the kinks ... practice won't make perfect ... but it will make it a little easier when we shoot for real.

Love, E.

P.S. Kenneth and Gloria are always a little hush-hush when I mention you. You never told me how well you knew them—I want the spicy details. Maybe next time. Both said that David seemed nice but that's all. Gloria seemed to think he looked familiar.

Jill's E-mail to Ezra

You still out in the wilderness? When are you coming home? Constant seems grumpy. You better get here soon—I don't want her poisoning my food. ;)

BTW: My friend David has arrived. I've introduced him to Elliot and Wiley. I've told him only what I know about the Yahi, but I haven't told him your story. I will leave that to you.

Hope to see you soon ... safe and sound!

Ezra's E-mail to Jill

Actually, I got in about an hour ago. It was a good trip. My client was a green rookie but he was eager to learn and good company. Constant is cooking dinner and we'll stay in tonight. Tomorrow I've got to do laundry and need to clean my gear and repair a few things—so why don't you bring David around sometime in the afternoon.

I have news.

Chapter 22

Maxwell and Elena Cross

Jill was driving the red Miata west on Tehama Vina Road. She had just crossed the double-span bridge over the Sacramento River and was turning left on Second Street.

"You are in for a treat," she said to David. "Not many people get to eat real, authentic Indian food."

"Again, do you mean Indian or Indian?"

"I'm not doing that again."

"I'm just asking for clarity."

"In that case, the latter. I assume you've eaten the former."

"Excellent! I was hoping that's what you meant."

Ignoring further silliness, Jill cruised silently down Second Street, crossing E, F, G, H, and I streets. When she reached East Gyle Road, she parked in front of a modest two-story, vinyl-sided house, whose porch was decorated with shell chimes, windsocks, and dreamcatchers.

"This is the home of Maxwell and Elena Cross," Jill said.

David looked all about. The Sacramento River was behind them. The home was the only house on the street. "How did you find this place? There's no signage at all. There's nothing that says restaurant."

"It's not an official restaurant."

"They have a license to serve?"

"I doubt it."

"They have a menu with posted prices?"

"Nope."

"They charge sales tax?"

"They don't charge anything."

"I love this place. You been here before?"

"Just once, with Ezra. I think he and Maxwell did some work together years ago. Ezra brings them animals that he's trapped or shot with a bow. They won't accept any animal killed by gunshot."

"Is that a law or just one of their core principles?"

"Maxwell and Elena are both part Maidu. They like observing some of the old ways—especially when it comes to preparing and cooking food. Which is why we're here tonight."

"Is this place open to the public?"

"Not exactly. It's not illegal or underground or anything. Maxwell and Elena just like cooking for their friends—and friends of their friends. If you're part of the loop, you can give them a call any afternoon to see if they are serving dinner that evening. But they don't do it every night."

"Too much work?"

"For sure. They're nearly eighty. It's hard to gather all the food they need to eat—and they certainly don't do their own hunting anymore. But most of the people who eat here are Indians, and instead of paying with money they bring berries, nuts, or fish that can be used for the next person's meal. I know Ezra keeps them fairly well supplied, and he brings fresh meat, too. But Ezra is a special case."

"Why?"

"That's part of his story. We'll get to that soon."

Jill and David stood on the porch, looking all about. A strong breeze blew off the river, tinkling the chimes and filling the windsock.

Jill struck a regal pose. "How do I look?"

She wore casual jeans; a simple, white, long-sleeve blouse; and a modest turquoise bracelet.

"Beautiful. Like a Maidu queen."

Jill smiled, then turned to rap lightly on the doorframe. "Hei!" Turning back to David, she whispered: "That's Maidu for *hello*."

The door opened and both Maxwell and Elena were there to greet them. David thought they looked oddly normal, like someone's grandparents: small, old, proud, and happy.

"Good to see you. Please come in," they said.

Jill and David stepped into the kitchen. All about were pots and pans, hanging utensils, large and small appliances: all the kitchen appurtenances and accessories any modern American family might be expected to own.

David was disappointed by the lack of Indian authenticity, but Maxwell and Elena lead the way to the dining room, which provided a very different experience. On the left side of the room, where there must have once been a traditional fireplace, there was now a deep fire pit surrounded by a set of stone, food-processing tools. As this was Elena's purview, she explained to David the purpose and technique associated with each pair of implements: the bowl mortar and pestle, the metate and mano stone, and the hopper mortar base and basket. She had just finished speaking when there was another knock on the door. David's eyes went to the dining table, which was set for six.

If Looks Could Kill

Maxwell and Elena went to the front door and returned with the newly arrived guests. Maxwell handled the introductions.

"Morgan, Simon, I'm sure you know Jill Black. And this is her friend, David Grossman. David, this is Morgan Crabtree and Simon Lescault."

Morgan moved first, clasping David's right hand in both of his/hers. "So nice to meet you." In turn, Simon answered David's proffered hand with a viselike grip that made David wince.

"Come," said Elena. "Dinner's almost ready. Please sit."

With the usual scuffling and shuffling, the six diners arranged themselves at the rectangular table. Maxwell and Elena occupied the end seats; Morgan and Simon faced Jill and David.

Everyone looked happy except Simon, who stared across the table with a baleful glare as hot as the flames in the fire pit. Jill had not anticipated his arrival but was quick to respond.

"David is a writer. He's researching local Indian history and cultures for a new book."

"How interesting," said Elena. "What have you written?"

"I've written many things, but I've published only one novel."

"Ooooh a novelist—how exciting. I don't think I've met a famous writer before."

"Well, I don't know how famous I am."

Morgan smiled. Simon smirked.

"David's being too modest," said Jill. "His book was a number-one bestseller in two Amazon categories."

Simon intensified his glare.

"Congratulations," said Elena. "May I ask the title?"

"*Forty Years Later.*"

"I like it. Does it also take place in California?"

"No. Most of the action takes place in New York City and in the Catskill Mountains."

"The Catskills—wonderful!" said Elena. "I believe the Mohican and Munsee are from those parts—or were, at one time."

"Chingachgook—last of the Mohicans!"

Elena looked at her husband and shook her head. "That's just a story, Max."

Jill caught Elena's eye. "David and I met in the Catskills. We're from the same tribe."

"I didn't know you are Indian," said Elena.

"We're not. We're Jews—historically from twelve tribes—but please don't ask me to name them. Haven't a clue."

"That's too bad," said Elena. "It's important to remember your people's history and to pass on what you know."

Everyone nodded at the wisdom of Elena's words.

"We're Maidu," Elena said, clearly referring to herself and Maxwell.

"I'm Rancheria," said Morgan.

"I'm Maidu and Wintu," said Simon. "But I also have Yahi blood."

"Ishi—last of the Yahi!"

"Max, you make that sound like a happy boast. It's not."

"Of course, dear. Just adding to the talk."

Elena turned back to Jill. "How did you and David meet?"

"We were young. He was sixteen. I was fifteen. We met in a bungalow colony in the Catskill Mountains. We watched the first Moon landing together."

"Wasn't that the year of Woodstock?" asked Morgan.

Jill and David nodded but said no more on the subject. Suddenly self-conscious, David remembered he was wearing his wedding ring and slowly withdrew his hand from sight. Too late. Everyone had noticed the ring but no one commented, not even Simon, who was sorely tempted.

"What brings you to Los Molinos, David?"

"Ellie, you ask too many personal questions," said Maxwell. "He is our guest."

"Actually," said David in a bright tone that suggested he was fine with the question, "I went to school near here."

"Really? Here?" asked Elena.

"Well, close. I studied at Chico State College for a summer semester after my freshman year. I worked on an excavation of an ancient Maidu site."

"Maidu!" exclaimed Ellie. "That's us! How wonderful!"

"Yes, I loved it. It was an extraordinary experience. As soon as it was over, I started writing a novel about that summer—and about Ishi. But I was young and lost the thread. I'm older now.... Things change.... I thought I'd come back to see if I could pick up where I left off—or find a new scent to track down."

Simon looked daggers at both Jill and David. He saw them as complicit in some vague, dark betrayal. He wanted to kill them both.

"David, I thank you for helping us remember our history." Elena lifted a half-filled wineglass. "To David. To the success of your new novel!"

Everyone lifted a glass, but only Simon put his down without taking a sip.

Elena made eye contact with all the diners to make sure she had their attention. "It's so important to carry on our traditions," she said. "That's why I still cook these occasional meals in the old ways.... But I have a secret."

"Don't say it!" said Maxwell in mock horror.

"No, my dear. I must bare my soul. The truth is ... I don't always grind my own acorns anymore. Sometimes I ... use the electric coffee grinder!"

Everyone laughed.

"Vile sinner!" said Maxwell.

"Repent!" said Morgan.

The laughter soon died.

Morgan turned to Elena: "All kidding aside, don't be too hard on yourself. You have taught many people about the old ways—you have done your part."

"Thank you, Morgan. You are kind. And on that note, I say: Let's eat!"

Elena stood and began to organize the serving. Jill followed her, and her assistance was silently accepted. The others remained seated, including Morgan. David wasn't sure if he should offer to help. Finally, he made a half-hearted attempt to stand, but Jill passed by and deftly pressed him back into his chair. Morgan, Maxwell, and Simon stared at David with critical curiosity.

The meal itself was a big success. Everyone agreed the acorn and apple soup was delicious. David, who knew acorns only as the staple of squirrels and the bouncy nuts that covered the tennis courts in the late Fall, thought they tasted like a cross between hazelnuts and sunflower seeds. Even more successful was the main course, a fresh, broiled salmon that had been squirted with lemon, left to stand for an hour, and then seasoned with salt and pepper. The dessert was acorn bread, which had sounded boring to David but proved to be a deliciously sweet, crumbly cake.

The after-dinner conversation was a circuit of topics familiar to all the guests. There was talk of Ezra and his relationship with Constant. Maxwell rued the fact that he was no longer able to go with Ezra into the wilderness to hunt and fish with bow and spear. Morgan—more than a little tipsy with wine—said he'd be willing to barter a full-body massage for one of Constant's three-course meals. The remark drew a swift reproof from Elena, which silenced Morgan for about ten minutes.... There was much discussion about the hotel: how it could not continue as it was—how a big infusion of tourist dollars was needed to save it. Talk of the hotel's demise upset Elena. "If it does die," she said, "the number of Indians who come to Los Molinos will dwindle. Eventually, there will be no more dinner guests at our table." For several long seconds everyone looked down in sadness.... The conversation brightened with Max's mention of the continuing great weather and improved further when Elena noted that PBS would be reshowing the film *Ishi: The Last Yahi Indian* as part of its American Experience series. Everyone shared in this part of the conversation except Simon, who continually clutched his heart as if suffering from acute angina.

Driving back to the hotel, David and Jill shared their impressions of the evening.

"What's up with Simon?" asked David.

"He's angry."

"I gathered that much. But why?"

"He took me to lunch and I didn't sleep with him."

"That's it?"

121

"And now he sees me with you."

"So?"

"He feels slighted, insulted, and ..."

"And what?"

"I'm sure he assumes I told you about the surviving Yahi."

"But I know nothing, except that they exist."

"I think he knows that we're closing in on the whole story—and he doesn't want that to happen."

"How does he know that?"

"Because he sees me getting closer with Ezra."

"And Ezra knows all?"

"Ezra is the key. To the Yahi, Ezra is like Moses. He's going to lead the Yahi out of the darkness."

"And Simon is opposed to this?"

"I don't know all of Simon's reasoning. I'm sure it's more complicated than I understand. But I know he doesn't want Ezra to play the part of Moses. And he certainly wouldn't want me to make a film about it."

"What about me writing a book about it?"

"He'd kill you for sure if he knew."

David was stunned silent for several seconds.

"What's with all the biblical references to the Ishi story?"

"Like I said, Ezra proposes to play the part of Moses. Ishi is like Christ in that he sacrificed his life so the Yahi could live."

"Moses and Christ. A story of biblical proportions."

Jill closed her driver's side window so her words would not be lost on the wind.

"The story of the American Indians is similar to the history of the Jews."

"How so?"

"Both stories include big chapters about exodus and genocide."

"I don't know much about the Indian genocide," said David.

"Not surprising. It's scrupulously avoided in American textbooks. It's a terrible travesty. The events and the cover-up."

"I know about the Cherokee Trail of Tears."

"That's one token story. There is a long, suppressed history of official genocide."

"And this affected the Yahi?"

"It nearly wiped them out."

Chapter 23

Genocide

Following the discovery of gold in 1848, dreamers and thrill-seekers rushed to the Sacramento Valley as if it were the Promised Land. In the time it takes to sharpen a pelt knife or load a rifle, indigenous tribes and whites came into bloody territorial conflict.

"We hope that the Government will render such aid as will enable the citizens of the north to carry on a war of extermination until the last redskin of these tribes has been killed. Extermination is no longer a question of time—the time has arrived, the work has commenced and let the first man who says treaty or peace be regarded as a traitor." —Yreka Herald, 1853

"Little children and old women were mercilessly stabbed and their skulls crushed with axes.... Old women wrinkled and decrepit lay weltering in their blood, their brains dashed out and dabbed with their long grey hair. Infants scarce a span long, with their faces cloven with hatchets and their bodies ghastly with wounds.... No resistance was made, it is said, to the butchers who did the work, but as they ran or huddled together for protection like sheep, they were struck down with hatchets. Very little shooting was done, most of the bodies having wounds about the head." —Francis Bret Harte, 1860

The local authorities encouraged the war of extermination, citing the spirit of Manifest Destiny to sanction the theft of valuable Indian lands and resources. As to the systematic brutalization and murder of innocents, it was easy enough for white society to look the other way. After all, there was much bloodlust in their own histories to countenance the conquering of Canaan and the launching of the Crusades.

THE ISHI AFFAIR

Bottom line: After decades of rape, scalping, kidnapping, and forced labor, the Indian population of California had been successfully reduced by about ninety percent. As many as 150 Indian communities had been destroyed. Most of those that survived either intermarried with whites or, as in the case of the Yahi, removed themselves farther and farther from threat until they dwelled in rough regions without even enough nuts and berries for sustenance.

Chapter 24

Another Chance

I have news.

That last phrase from Ezra's e-mail thrilled Jill to the depths of her soul. It felt like a heavenly reward for her recent sobriety.

She'd been moderately soused when she'd first met Simon and had continued drinking with him throughout their lunch. But drunk as she was, she was not so far gone as to sleep with him. His response was to drink himself past the pain of rejection. But at some point he felt the need to fan his feathers, and it was during this time that he told her about Ishi and the living Yahi ... and still she wouldn't sleep with him, which led him, after yet another hour of drinking, to threaten her life if she ever repeated what he had said.

Jill was not sorry for the experience. Simon's revelation had excited her dormant imagination. She'd heard his words as *untold story*—an opportunity that seemed to speak directly to her. It wasn't a leap for Jill to imagine that everything in her life had led to that moment ... that she'd been destined to learn about Ishi and the Yahi and to bring their story to the world.

Still, Simon's threat had upset her. She knew he was dead serious. *What to do?* She couldn't think straight. So she slunk back to La Cantina, where she could drink without having to think at all. As usual, some Goth chick in camo pants and sleeveless black tee appeared behind the counter, but this time—before she could order a drink—Jill's face convulsed in a cycle of heaving sobs. After about a minute, the Goth chick disappeared. Feeling she'd just been abandoned by the last person on earth who might have helped her, Jill sobbed to bust her guts. She was about to muster a wail to end all wails when the Goth chick returned, holding a delicate teacup filled with honeyed chamomile. Jill accepted the gift and sipped the honeyed tea until it calmed her. After a few minutes she felt the need to talk. She told the Goth chick the story of her life, ending with the threat from Simon. When Jill finished speaking, the Goth chick said to her: "I want you to meet my boyfriend Ezra and tell him what you told me."

Jill met Ezra a few days later (he had been working in the Wilderness as a guide) and repeated everything she had told Constant, ending with the part about drinking with Simon and learning about Ishi and the living Yahi. When she told Ezra about Simon's threat she started crying again. She said she was scared but wanted to stay.

"What kind of writer are you?" asked Ezra.

"I'm the good kind," Jill said, smiling and wiping away her tears. "I tell the truth."

"What kind of movies do you make?"

"The last movie I made was about these middle-aged women who tell each other hard, painful truths. But it was taken away from me.... I'm very good. I deserve another chance."

"I will try to protect you," Ezra said. "But it may not be easy. Simon told you the truth. The Yahi do live. The Stone Age is alive—though not so well. Because you know this, you may be in danger."

"Should I leave?"

"No."

"Then what should I do?" she said, her eyes welling again.

Ezra was silent for maybe ten seconds. "For me to help you, I think we must work together."

"What can I possibly do for you?"

"You can tell the truth about the Yahi. You can make your movie."

Early Plans

Over the next several days Jill listened to Ezra's remarkable story. Several times Ezra took her into the Ishi Wilderness

127

to familiarize her with the landscape. He told her details about Ishi's life that could not be found in any article or textbook. He told her about the Stone Age Yahi and how they had survived and secretly adapted. Jill recorded Ezra's words using a microphone app on her smartphone. At night she listened to the recordings and took notes. When she wasn't with Ezra she read relevant books and articles on her laptop.

Jill started planning her strategy. Sitting in La Cantina (not at the bar, but at one of the small, half-dozen tables), she wrote to Elliot about her idea for a film collaboration. She then wrote to Wiley to let him know that she had stopped drinking and was happily involved with a new project, which she described in broad outline. Next, remembering that her lifelong sweetheart David Grossman had been to Chico as a teenager and had written something about Ishi, she began thinking how she might inveigle him to join her. These thoughts led her to think of David's brother-in-law, Bill Manes, and it was not long before she learned that he'd left his wife and had been working in a Vegas casino but was now out of a job and looking for work. *Perfect,* she thought. Bill could be useful to her in several ways, including as a hook into David.

A few days later, she got into her car and began her cross-country trip to New York. It was anything but a direct route. Often fearing that the car in her rearview mirror was tailing her, she made many sudden detours, which seemed to lose her tail—at least for a while—but added a couple weeks and much expense to her trip. But these delays did not disturb her; in fact, she welcomed them. It had been four years since she last spoke with David; four years since they'd danced together in the midnight woods behind Yasgur's farm. She needed time to plan how she would meet him and what she would say to him. She was sure of only one thing: The time seemed right for their second reunion.

Chapter 25

Trapping the Wilderness

Such was Ezra Winship's reputation as a trapper and wilderness guide that the hotel gave him two adjoining rooms for free, board included. Ezra was a draw for the hotel, attracting almost as many overnight customers as did the casino. Throughout the year, people seeking master-class survival skills hired Ezra as a field guide and mentor, reserving his time through his well-known website *Trapping the Wilderness*. Sometimes business was brisk: customers came as individuals, couples, or even entire groups. Most often, customers stayed at least two nights in the hotel: the night before a trip into the wilderness and the night following their return. (The maximum number of people Ezra allowed in a group was ten. In Ezra's mind the number was significant, representing the minimum number of righteous people that would have stayed God's scorching punishment of Sodom and Gomorra. Regarding his max-group excursions, Ezra liked to say that if he had ten sinners going with him into the wilderness, he'd have ten who were much improved when he returned them to their worldly lives.)

One of Ezra's two adjoining rooms was his home and the other was his workspace. His home was like other standard rooms in the hotel, except there was no television or minibar. Ezra filled the extra space by adding a second large bureau for his clothing. On the standard desk he kept his laptop. He never took it with him on his wilderness excursions; same for his cell phone.

On either side of his queen-sized bed was a nightstand. On the left stand was the King James Bible; on the right was the Good News Bible. Both were well thumbed and highlighted.

Ezra did not like guns and rarely carried one. Still, he owned three identical Desert Eagle .50 caliber pistols. One he kept taped to the bottom of his mattress, on the right-side where he slept. One he kept under the driver's seat of his pickup truck. The third he kept inside the cabin he'd built in the Wilderness, behind the woodpile near the stove. Constant deplored guns, trembled even at the close sight of one. Ezra said he would never use them to kill animals. "At least, not the four-legged kind."

It was mid-afternoon. Ezra was mending a fishing net while waiting for Jill to bring David to his office to meet him. Jill had told Ezra a lot of good things about David, but Ezra liked to make up his own mind. For example, he had already met Bill and liked him. He knew Bill had a shady past, but he sensed that Bill would be a strong and loyal ally. Ezra had also met Wiley and liked him too, but could not entirely look past his homosexuality, which he believed was wrong. Ezra did not consider himself mean or unloving. But the law was the law. Ezra knew by heart those Bible passages (particularly Leviticus 18:22, 20:13, and Romans 1:26–27) that were the first and last words on the subject.

Jill and David arrived a little after two o'clock. As planned, Jill excused herself after making introductions. She'd already told Ezra she'd wait until after the meeting to discuss his news: "I'll leave you guys alone to get to know each other." Before turning on her heel and walking away, she put one hand on David's shoulder and the other on Ezra's. "What we're doing is important—and scary. Really, I am so grateful to both of you." She left while her face was still composed.

As soon as Jill was gone, Ezra spoke: "It's nice to meet you, David. Just give me a second. Have a look around—just don't touch anything."

David had never been in an "office" like Ezra's. There were no files or papers. All of Ezra's billing and correspondence were done electronically from his laptop in the other room. In this room Ezra created, maintained, and repaired his field tools. Against each of the four walls was a worktable, and above each table was a poster, save for the far wall, which was mostly window. The three posters were unframed. They weren't even printed. Each was a hand-painted quotation on a piece of white cardboard. Moving left to right, David examined each poster:

The wrongdoing of one generation lives into the successive ones.
—Nathaniel Hawthorne

Everything on the earth has a purpose ... and every person a mission.
—Mourning Dove, Salish

We shall live again; we shall live again.
—Comanche Ghost Dance Song

The quotations were rendered in thin, rusty-red brush-strokes. David (who'd learned about pigments from his wife Allison, the painter) thought the poster-maker must have used a red iron-oxide pigment or, perhaps, real blood.

"So," said Ezra, ready to focus his full attention. "Jill tells me you are a wonderful writer with a lifelong interest in Ishi."

David shrugged modestly. "I learned a little about Ishi when I was at Chico State College—I'm sure Jill told you."

"She did. She said you began to write about Ishi and the Yahi when you were seventeen."

"It's true. I tried to write a book about the Yahi who secretly survived ... but I was a kid. I had no facts or understanding. I thought I just made it all up. In any case, I was in way over my head and eventually put the book aside."

"You weren't ready. The time wasn't right. But God was preparing you to tell this story."

"Perhaps. But, to tell you the truth, I hadn't thought much about it until Jill came to New York to reconnect with me—again."

"She told me what happened at St. Patrick's Cathedral."

David laughed. "Yeah, that was an attention-grabber."

A few seconds of silence.

"I know you're married."

"Yes," said David.

"I asked Jill not to tell me much. I really don't want to know."

"Okay," said David. "Sounds wise."

"None of us are perfect. We're all sinners."

"No argument from me."

Ezra nodded. "I'm with Constant—as I'm sure you heard. We're not married, so I'm in no position to cast stones."

"Good. You probably have great aim—and I have thin skin."

Ezra laughed lightly. "I know Jill has been teaching you about Ishi and the Yahi. I have some things you might want to read. Not too much. This isn't an academic kind of thing."

"Thanks. I would like to learn more."

"Good. Also, we'll be making some trips into the Wilderness. Jill thinks you could use some training."

"I'm not in woeful shape. I play a lot of tennis."

Ezra laughed. "Sorry, it's just … you know, if someone is chasing you through the woods or across a ravine, you don't get to stop for a second serve or sit on a bench, drinking bottled water."

"Why would someone be chasing me?"

Ezra bent his head a little closer to David and lowered his voice: "I'm helping the Yahi come out of the dark and into the light. Some people don't like the idea."

"Like Simon?"

"And others, who have been alerted by Simon."

"But why would anyone oppose the Yahi living free?" David asked.

"Different people have different reasons," said Ezra. "Some people have a vested interest in maintaining the idea of 'Ishi, Last of the Yahi.' This is their brand, their business model. They have books and documentaries and school curricula—and more planned. Ishi is their cash cow. If we show the world that

Ishi wasn't the last of the Yahi—it changes everything for them—and for the buying public. Ishi wouldn't be the focus any more. The newly freed Yahi would be the story. And that would be fair game for anyone to write about."

"Including us," said David.

"Yes. We will be the first. As of now, no one else knows the whole story but me ... because I was destined to play my part."

For several seconds David remained silently skeptical. "Why does Simon oppose us?"

"Simon is another story. Like so many Indians, he's lived with a lot of white crap but remains proud. Because he's been lied to and short-changed, he holds on very dearly to what he has."

"You mean history and tradition—with Ishi at the heart of it?"

"Absolutely. And he resents further white interference. Which is why he doesn't like the idea that I will be the one to lead the living Yahi to freedom. He feels it should be an Indian honor—not a white man's."

"How do you feel about it?"

"This isn't my doing. This is God's plan. That might sound silly to you—but I haven't yet told you my story. You'll see. And you'll also see that this is what the Yahi want. They know about Ishi's sacrifice and his prediction that they would remain hidden for one hundred years. You see, I'm not interfering. I'm just playing my part. It was destined that all this would happen on my watch."

"Your watch?"

"Yes, my watch. Soon you'll understand."

"I guess Simon wouldn't embrace the story of your watch?"

"Not likely. But, from his point of view, white words are responsible for Ishi's death, the story of Ishi's brain, and Ishi's secret reburial. It's all related."

133

"I don't quite follow."

"Of course not. But you will. I'll tell you the whole story in a minute. First, let me show you around my office."

"I read your posters," David said, pointing to the nearest one.

"Words I live by. Soon you'll see why. But first, take a look at this." Ezra led David to the nearest worktable, which was covered with fishing nets, large and small. "Some of my tools are store-bought. But I like to make as many things as I can according to the Old Ways."

"Like Ishi."

"Yes. And like Ishi I've known Stone Age people for most of my life."

David opened his mouth to ask a question—but Ezra stopped him. "Wait until you hear the story. Then you can ask as many questions as you like. For now, let me show you some of the tools I make by hand."

Ezra began by explaining how Ishi fished. "You see, it depended on the season and whether it was river or creek fishing. When fishing for salmon, Ishi used a harpoon made of bone and wood like this one—and would usually thrust, not throw." Ezra also explained how the Yahi used a weir or seine and demonstrated how a smaller hair snare or dip net was used to catch trout and small fish.

"Is this how they still fish?" David asked.

Ezra did not answer. "Come," he said, leading David to the next table. "Take a look at this." On the next table was an unfinished, unstrung bow. "It's exactly forty-four inches," said Ezra. "It's modeled after one of Ishi's own bows. When it's done, it will have a thin backing of rawhide and a woolen hand-grip."

"And strings too, presumably."

Ezra ignored the joke. Instead, he lifted the bow as if taking aim. "Ishi's favorite wood was mountain juniper but other tribes used yew to make their bows. Ishi didn't like that as much, I think, because he knew the leaves are poisonous."

"May I hold it?" asked David.

Ezra handed David the unstrung bow. David took aim, drew an invisible string, and released it with a sound-effect *"Whoosh."*

Ezra took the bow from David. "Bow-hunting is serious and very different from archery. Archery is a game, a target competition. Modern archers use compound bows with gears and pulleys, stabilizers and sights. I'd never use a bow like that to take a life. It doesn't seem fair. If I'm the animal, I don't think it would feel like a good death."

"You think the animal cares how it was shot?"

"Yes, I do. Of course, the animal isn't thinking human thoughts—but I think there's some spiritual reckoning. Besides, it matters to me. My bows aren't made in a factory out of aluminum or carbon or whatever. I cut the branch, I season the wood, and I shape it. And when that's all done, I make strings out of animal sinew—from one of my own kills."

"That must take a lot of time," said David.

"It can take a couple weeks—and we haven't even discussed the arrows and the quiver. But the real hunter is committed—and fair. I think it makes a big difference to the dying animal who the hunter is and what kind of bow and arrow he used to take its life."

There was a sharp edge to Ezra's words. David was smart enough not to disagree or make any more jokes. Ezra reminded David of Billy Jack, the part-Indian, army-vet movie character who kicked bigot ass in the '70s. Like Billy, Ezra was under six foot but stocky strong and highly principled; hard to provoke, but—once ignited—explosive in temperament.

Ezra led David to the third worktable. "Here's where I make my cordage." On the table, and on a pegboard leaning against it, David saw various lengths and weights of untreated

135

string and rope and a number of bone needles with sharp points and precision eyeholes.

"On TV, I once saw a survival expert make string from a yucca plant," David said.

"Nature provides," said Ezra. "Depending on where you are, you can make string from tule, bulrush, beargrass, or even your basic reed."

David lightly touched the strings and needles but did not pick any up.

"I use plant cordage to make nets and snares, and for sewing repairs," said Ezra. "But I find sinew is best for bow-strings."

Ezra sidled over to the fourth and last of his worktables. "I think this may be my favorite work."

Above the table was a shelf of empty beer bottles, mostly green or amber-colored glass, a few that were cobalt blue. On the table sat two beautiful stone bricks like a pair of prized sculptures.

"Can you guess what these are?" Ezra asked.

No other materials or tools were on the table. A large, closed, cardboard box was nearby, on the floor.

"May I touch them?"

"Sure. Just be careful."

David lifted the first stone as if it were a venerated ingot from King Solomon's mines. It was caramel brown, with black striations that looked like fuzzy tiger stripes. After rubbing his fingers on all its sides and even smelling it, he replaced it care-fully. He did the same with the second stone, which appeared to be two horizontally enjoined stones but was actually a single blue stone with a naturally occurring yellow seam.

"No idea. What are they?"

"Care to guess?"

"Give me a clue."

"Both stones were gifts from Constant. The first comes from the legendary Honyama mines in Kyoto, Japan. They closed in 1967, which makes this stone increasingly rare. The second is from a quarry in the Belgian Ardennes."

David shook his head. "I come from the Bronx. The only stones I know are building bricks."

"Give up?"

"Uncle!"

"They're whetstones, two of the best and most beautiful in the world. I use them to sharpen my steel blades."

"Surprising," said David. "I pegged you for an obsidian man."

Ezra laughed. "I love obsidian. I use it for my arrowheads and spearheads. When it's flaked and polished well, there's nothing sharper. But it's relatively brittle. For hard work, my knives and axes—and, of course, my machete—have to be steel."

"You have a machete?"

"My most-indispensable tool."

David nodded. "All my friends have machetes."

"They do?"

"We work in Manhattan. It's a jungle out there."

Ezra laughed hard. He was liking David more and more.

"See these empty beer bottles?" he said, pointing to the shelf. "I find them everywhere. I use them to make my arrowheads."

"They look nothing like arrowheads. How do you do it?"

Ezra reached for one of the bottles. "I break the bottles carefully, then knap off everything except the circular bottom, which is flat and thick. I then use my stone and bone tools to flake the glass—until I have my arrowhead."

"You're like Michelangelo," said David. "He looked at a marble block and saw a Pieta. You look at a beer bottle and see an arrowhead. Same concept."

Ezra smiled again. "For the record," he said, "the older Ishi preferred glass to obsidian for making his arrowheads."

"For a Stone Age Indian, Ishi was a thoroughly modern man."

Ezra smiled. "I think it's time you heard my story."

Chapter 26

Ezra Through the Ages

Willows, California, was (and still is) a small town due east of Oroville, a home to some regional government offices. In November of 1908, Willow's Oro Light & Power Company hired a team of engineers to conduct a land survey in preparation for building a local dam. Tobias Winship worked for the company as a bookkeeper. He'd had two sons, but the elder was killed in a road-building accident the year before. The company might have had some culpability but did its best to ignore the situation. When Tobias' wife died of consumption, he had to decide what to do about his son Ezra, only twelve. *[Ed. Note: The young Ezra described here is Ezra's great-grandfather.]* The boy could read and cipher like a schoolteacher but had an explorer's spirit that could not be chained and was thus unsuited for school or office work. When Tobias heard that his company had hired a group of land surveyors, he asked if his son might join them as an apprentice. The company gladly interceded on his behalf, believing it would end any speculation of its possible wrongdoing in the death of his elder son. And so young Ezra, tall and strong for his age, became a surveyor's assistant, serving mostly as a caddy—carrying transit rods and reels of steel tape, which (lucky for Ezra) had replaced the heavier link chains that had for many years been the traditional means of measuring distance on land.

One day, a party of four (three surveyors and young Ezra) were in Deer Creek Canyon, walking along the shore of the creek, judging whether its rushing waters might be harnessed and made into hydroelectric power. Despite his heavy load, Ezra liked taking the lead, pretending he was a scout. He'd just come around a bend when, no more than fifty feet in front of him, he saw what looked like a loin-clothed Indian, standing mid-stream, poised to harpoon some migrating salmon. The Indian was intensely focused on the blue rushing waters. He had not seen

Ezra (and likely could not have heard or smelled his approach). Ezra wasn't frightened. In fact, some instinct told him that he should warn this Indian of the surveyors' imminent arrival. He dropped his steel tapes with a crash and gave a startling yell. Reflexively, the Indian turned his head and his arms flew up, including the one holding the spear. Just then the three surveyors arrived.

Seeing a half-naked Indian with a raised spear, the three surveyors fled in fright, without any concern for young Ezra. For his part, the boy calmly picked up the reels of steel tape and watched while the Indian leaped out of the stream and into the nearby woods.

Whether the Indian had been surprised or had aggressively brandished his spear is a matter of debate. It's all in the telling. By the time the three surveyors returned to their camp and were sitting around their evening fire, they had conjured a rollicking tall tale.

The next day, still infused with high color from their "brush with death," the three surveyors, along with their local guides, returned to the spot where the Indian had been seen. This time the men were unencumbered with equipment but well-armed. Not surprising, the Indian was gone. Somewhat surprising, no trace of the Indian was found: no sign of fire, not even a footprint on a sandbar. While the men searched for signs, Ezra stood to the side. No one asked him anything, even though he'd had the first and last sight of the Indian. Had they asked, Ezra would have kept his thoughts to himself, intuiting that his silence would help protect the Indian.

The guides fanned out to see if they could track the Indian's scent. After several minutes they announced they were on to something. Whether it was the lingering wisp of a foot-crushed leaf, a trail of toe-heel depressions in a bed of pine needles, a drop of the fleeing Indian's perspiration or some spatter from his urine, they didn't say. Keen to know but too shy to ask, Ezra shadowed the man who seemed to be the head guide, a man named Jack Apperson. When Jack looked down at a broken pine cone or some recent scat; when Jack stared at windblown treetops and the height of flying birds; when Jack notched a tree bark or knotted a spindly branch, Ezra noted all and yearned to understand why.

Jack led the group in a mostly steep ascent through densely thicketed woods. They had just reached a canyon ledge, about five hundred feet above Deer Creek, when they saw two Indians running to higher ground. One was a female of indeterminate age and the other appeared to be an old man who ran with a limp. The men might have chased the fleeing duo if Jack had not caught the scent of some familiar cooking. Following the scent, he discovered a former bear den that reached fairly deep into the granite hillside. Pushing aside some brush cover, Jack entered cautiously, Ezra right behind him, followed by the other men. Just past the den's penumbral shadow, Jack discovered a pot of boiling acorns and the signs of at least two other residents, possibly three.

From the deeper shadows came a human sound—an unmistakable moan. Leading the way, Jack found a small, prone body. He approached carefully, prodding it with the toe of his boot. Another groan. Jack bent towards the body and slowly pulled back a threadbare blanket. The surveyors drew their guns and aimed. "It's an old woman," Jack said, relieved. "Put away your guns. Ezra, push aside the rest of that brush. Let's get some more light in here." Ezra, who had been at Jack's side, eased through the clot of men and moved away more of the concealing brush. His work was swift and effective. The entire den filled with warm sunlight. Feeling proud (not only had he been useful, but Jack had referred to him by name), Ezra insinuated himself back through the crowd to stand at Jack's side. At his feet lay an old woman: withered, weak, and very sick.

"I'm thinking this was a family," said Jack. "The Indian you saw yesterday was prob'ly the son. This must be his ma. No tellin' for sure about the other two."

Ezra stared at the woman. She reminded him of his own mother. For months he'd sat at her bedside while she wheezed and spat blood. His father was usually at work or drinking in town. His older brother was dead and likely in heaven. That left Ezra in charge of his ma's dying.

The woman moaned, a long arc of agony. Ezra dropped to his knees and embraced her. With her lips close to his ear, she spoke a language he had never heard.

"She's thirsty," he said. "She wants a drink of water." Without asking anyone's permission, he opened his canteen and canted it towards her dry lips. The men had already lost interest and were looking around for souvenirs.

Ezra whispered some soft cooing things. And then he thought of his mother's favorite hymn and sang it sweetly, not caring if the men heard him. The old woman seemed to like the lilt of the final verse, so he repeated it several times:

This is my story, this is my song,
Praising my Savior all the day long;
This is my story, this is my song,
Praising my Savior all the day long.

When he finished singing, the woman showed Ezra her closed fist. Slowly, her fingers opened, one petal at a time, and in the center of her palm was a perfect circle of black obsidian, like a coin or medal. She held her hand aloft until Ezra took the gift.

Meanwhile, the men were grabbing whatever seemed interesting or useful. When they finally left, they had gathered three fur capes, fishing nets, arrows, mortars, and baskets. They left the old woman's rags and blanket. Ezra did not mention the perfect circle of black glass, hidden deep in his pocket. He was angry and sad. He knew the other Indians would come back for the old woman and find that all their clothes and supplies had been taken. He imagined them huddled in the hillside den, hungry and cold.

Jack led the way back to the camp. This time, Ezra brought up the rear. He didn't want the men to see his tears.

That night, Ezra had dinner with his father. His father was particularly tired and went to bed early, right after sundown. As soon as his father was asleep, Ezra began collecting useful items he did not think his father would miss. He found some extra rope, a broken knife, two of his brother's coats, some shirts of his own, and a coat that had belonged to his mother. He packed all into an old sack. He figured the bear den was nearly six miles away ... the last half mile through densely thicketed woods ... and then a steep climb up a rocky hillside. He knew he would remember the trail.

Maybe three hours later, Ezra was within fifty yards of the canyon ledge. He thought it best not to seem sneaky, so he rattled branches and kicked stones as he approached. About fifty feet from the bear den, he laid the sack down. If the Indians were there, it surely would be visible. He was about to leave when it occurred to him to add a special signature to the moment. And so, with a voice as sure as he could muster, he sang the verse from his mother's favorite hymn that the old woman had seemed to like:

This is my story, this is my song,
Praising my Savior all the day long;
This is my story, this is my song,
Praising my Savior all the day long.

Feeling satisfied and complete, he made his way home.

The next morning, the surveyors and their guides decided to return to the bear den for a last look around. Ezra began the trek at the back of the single-file march, hoping to hide his crisis of conscience. He worried what the men would say if his gifts were discovered. Knowing they harbored anti-Indian prejudices, he was sure they would condemn him, rather than congratulate him, for his Christian charity. But as they hiked,

Ezra thought of the poor Indian family, hungry and huddled, and with each step his resolve strengthened and his pace quickened. One by one he passed the men ahead of him until, once again, he walked directly behind Jack. By the time they reached the canyon ledge, Ezra was resigned to his fate, ready to accept his punishment, no matter how painful or public. As it turned out, the old woman was gone, along with his sack of gifts. There was no apparent trace that the Indian family had ever been there....

Ezra continued his work as a surveyor's apprentice. A quick study, he was appointed assistant surveyor two years later and told that he should take the official licensing exam as soon as he was of age. Meanwhile, Ezra kept his association with Jack Apperson, who was widely regarded as the best guide in the area. He told Jack he'd work as his damn pack mule if Jack would teach him everything he knew. Jack smiled. He liked the boy's spunk. Ezra learned a great deal from him over the next couple years.

There was no more talk about Indians until late August, 1911. On the morning of the 31st, following his breakfast of coffee, biscuit, and an apple, Ezra was struck by a headline on one of the newspapers on a colleague's desk: "LEAST CIVILIZED MAN TELLS HIS TALE BY SIGNS." To the right of the headline was a side column with its own headline: "Aborigine Whose Tongue No Man Can Understand." Below that headline was a photo of the Indian he'd last seen leaping out of Deer Creek and into the woods. But this Indian seemed vastly changed. He faced the camera with a stunned expression, a cross between zombie and supplicant. He wore a shabby dark coat over a collarless white undershirt. He did not appear to be wearing pants or shoes. His hair was short—modern-looking, thought Ezra. (He could not tell that the Indian had roughly cut and singed his hair as a sign of his grief and sadness.) Ezra read the opening paragraph slowly:

THE ISHI AFFAIR

"OROVILLE. Aug. 30.—In the weird pantomime which has in all ages been the medium through which people of different tongues converse, the Indian found Monday in the mountains near Oroville today told the story of his wanderings."

Ezra continued reading. He learned that the Indian had uttered sounds (presumably words from his native language) but mostly had relied on a kind of universal sign language to show that there had been but four in his party and that two had drowned while crossing a fast stream. With hand gestures and facial expressions, the Indian showed that he had dug two graves and chanted a mournful song for the dead. Then he indicated that he and another had continued wandering until his "mahala" became sick. It was thought that *mahala* meant woman. Though it wasn't certain if the mahala was his mother, wife, or someone else, what happened was clear: he had gone for water while she lay sick and when he returned she was dead and coyotes had attacked her body. The Indian imitated the barking of coyotes. He then mimed digging another shallow grave, placing the mahala there, and chanting the song for the dead once again. Towards the end of the article Ezra read:

"From there, raising one finger and pointing at himself, he showed that he had proceeded alone, that there were no others for whom the officers could look, nor was there any place to which he could lead them."

It was a terribly sad story, a tragic story, from this man, referred to as the last of the Deer Creek Indians. But Ezra wasn't buying it. Something about the Indian's story did not seem right to him. The details seemed too complex (persons drowning, coyotes savaging, aggrieved chanting) to have been spontaneously mimed by a hungry, exhausted, and (presumably) frightened Indian. It seemed to Ezra that such successful miming would have required much forethought and practice.

Ezra read the article a dozen times. He found other newspaper articles, which essentially repeated the same story: The Indian had been part of a tribe that had been hunted for many years. Reduced to a paltry few, its last members had died of privation or accident until only one remained, the last of his people. This was another thing that bothered Ezra. The more he thought about it, the more certain he was that the Indian had not told the whole truth. Ezra thought it was much more likely that at least a few of the Indian's people still lived. But if that were true, *Why did he give himself up? Why does he insist he is the last of his people?* Ezra considered that the Indian might have sacrificed himself. This led Ezra to think about Jesus. Jesus had sacrificed Himself to save the souls of sinners. Jesus died so others could live forever. With this thought echoing in his brain, Ezra began to think that the Indian might have sacrificed himself so that his people, the Yahi, might be left alone—so that they could live forever.

Ezra followed the story of the Indian's life in the newspapers. "Last of the Yahi" was becoming a popular phrase. It seemed to Ezra that any idea repeated often enough could be regarded as truth, irrespective of the facts.

But the facts mattered to Ezra. He couldn't commit to his belief about the living Yahi until he knew for sure. He figured there were only two ways he could clear up the mystery. He could search for the living Yahi until he found them—or he could meet with the Indian and hope to learn the truth. He thought the latter was the most direct path and decided to pursue it.

In the several months since the Indian had been found cowering by the slaughterhouse corral, he'd been escorted by railroad to San Francisco and installed in the university's new museum as its greatest attraction, a living and breathing Stone Age Indian. Ezra had learned that the Indian now had a name. He was called *Ishi,* the Yahi word for "man." It was presumed he had another name—but he wouldn't say. According to the newspapers, Sunday had recently been added to Ishi's weekly schedule of public appearances, during which he greeted museum guests and demonstrated his Stone Age skills, like fire-building and arrow-making.

For months, Ezra had been anxious to make a trip to San Francisco to see Ishi, but he worked Monday through Saturday and had no vacation time. Ishi's Sunday show made Ezra's goal possible—but came with its own conflict. Six months earlier, Ezra had volunteered to help build a new church on the south side of town. It would be a poor church, built mostly from discarded lumber from local lumber mills, where many of its Negro members worked. These Negroes and their families did not feel warmly welcomed at the other Oroville churches and wanted their own house of worship. Ezra believed they ought to have their own church and volunteered to help in its construction. The Grace Mission Holiness Church of God of All Nations opened its doors on the second Sunday of March 1911. Ezra was the only white person invited and had accepted the invitation because he thought it would be impolite to decline. As it turned out, he loved the spirited service, the singing, and the talk of saints. He returned the following Sunday, and every Sunday thereafter, until he'd read about Ishi's Sunday meet and greet at the museum. The question of whether to skip a Sunday service was a moral quandary for Ezra. Ultimately, he decided that learning the truth about the Yahi was more pressingly important. He thought that if the Yahi lived, they likely could use his help.

On the train to San Francisco, Ezra prepared for his meeting with Ishi, rehearsing the few Yahi words he had learned from the newspapers and how he might combine them with his own attempts at sign language.

Despite lingering signs of devastation from the '06 earthquake, Ezra's trip to San Francisco was thrilling—but ultimately disappointing. Ishi's Sunday show had become a smashing success; by the time Ezra arrived in mid-afternoon, there were more than a thousand people on line ahead of him. Though the line moved briskly at times, visitors watched Ishi from a distance of fifteen feet and only for a few minutes. A private audience was laughably impossible.

Ezra's disappointment eased as the train made its way back to Oroville. Ezra thought Ishi had looked happy. Perhaps he'd been wrong about the surviving Yahi. Or, perhaps Ishi was happy because his plan had succeeded and his people were no longer hunted. Either way, thought Ezra, it was in God's hands.

In the summer of 1914, three years after leaving Oroville for San Francisco, Ishi agreed to return to his Deer Creek homeland in the company of Alfred Kroeber, Thomas Waterman, and Saxton Pope, his three closest museum associates.

As soon as Ishi agreed to go, Kroeber began outfitting the expedition. To help with the planning and to serve as guide, Kroeber hired Jack Apperson. Jack casually mentioned it to Ezra. He believed the boy still bore him a grudge for stealing from the Indian's family and thought he could square it with Ezra by inviting him to be his assistant. Ezra was extraordinarily grateful and thanked God for the opportunity—for he saw God's hand in the arrangement, not Jack's thieving one.

As the launch of the expedition neared, Kroeber and his associates became increasingly excited. It was one thing to observe Ishi within the confines of a university museum—but it would be another, miraculous thing to observe Ishi in his native habitat.

To their credit, Kroeber and his associates were concerned that Ishi would be revisiting places of unspeakable tragedy. Even so, they believed Ishi would handle it in his steady, cooperative way. In fact, Ishi did his best to satisfy their every request. He helped them map the area, noting the best fishing pools, deer runs, salt licks, and mineral springs. He named hundreds of varieties of plants and their uses. He explained the Yahi's peripatetic lifestyle, describing how the seasons dictated their travel between valleys, foothills, and high country. He demonstrated how they had hunted and fished, bathed and prayed, raised their children and honored their dead ... in effect, how he and his people had once lived.

All this was both fascinating and exasperating for Ezra. Days passed and he'd had no opportunity to be alone with Ishi. It seemed everyone was always wanting Ishi's attention. Ezra began to despair that he would never learn the truth about the Yahi.

One day, knowing that Ishi liked to wander off after a meal to urinate alone, Ezra followed him towards what the men called the camp's "watering hole." When they arrived, Ezra peeled off to stand ten yards away by his own private bush. While they both did their business, Ezra sang the chorus from his mother's favorite hymn. He thought that Ishi might have heard about his singing. When Ezra began walking back to the camp, Ishi approached him, looking him over without saying a word. To break the silence, Ezra pointed to himself and said his own name. Ishi just stared. Eventually, Ezra reached into his pocket and withdrew a closed fist, which he opened slowly, one finger at a time, to reveal the perfect circle of black obsidian that Ishi's mother had given him. Ishi stared back and forth between the black stone and Ezra's eyes. Ezra then moved his hand towards Ishi and said simply: "For you." Ishi took the stone and pressed it to his heart and kept it there while mumbling something Ezra did not understand. Ishi then placed the stone back into Ezra's hand and closed Ezra's fingers around it. He then turned and walked away, gesturing Ezra to follow.

Ishi led Ezra to a circular grove of tall manzanita bushes that grew in relatively arid soil. Ishi slipped inside the grove and Ezra followed him to its center, where there was a relatively smooth and sandy patch of ground. Immediately, Ishi dropped to his knees and began drawing with his right forefinger in the sand. While he drew, he used his limited English and his great miming skill to indicate he was drawing a map route. Ezra's heart pounded fiercely. He understood Ishi's symbols for hill, mountain, stream, valley, cliff, and cave. A few times he asked for clarification, and Ishi's responses were always very clear. It seemed to Ezra that Ishi must have practiced exactly how he would convey this information.

Ezra understood his mission: He would find the living Yahi and do what he could to make sure they thrived. When Ishi was sure that Ezra had understood, he wiped clear all the lines in the sand, stood up slowly, and walked back to the camp. Ezra remained awhile in the circle of bushes. He felt like he was in a sacred place and had just been charged with a holy office. When he calmed, he walked slowly back to camp and took his usual place beside Jack.

No one had noticed that he had been gone. Why would they? He was just the guide's assistant—so unimportant that his name and function had never been recorded by anyone who had ever written about the expedition.

Chapter 27

David's Response

"That was your grandfather?"

"My great-grandfather," said Ezra.

"Ishi told your great-grandfather where to find the living Yahi?"

"Yes. He drew him a map."

"And today's Yahi are Stone Age Indians, just like Ishi was?"

"Yes. In some ways even more primitive and isolated."

David drew a deep breath.

"Jill knows all this?" David asked.

"Yes."

"What about Simon?"

"Simon knows the Yahi live. But he doesn't know where."

"What's his plan?" David asked.

Ezra thought awhile before responding. "I don't think he has a clear plan. I think he has two vague goals. One: Find the Yahi himself and lead them to liberty. Two: Stop us from doing it first."

"Would it be so bad if Simon lead them out first?"

"Yes. It would be terrible."

"Why?"

"News of an American Stone Age people will turn this place into a media circus."

"But that will happen whether Simon leads them out or you do."

"That's right. But Simon will do it as soon as he can, just to make sure he's the one to do it. The sooner he leads the Yahi to freedom, the sooner he'll be in the spotlight and feel important. He wants to have his name in the history books. He wants to be remembered."

"He's not the first person to feel that way," said David.

"Just because his motives are understandable, doesn't make them right. I get where he's coming from. He's always been poor and he's tired of it. He's tired of feeling second-class and asking for help. He knows that being credited for discovering the living Yahi will make him famous. He also knows that the buzz will draw a lot of people here, which will bring a lot of business to the casino, which will also benefit him."

"Simon's plan doesn't seem so terrible to me," David said.

"You're not seeing the big picture," said Ezra. "Simon will just plow ahead without thinking anything through. When Ishi was brought into the modern world, the response was crazy. Imagine what it will be like when a whole tribe of Stone Age American Indians are thrown into the twenty-first century."

David imagined....

"I need to protect the Yahi," said Ezra. "I need to prepare them for their introduction into society. Before that happens, we need to have them recorded as they are—before they are polluted and mainstreamed beyond recognition. Jill and her team will do as much filming as possible. You should start writing."

"I already have," David said proudly. "I began with a dream I once had about Ishi's brain and then started sketching out the story, beginning with Jill coming back to New York and calling me from Bellevue. I'm writing notes as the story unfolds."

"That's great. Of course, it's impossible to predict how it will go."

"That's true in fiction, too."

"I trust that you and Jill will get the story straight. For my part, if I don't manage this right, the Ishi Wilderness will be wild with a million curiosity seekers."

"It's a huge story. Can you blame them?"

"No, I don't blame them. But I need to manage them. I need to do what's best for the Yahi."

"You're the man," said David.

"I've been thinking about this my whole life. I've been trained to do it. I was born to do it."

"Born to do it? Really?"

"Yes. You need to know the rest of my story."

Chapter 28

Ezra through the Ages (part 2)

Regrettably, there is no picture of Ezra Winship's great-grandfather and Ishi together. A picture of Ezra (1) and Ishi would have been venerated by the surviving Yahi more than any other object. Alas, there was no other opportunity for Ezra to be alone with Ishi, much less to be photographed with him. Ishi never spoke to Ezra again after their first and only meeting. He would not even look in his direction. And yet, all the while Ezra was part of the Deer Creek expedition he felt Ishi's eyes upon him. In fact, even after Ishi's death in 1916 and until the hour of his own death in 1968, Ezra (1) always felt Ishi's watchful presence and the weight of the holy charge he had wordlessly accepted.

Ezra (1) did not seek out the Yahi until after Ishi had died. Even then he was hesitant to fulfill his charge. He never doubted he would find the cave where the Yahi lived. He never questioned why God had chosen him for the special honor. He only doubted his readiness. He knew the time would be right when he saw the signs.

The next spring, more than a year after Ishi's death, when the birds were singing and the flowers blooming, Ezra celebrated his twenty-first birthday. The following week he passed the exam to become a licensed surveyor. The week after that a fire severely damaged the church he had helped build. The pastor announced that Sunday services would be held outdoors—weather permitting—until repairs could be made. Ezra imagined the uncharred pews and benches arranged on the back lawn: the foothills, mountains, and sky serving as nave, altar, and pulpit. It occurred to Ezra that the wilderness was his true church.

When Ezra (1) was twenty-one he went in search of the Yahi. With a surveyor's license in his pocket and Ishi's map route in his memory, he was ready to find them. He used all his skills and knowledge to track the way. When he came to a stream or hill or valley that Ishi had mapped in the sand, it was confirmation of the landmark he saw behind his eyes.

With amazing directness Ezra approached the cave where the Yahi had been living secretly for more than six years. He stopped when he was about a quarter mile away, suddenly fearful he might be shot by an arrow or speared by a Yahi sentry. He wished Ishi had provided him with some password or bird-call or drumbeat to guarantee his safe arrival. But he was hardly unprepared. In his rucksack he'd brought an envelope filled with newspaper photographs of Ishi. In his memory he'd stored a couple hundred Yahi words. He also carried a powerful totem: the perfect circle of black obsidian given to him by the old woman, likely Ishi's own mother. Ready, Ezra (1) went to meet his fate.

Chapter 29

David's Interruption

"Hold on! Let me get this straight. Your great-grandfather actually found the surviving Yahi. And the same Stone Age people still live today."

"Their descendants live today—but yes."

"Wow. Really, wow…. And I'm going to meet them."

"You and the rest of the world," said Ezra.

"Has anyone else met the Yahi in the last hundred years?"

"No. They've been isolated and protected. Other than my great-grandfather, grandfather, and father, they've met no one else … other than me and Constant."

"Your girlfriend?"

"Yes, though I hope to marry her when all this craziness settles down."

"How'd the Yahi meet her?"

"The Yahi know their isolation is coming to an end. Lately, they've been asking more questions about 'the other world,' as they call it. One of them—a young man named Branch—asked me if I had a woman. He used the word *mahala*. I assumed he meant 'wife.'"

"A normal question."

"Exactly—and it gave me an idea. I'd been thinking of ways to transition the Yahi, so I told him I have a mahala and asked if he and the others would like to meet her."

"How'd that go?"

"At first, not well. My suggestion was a bigger deal than I realized. Branch and some of the other Yahi started arguing."

"What'd they say?"

"They spoke so fast I couldn't follow what they were saying."

"They speak English?"

"They speak Yahi."

"You speak Yahi?"

"I know about three hundred words, and they know about the same amount of English, so we can communicate pretty well—unless they speak fast—and then I'm lost."

"What'd they say about Constant? I guess they agreed to meet her."

"At first, they were very nervous. What I suggested had never been done before. But they knew it was time ... and they trusted me."

"How'd it go?"

Ezra paused. "The next time I came to visit them—I try to visit at least once a month—I brought several photographs of Constant, including a few that show us together. The Yahi passed the photos around, talking low, so I couldn't really hear. They seemed happy. And then they took the photos to a room I call the Gallery, and they added the photos to their wall collection."

"They have a photo gallery?"

Ezra laughed. "I suppose—Stone Age style. They live in a cave."

"One big cave?"

"Actually, it's an ancient lava tube. It looks and feels impressive, but it's porous and a thousand years of seeping rainwater has compromised its integrity. It won't last forever. Anyway, this tube is naturally divided into sections, like rooms, and one of the larger rooms is where they pray and chant. On one side of this temple-room—this Gallery—they display all the photos of Ishi they've collected over the years. On the opposite side of the room they display all the photos they have of my fathers and me."

"And Constant."

"Yes. I hadn't expected that. It's unfortunate."

"Why?"

157

"The Yahi regard their photos as holy. I think they see the images as immortalized souls. Introducing Constant through her pictures was a bad idea. All I did was give the Yahi another person to venerate."

"Another person? They venerate you?"

"Yes. They see me as the last in a line of prophets. I'm the Moses who will lead them out of darkness and into freedom."

"They use that name? I mean, they refer to you as Moses?"

"No. They call me Ezra, but they think of me as Moses."

"Your line of fathers taught them some Scripture?"

"A little. Some basics. I don't know if it was right. Don't ask me to defend it or deny it. But each of my fathers, as you call them, had a missionary zeal."

"Passed down, father to son."

"Yes. We are each our father's son: all surveyors ... all expert outdoorsmen ... all believers in God and Jesus ... all sworn to protect the Yahi."

"Were they all named Ezra?"

"Yes, beginning with my great-grandfather, Ezra 1. I'm Ezra 4."

"You're the last of the Ezras."

Ezra paused. "I never thought of that. But you're right. I'm the last. Even if I marry and have a son, I will not name him Ezra. After I free the Yahi, our job is done."

Chapter 30

Jill's Debriefing

As planned, David knocked on Jill's door after his meeting with Ezra.

"Hi, it's me."

Jill answered from the other side: "I'm not decent."

David pressed his mouth close to the door. "I can come back when you're dressed."

The door swung open. Jill stood before him, fully clothed.

"I didn't say I was undressed—just not decent."

David looked her over. She looked sexy. "What's the difference between *indecent* and *not decent*?" he asked.

Jill paused to think. "*Indecent* is a temporary state of depravity. *Not decent* is a permanent state of bad."

"Which are you?" asked David.

"I lack basic decency," said Jill.

"But are you still a good person?" David asked, smiling.

"I don't know," said Jill. "Is it possible to be good if you're not decent?"

"Not sure," said David. "But while we're at it: Where have all the flowers gone?"

"Good point," said Jill. "And by the way: What becomes of the brokenhearted?"

With that, Jill drew David into her room, closing the door behind him.

[Twenty minutes later]

"What did you think of Ezra and his story?" Jill asked.

"Perfect," said David.

"*Perfect?* What does that mean?"

"It means if I were writing a story about a social outlier who has sworn to protect a tribe of Stone Age innocents against person or persons who are selfishly ambitious and possibly violent—I'd use Ezra as my protagonist. In fact, you may want to use him as the leading man in your film."

"He does fit the bill."

"Absolutely. Ruggedly handsome. Principled but practical. Orthodox but individualistic. Equal parts evangelist and commando. I can't wait to describe him in my book."

"Have you already started?"

"Yes, I told Ezra I started with a dream I used to have about Ishi's brain. It's a nice narrative hook ... and then I move into my latest reconnection with you."

"Doesn't your wife mind when you tell all in your fictional tell-alls?"

"I usually change the names to protect the guilty."

"That's comforting. But really: Aren't you worried what your wife will say?"

"It's fiction, I tell her. If that doesn't work, I deny. If that doesn't work, I lie."

"If that doesn't work?"

"I run for cover."

Jill shook her head. "Nice plan. I hope she doesn't find you under my covers."

"That reminds me, I should write her an e-mail today."

"Send her my regards."

"Really?"

"No, you idiot."

Chapter 31

David's E-mail to Allison

Hi Honey—hope all is well! Things are fine here. So far, babysitting Bill has been a good job for me. Once in a while, when I think he might be drinking too much or getting too cozy with undesirables, I do what I can to redirect, if you know what I mean. But basically he's been behaving. I'll report to Sandy later today.

I want you to know that I've been eating pretty well. I grab most of my meals in a cute little cantina in the hotel. It's actually called La Cantina. I can't say it's as wholesome as Saffron, but the food is really good—although you might be surprised if you saw the chef. She's a young, tattooed Goth chick in army fatigues and ballet slippers—a little weird, but she can flat-out cook. Sometimes, for a change of pace, we pick one of the local restaurants in Los Molinos or we drive to Chico.

By the way, my trip back to Chico turned out to be a great idea. It brought back so many memories and really helped me reconnect with my past. Most importantly, it got me thinking about Chico, my first novel—my unfinished, teenage attempt to write about Ishi, the Stone Age Indian. Well, here I am again, forty-five years later, and some new ideas have reignited my interest. I'm sketching out an entire new plot. I won't be able to call it Chico anymore. That title fit when I was seventeen and imagined myself as the first-person protagonist. The following year is when I met you. We were both only eighteen—a lifetime ago!

I love you very much.

David

P.S. How did the dental and car repairs go? I'm sorry I'm not there to help you take care of all that. And how's your freelance job going? Not too much stress, I hope. Have you been receiving my salary payment from Sandy? She was supposed to wire the money into our account every week. Let me know if there's any problem.

Steven Jay Griffel

Allison's E-mail to David

Good to hear from you, my love! I miss you! When I don't hear from you for a few days, you know what I do? I go to Google Images and look up all the places you've been visiting. If your job lasts a long while and we've saved up some money, I want to come visit you for a few days. Wouldn't that be fun! You can show me around!

As for the car and my teeth and all the other bills … what can I say? It's only money—if only we had a little more! On that note, let me offer a heads-up: I spoke to Sandy just yesterday. I think she wants to hear from you a little more often. And I think she'd like your reports to be a little more specific. I mean she's paying for them—so give her what she wants, right?

Write soon. Also, let's talk on the phone. I need to hear your voice, my love….

David's E-mail to Sandy (Bcc to Allison)

Hi Sandy—hope you are well and profitably busy. Life here is okay, but very slow…. Los Molinos could be renamed Los Molasses.

From what I can tell—and I watch him a good part of every day—Bill is staying out of trouble. He's usually up at the crack of noon and has a slow brunch in the cantina—the only restaurant in the hotel, though it's really just an extension of the bar. He likes his coffee black, his eggs scrambled, and his home fries burnt. Don't know if there's any change there.

From everything I've seen—and everything I've heard—Bill has been a solid employee. Whenever I see him in the casino he's always working or shooting the breeze with a customer—point is: I never see him gambling. Because the casino biz is slow—Bill sometimes helps out in the bar or cleans up, wherever he's useful. I haven't heard him complain. One thing, he hasn't asked me for any money, which is a good sign.

We have some interesting characters here: the cook is a tattooed Goth commando-ballerina; her boyfriend is an evangelist-wilderness expert. We have an Indian massage therapist named Morgan whose gender is impossible to tell without bending him/her over and taking a good look—and I'm not going there. We have a front desk clerk named Ellie who is part

162

Wintu Indian and who can talk nonsense for an hour without drawing a breath. And then there's this other Indian, a surly guy named Simon, who might be trouble. I'm not exactly sure what the story is, but it seems there's some ancient tribal blood-feud between Simon and some of the others. I don't think Bill is involved—but I'm watching.

By the way, do you know if Bill owns a gun? If so, is it licensed? It may be nothing, but Bill and a friend went into the desert the other day to do some target practice. Perhaps no big deal—just wondering.

Hope this report suffices. Let me know if there's something specific you'd like to know.

Love—

Bro

Sandy's E-mail to David

I was just about to write to you. I'm worried.

Two days ago our lights and elevator went out. I thought it was a power issue and called the building manager and he mentioned the word generator. Anyway, I was late for my yoga class and had to take the stairs down seven flights to the basement parking garage. It was dark as hell down there. So I get into my car, start it up, put on the headlights—and I see a piece of paper tucked under my windshield wiper. Now I'm really pissed. I'm thinking: I'm paying for a luxury hi-rise: No Solicitors! So I get out of the car, grab the paper, get back in the car, and I'm about to toss it, thinking it's an ad for carpet-cleaning or a Chinese menu—but I see it's a handwritten message on an index card—bold, like written with a Sharpie: "Your husband owes us money. We're looking for him. We'll find him. One way or the other, we expect to be paid."

I almost screamed. I felt like some thug was in the car with me. I was so flustered, I backed out quickly, scraped a fender, and drove outside. I was so scared I couldn't even go on. I just pulled into an open spot and just sat there, trembling. I mean someone in the dark was almost in my car! It felt like the Psycho scene—like I was alone in the shower and someone rips open the curtain and starts hacking away with a knife. That's how I felt! I don't usually fluster too easy—but this got to me. And now you say he has a gun! He's never had a gun. I've never even seen him hold a gun. I'm call-

ing Murray Levine, my lawyer. He'll have some ideas. Meanwhile—you be very careful! I don't know what else to say. Watch out for Bill—and watch out for yourself too!

    Love—

    Sis

David Forwards Sandy's E-mail to Allison

    Honey, I just got the e-mail below from my sister. I'm fine. Bill's fine. But you might want to give her a call. She's been good to us, and I think she could use some support. Let me know if you learn anything new.

    Love ya!

Chapter 32

Fraternal Order

Bill walked into La Cantina and approached David, who was sitting at one of the few tables. Constant was behind the bar.

"Is that white wine you're drinking?" Bill asked David.

"Nope."

"Ginger ale?"

"Nope."

"Sarsaparilla?"

"Is that like root beer?"

"I think so," said Bill.

"Nope."

"Hmmm. Are you drinking regular beer?" Bill asked.

"Yup."

"Constant, I'll have what he's having. Add it to his bill."

David pulled back the chair beside him. "Please, join me."

"I hate to impose."

"I insist."

"Thank you, mon frère ... just for a bit, while I slake my thirst."

Bill settled in and Constant brought the beer. Bill lifted his glass of beer and toasted his brother-in-law: "Liberté, égalité, fraternité!"

"Same to you, brother!" David said, clinking his glass with Bill's. "L'chaim!"

The two men settled in for a talk.

"I heard you met with Ezra yesterday," Bill said. "He tell you the whole story?"

"Chapter and verse."

"Touché!"

"I gather you know the tale," said David.

"I got the Cliff's Notes version. I don't need all the minutiae."

"You're a Big Picture guy."

"That's flattering. Truth is: I do what I'm told, when I'm told."

"Whoa. No need to sell yourself short."

"On this job, I'm not being paid to think," said Bill.

"What are you being paid for, if you don't mind me asking?"

"To protect your ass—and Jill's too."

"We need protecting?"

"Look," Bill said, lowering his voice. "I don't know what's going to happen. But I do know that Simon has formed a group of outside friends—mostly other Indians. He wants to free the Yahi. He's determined to stop anyone else from doing it first."

"That much I understand," said David. "But why does he need a group? Why doesn't he just do it himself?"

"For one thing, he's paranoid. He thinks people are out to stop him."

"He's right."

"Well, he's a smart paranoid. But he also doesn't know what the hell he's doing. He needs a team."

"An advisory board."

"Precisely."

"I meant to ask Ezra, but maybe you know: How did Simon discover that the Yahi exist?"

"Pure dumb luck," said Bill. "As I heard it, he took some woman hiking into the Ishi Wilderness. Cheap date. Anyway, at some point he wanders off to get some firewood or to take a leak—whatever—and the dumb bastard gets lost and separated from the woman. He wanders around—probably walking in circles—only Indian I ever heard of who gets lost in his own backyard. Eventually, he comes across another Indian who was hunting or gathering or something. This Indian is dressed in a loincloth and has a bow and arrow. Simon gets all excited, thinking this Indian must be the Second Coming of Ishi. And this Indian, a strong, young-looking fellow, doesn't run away. In fact, he isn't even shy. Even more amazing—he knows some English."

"Like three hundred words of English," said David.

"You see where I'm going with this."

"Keep going."

"So Simon and this Indian have a little chat, and it doesn't take long before Simon understands that this Indian is a kissin' cousin of Ishi's."

"One of the living Yahi."

"Glad you understand my French."

"Oui."

"Back to Simon: It's getting late and the other Indian indicates he must go. Simon explains that he's lost and has no idea how to get back. So the other Indian gestures for Simon to follow him and in less than thirty minutes he leads Simon to a trail and points which way he should go."

"That's it?" asked David. "What happened to the woman Simon was with?"

"She left him and found her way home. But Simon, he's torn. On the one hand, he's in a hurry—the sun's going down, he doesn't want to get lost again, he's in the wild, there are bears and big cats out looking for dinner—but he also wants something from the young Indian, some proof of their meeting."

"They strike a deal?"

"Neither of them had a lot of bargaining chips. But each had something the other wanted. Want to guess?"

"No, just tell me."

"Simon asked for the beaver quiver—with a few of the arrows thrown in to sweeten the deal."

"What did the other Indian want?"

"Simon emptied his pockets and told the Indian he could pick what he wanted.... Sure you don't want to guess?"

"No. You're killing me. Just tell me," said David.

"The Indian pointed to two things: a nearly full pack of cigarettes and … last chance to guess."

"Tell me!"

"The cell phone."

"Simon gave him his cell phone? A Stone Age Indian is walking around with a cell phone?"

"Truth is stranger than fiction, bro. Isn't that what you told me?"

Chapter 33

Simon Says

Simon had been an angry boy who grew up to be an angry man. If a Native American sat beside him on the bus, he might tell the stranger why he was angry. With everyone else he maintained a sullen distance.

Simon believed, with all his heart, that he had good reasons for his dark broodings. He wouldn't say he'd been conditioned. That wasn't a word he'd use. He'd say screwed, stifled, cheated. Outside the community of Indians, he saw himself a stranger in a strange land; a man without a country. For years he wore such feelings with anger and shame, the way Jews in the Third Reich wore a yellow Star of David. But over time his perceived badge of shame became an occasional badge of honor. Over the years it became increasingly cool to be Indian.

Simon was a little boy when Theodora Kroeber (Alfred's much younger second wife) published two books about Ishi in the 1960s. By the time Simon was a teenager and had read the books, Ishi had regained iconic status, especially in California where his story was familiar to most school children.

Understandably, Native Americans felt they owned Ishi. Though millions of people—and not only Americans—were inspired by Ishi's tragic story, Native Americans could reasonably claim that they understood him best.

Simon felt Ishi's story very personally. His maternal great-great-grandparents were northern California Indians, Maidu who had met during their own Trail of Tears (a forced march back to the Round Valley Reservation in 1863, just two years after Ishi's birth). Though Simon's parents survived, many aunts, uncles, cousins died of stress or were murdered. Simon's connection to Ishi was also a matter of blood. While it is true that the Yahi and Maidu were enemies, it is also true that the two tribes sometimes intermarried. Members of Simon's family loudly insisted that they were equal parts Maidu, Wintu, and Yahi. In fact, by the time Simon reached full adulthood, it was commonly pointed out that he bore a striking resemblance to Ishi. Finally, in Maiduan languages, *maidu* means "man," just as *ishi* means "man" in Yahi.

Throughout his hardscrabble life Simon clutched to these special connections. But it wasn't until he was middle-aged and half addled with alcohol and anger that he saw an opportunity to make his own mark that would tie himself to Ishi for all eternity. These thoughts were floating in his mind after he'd he met the young Indian in the Ishi Wilderness and was trying to find his way home in the darkening twilight.

For his part, the young Indian (who'd been out past curfew, burning off his frustrations after having laid eyes on a beautiful woman—and not just any woman, but Ezra's woman) had also been thinking about the plans to free the Yahi and what he might do to draw Constant's attention and to create his own everlasting legacy.

Chapter 34

Front Desk

Having updated the rough draft of his new novel to include some notes about Branch (the Stone Age Indian Simon had "discovered" in the Wilderness), David moseyed to the hotel's lobby to chat awhile with Ellie who was, as usual, working behind the front desk.

"Quiet around here."

"Usually is," said Ellie.

"Makes me wonder: Why'd they build the hotel here?"

"Why not?"

"I mean, it's off the beaten path, don't you think?"

"It's right off the highway."

"Still ... it's out in the sticks."

"That's part of its charm. Besides ..."

"Besides what?" asked David.

"It's not far from where Ishi's buried. I think that was the idea—to make the hotel a kind of tourist magnet."

"I didn't realize Ishi is buried so close to here."

"I didn't say he was."

"I thought you did."

"No, I said it isn't far."

"So, you're saying the casino was built here because it isn't far from where Ishi is buried."

A few seconds of silence.

"The burial site is a secret," said Ellie. I shouldn't be talking about it. Especially with you."

"Because I'm not an Indian?"

"Yes. No offence."

"None taken."

"Good."

A few seconds of silence.

171

"Sorry," said David. "I didn't mean to make you uncomfortable."

"You didn't."

"Good. I like talking to you. I'm just curious."

"I like talking to you too. It gets lonely here."

"Can I ask another question?"

"Depends."

"Okay. Can you tell me when Ishi was reburied?"

"Sure," said Ellie. "That's not a secret. He was reburied in August of 2000."

David paused to calculate.

"That's almost eighty-five years after he died. Why'd it take so long?"

"They had Ishi's ashes. But they didn't find his brain until January 1999."

"Had they been looking for it?"

"No. No one knew it was missing. No one knew it existed. But then someone found out that the brain had been saved. To bury Ishi right, we needed his brain and the ashes of his body. We needed to bury them together in a real Indian ceremony."

"Where'd they find the brain?"

Smithsonian Brain Tank

Alfred Kroeber had made it clear that Ishi should be buried in a manner that respected both Yahi custom and Christian tradition. He was opposed to an autopsy, noting that scientific collections already contained hundreds of Indian remains that nobody came to study. Kroeber wanted—and expected—Ishi to be cremated, according to Yahi custom.

When Kroeber returned from a sabbatical in New York to find Ishi's brain on his desk, floating in a glass jar like a giant paperweight, his repugnance was incalculable. After an exchange of letters with Ales Hrdlicka, Curator of the National Museum, Kroeber had the brain pickled in formalin and shipped to Washington in the hope that it might be put to some scientific use. The brain was received by the Smithsonian and given accession number 60884 and museum number 298736.

For sixty-four years Ishi's brain, weighing in at exactly 1300 grams, was stored in a ground glass jar in the Division of Collections of the Physical Anthropology Labs on the third floor of the Natural History Building. Ishi's brain wasn't alone. It was surrounded by hundreds of other nameless Indian brains, all ID'd with accession numbers and museum numbers, the equivalent of scientific toe tags. In 1981, the soft tissue collections (non-skeletal remains) were re-preserved in ethyl alcohol and transferred to stainless steel tank #6 in Hall 25 of a Maryland storage facility. In 1994 Ishi's brain was moved to Third Pod, Museum Support Center. And there it remained, unnoticed, until someone thought to ask about it.

Chapter 35

The Wilderness Cabin

Ellie had excused herself to go to the bathroom and while David deliberated what to do next, Ezra entered the lobby.

"Just the man I wanted to see," said Ezra.

"I'm flattered. What's up?"

"Let's go for a ride."

"Okay. Where we headed?"

"The Wilderness."

The two men walked out the main entrance and towards Ezra's pickup truck in the parking lot. There were only four other cars in the lot.

Ezra turned on the ignition and drove towards the back of the hotel and onto the western terminus of the Lassen Trail.

"You're driving," said David.

"You have a keen eye for detail. Good thing for a novelist."

"I read somewhere that this was a pioneer trail. No vehicular traffic allowed."

"You read right. The trail was paved by hoofbeats, wagon wheels, and stamping boots. Now it's part of Lassen Park—no vehicles allowed."

"And yet you're driving."

"I have a special license."

"Like Papal Dispensation?"

"Papal authority does not play here. This is U.S. federal land. I'm an assistant park ranger, in charge of the Ishi Wilderness."

"Really?"

"Really," said Ezra.

"You have a badge and a secret decoder ring?"

"I have a card. And a gun."

"Works for me. How'd you become a park ranger?"

"I'm an assistant. My father—"

"Ezra 3."

"Yes, Ezra 3. He was at a local ceremony when the government designated this section of Lassen National Park as the Ishi Wilderness Area."

"A local decision?"

"Actually it was an act of Congress in 1984. It was a nice tribute and the area is aptly named. It really is a wilderness. The terrain is rough, cut from volcanic rock, which keeps it relatively isolated."

"And protects the Yahi who still live there."

"Yes, but only my father would have known that. Anyway, a friend of his was one of only two rangers assigned to all of Lassen Park—that's 166 square miles—a lot of territory for one ranger on duty at a time. When the Ishi Wilderness Area was designated, my father went to his friend and volunteered to help him. He said he often made trips throughout the Ishi Wilderness and could help him keep an eye on things. The ranger was thrilled. He knew my father was a surveyor, an expert outdoorsman, and a good Christian—and was very grateful for his help. He was even able to get the Department of Parks to give my father a special license."

"Which allowed your father to drive in the area."

"Where possible. In most places the trail is too narrow and rugged. Even hiking can be a challenge—if you don't know what you're doing."

"You inherited your father's license?"

"I applied for it and was accepted."

"Like father, like son."

Ezra smiled. "The Department of Parks went one better with me. After 1999, when Ishi's brain was discovered floating in a steel vat in the Smithsonian, I volunteered to build a cabin in the Wilderness—at my own expense. With all the talk of which Indian tribe would receive the brain and oversee the burial, I suggested to the Department that there might be a surge in curious tourists that should be kept in check."

"Did you really think that would happen?"

"It was possible. Still is. The route to Ishi's gravesite would likely be a popular pilgrimage if the exact destination was generally known. But it's not. Even so, I think the idea of a pilgrimage is what inspired the building of the hotel."

David looked a little perplexed. "If the government thought the Yahi were extinct, how'd they decide which tribe would get the honor of receiving Ishi's brain and reburying it—along with his ashes?"

"That's a good question. It took a long time for the government to decide. And the final decision disappointed a lot of people. Especially Simon."

Next of Kin

In 1990 the U.S. Congress passed the Native American Grave Protection and Repatriation Act. This law and its amendments mandated that all federal agencies and museums receiving federal funds must return, when requested, human remains, funerary articles, and other cultural objects to proven lineal descendants and culturally related Native American tribes.

But what if there were no proven lineal descendants? What if there were many competing culturally related tribes?

Such was the case involving Ishi's cremated ashes and his scientifically preserved brain. To the government's best knowledge there were no surviving Yahi that would automatically inherit Ishi's remains. According to law, next in line would be the federally-recognized tribe (or their representatives) that had the closest cultural affiliation with the Yahi. But on what basis does one measure cultural affiliation? Federal authorities put together a committee that considered a wide range of kinship factors, including linguistic, folkloric, oral traditional, historical, geographical, biological, archaeological, anthropological, and whatever other relevant information and opinions the experts could gather.

The temperature among the competing tribes was heated. It would be an extraordinary coup to take possession of Ishi's ashes and brain, which had become treasured symbols of Native American heritage and loss, and now, hope for a better future.

At long last, the vetting committee decided to choose one of the Yana tribes for the honor. After all, Ishi identified himself as a Yahi-Yana (despite the assertion by some researchers that he might have been half Maidu or Wintu). But Ishi's self-identification aside, the most compelling reason for choosing the Yana was their distinctive language. Even with their different dialects, basic Yana is based on gender-specific patterns that had made it easy for Ishi to communicate with other Yana. Language, more than history or geography, was the deciding factor in repatriating Ishi's ashes and brain.

Because there were two equally deserving Yana tribes to choose from, the experts chose the Redding Rancheria and the Pit River tribe to share in the honor of receiving Ishi's earthly remains. Jointly, they planned a secret ceremony to consecrate ash and brain together so that Ishi's whole spirit might finally be at peace and join his ancestors.

Members of the Redding Rancheria and Pit River tribes were thrilled.

Simon, part Wintu and part Maidu, was bitterly disappointed.

Ellie, a Wintu, was mildly disappointed.

Morgan, the Rancheria Indian and gender-indeterminate masseuse, was quietly thrilled, lest her/his friend Simon be driven to some violent act of jealousy.

Chapter 36

Ezra's Traps

Ezra and David were still riding slowly and bumpily on the Lassen Trail.

"So, do you know where Ishi is buried?" David asked.

"No. I wasn't invited. But I know people who were there."

"Ever tempted to ask them?"

"Once."

"Only once?"

Ezra nodded. "I used to think the living Yahi had a right to know. And if that were true, I thought I should probably be the one to tell them."

"You didn't pursue that line of thinking?"

"No, I thought it would be too complicating. I decided I should just focus on preparing the Yahi for freedom—and then getting it done. Down the road, if the people who know about Ishi's burial want to share that information with the living Yahi—that's up to them."

"I see.... But weren't you tempted to find out, just for your own curiosity?"

"Not really. I think it would be insulting to the people who were honored by being there. They were entrusted with a hugely important secret. I respect that."

"You're a good man, Ezra."

"I've been blessed. It's been my great privilege to help care for the Yahi. And I'm grateful beyond expression that I've been chosen to deliver them to freedom."

"That's a lot of pressure though, isn't it?"

"There's no pressure if you're doing God's will. Besides, look how God has paved the way for my success: I'm the fourth Ezra blessed to help protect the Yahi. I've been able to become a surveyor. I have built a good business as a wilderness guide. I have a special license to drive my truck in the Wilderness. And I was allowed to build a cabin here."

"I guess you use the cabin when working as a guide and also to be closer to the Yahi when you need to be."

"Exactly. You're a quick study for a city slicker."

David smiled. "Is that where we're going now, to your cabin?"

"Yes, in fact we're almost there."

A half mile or so later, the ever-narrowing trail curved behind a large brown hill. The one-room cabin sat on the lee side, out of sight, huddled in the shade of tall, over-arching oaks.

"Home sweet home," said Ezra, parking the truck where it could not be seen from the trail. "Come on in."

Ezra opened the heavily timbered door and David had his first look inside. In the proximate center was a simple wooden table and four ladder-back chairs. On the left was a roughhewn platform bed covered with a quilted yellow blanket and a pair of plump pillows. On the right was a neatly stacked pile of firewood; beside it, a wood-burning stove, its black stovepipe rising through the ceiling and roof. Each wall had a single, double-paned window, bordered with a lacy curtain. A modest bureau, desk, and tool cabinet filled the room. There was no closet, sink, or toilet.

"Lovely," said David. "All the comforts of home— except for the comforts of home."

"There's an outhouse about thirty yards away."

"That's comforting."

"It's a cabin, not a hotel," said Ezra.

"The Michelin Guide gave it a deluxe rating," David said, smiling. "I'm canceling my subscription."

Ignoring the joke, Ezra checked the windows. Meanwhile, David walked about, taking a closer look at details he had not noticed with his first glance. On the right wall, two pots and a single black skillet hung from pegs. On the far wall, a narrow shelf displayed three bone-white plates with an encircling blue filigree.

David was about to remark how a woman's touch had softened this man-cave when he turned to observe the wall behind him. There, arranged with a kind of ferocious bravado, was a shocking display of leghold animal traps, their maws wide open.

David felt the weight of Ezra's watchful eyes.

"Be careful."

David approached the largest of the metal jaws: a monster's mouth full of sharp, serrated teeth.

"They bite?" David asked.

"Not anymore. I've removed the springs."

Very carefully, David tested the sharpness of the teeth with the tip of his forefinger.

"You use these to trap animals?"

"No. I use homemade snares and deadfalls to trap small game. I hunt big game with a bow."

"Where'd you get these?"

"I occasionally find them in the Wilderness. They're illegal, so I confiscate them."

"Constant doesn't mind them staring at her?"

"Not much scares that woman."

David pictured Constant out in the wild in her black tee and camo pants.

"I guess she can take care of herself."

"She's good with a bow," said Ezra. "And she can shoot. At twenty yards she can pop a beer can with a pistol."

David was processing this information when Ezra added, "Which reminds me: Jill asked me to teach you how to shoot."

"Why?"

"Because it's hard to shoot if you don't know how."

"I mean, why do I have to know?"

"It's an important survival skill."

"Shooting a gun is a survival skill?"

"It is, if someone is pointing a gun at you."

David could not think of anyone who might want to shoot him, expect, perhaps, Simon—and even that was hearsay.

"I don't know about this."

"I taught Jill and Bill. And now they're both pretty good."

David was shaking his head. "I don't own a gun. And I don't want to."

"You don't have to. Jill already bought one for you."

"What? No way!"

"Look, you won't actually own it. And you don't have to walk around with it. But there may come a time when you need it ... and then, believe me, you'll thank God you have it and know how to use it."

David was angry and he wasn't sure why.

"Is that why you brought me here? To teach me how to shoot?"

"Absolutely not. It's illegal to discharge a firearm in this park."

"Then why am I here?"

"I thought you might like to see the cabin. And I wanted to give you some tips about the great outdoors. I thought we'd take a hike."

"Survival 101?"

"Something like that."

David was intrigued. "All right. I can do that. How long do you think it will take?"

"Not long. I'll give you a crash course. I'll have you back in three days."

"Three days! Are you crazy?"

"I don't think so. Though Constant might say otherwise."

Chapter 37

Wiley's Phone Call to Jill

How are you, my lovely?

Great, Wiley! How are you?

I'm fine. Ralph's fine. Restaurant is doing well—all is right with the world. But are you really okay? I haven't heard from you in a while. I get worried.

Oh, Wiley, what a darling sweetheart you are! Yes, really, I'm fine. We're all fine. We're all working hard. Ezra is preparing the Yahi for their freedom. David is writing his book. Elliot is putting together the pieces for our film crew. All is good ... although, admittedly, I've heard some disturbing stuff about Simon.

What have you heard? What's going on?

Lately he's been meeting with an increasingly large group of Indians. We know they're plotting to spring the Yahi—that's how they see it— that's how Simon's been selling it—that the Yahi are being held captive by a white conspiracy and Indians have to band together to set them free. He's riling up some locals and there's no telling what they'll do. We're trying to prepare for what we see as two basic contingencies: Either Simon and his gang will get to the Yahi before we're ready ... which would be just disastrous for the Yahi's sake and ours ... or Simon and his gang will come after us directly ... to try to scare us off ... or worse.

Let me know if you feel threatened. I mean it. I'm less than an hour away. If I ride my Harley, I'll be there in no time. And I have friends. Plenty of them.

Oh, Wiley. I don't want you to worry. It's very possible that nothing will happen. We just want to be prepared. And I'm not alone. I have Bill and David and Ezra, and Constant too, if it comes to that.

And you have me. Don't forget that.

Oh, Wiley, I never will!

Good. Now, I want to change the subject. I'd like to see you and your friends. Have a little fun.

Wonderful! What do you have in mind?

Friday is dance night at Chaps & Scraps. Good food ... good drinks ... great music—live, kick-ass band.

Sounds great! We could use some fun.

Super. Come this Friday. Stop by any time after 8:00.

Oh, Wiley, this is great. I love you!

I love you too, Jilly. See ya Friday!

Jill's Phone Call to Elliot

Hi, Elliot.

Jill! How are you?

Fine. You still basking in the glowing reviews of your film festival?

It was great!

I knew it would be. You have good taste and good management skills.

Hah! You wouldn't have said that a few years ago.

I suppose not. But things change, don't they?

They sure do.

[Both laugh]

[Jill speaking] So, how are the arrangements coming along?

Everything is falling into place. I have all the necessary equipment and the personnel to make it work.

We ready for rehearsals?

I think we need just a single practice for logistics. Maybe two.

Really, that's all?

Here's my thinking: You're writing a script that relies on a lot of narration. I have actors to choose from, all with voice-over experience. We can record that in a single day. And it's best to do that after we have shot and edited all the film.

Makes sense.

Also, much of what we hope to capture on film will be live and un-scripted.

Can't rehearse that.

No, we can't. But here's what we can do: We can practice trans-porting equipment over the kinds of rugged terrains we're likely to face: hills, streams, rocky paths, woods … And we have to be able to shoot at night and in the darkness of caves.

You have people who can do that?

Short answer: yes. This is the plus side of using film students. They're strong and they're mobile.

And they're free!

[Both laugh]

[Elliot speaking] Absolutely. And they won't be prima donnas. What they lack in experience they'll make up for in exuberance. Besides, there's me and you—and Kenneth and Gloria. That's plenty adult experience.

That's for sure!

[Both laugh]

[Jill speaking] I'm so excited. This may be the one and only time in the history of our planet when an entire Stone Age community is filmed live! We do this right and it will be a big deal.

I can't wait to escort you to the Academy Awards.

What color gown should I wear?

Something that complements my tuxedo.

[Both laugh]

[Jill speaking] I still have one big question.

Only one?

[Both laugh, a little nervously]

[Jill speaking] Yes. I'm still not clear on the Big Scene. I mean, what's the climax? Is it when they all come out of the cave at the same time? Is it when we lead them to the trucks and vans that will take them to Oroville? Is it when they all arrive in L.A. and look around, all gaga?

I always assumed that would play out naturally. Did you ask Ezra's opinion?

I did. He said he's checking it out with the Yahi. He said he might be able to get us an incredibly dramatic scene to film. Something amazingly unique.

Did he say what? Is this something we have to prepare for?

He didn't really say. He just said it's a scene of biblical proportions.

Bill's E-mail to Sandy

I know you haven't heard from me in a long time and maybe you deleted this e-mail as soon as you saw it was from me but I hope you're still reading. Thing is, I want to make this short and sweet. We both know I left some gambling debts behind. Those things are not forgiven—and I don't mean by you—I mean by the people I owe. If they haven't yet contacted you again, I suspect they will. If they do, tell them anything you want. If that means you tell them where I am—that's okay. Eventually it's a score that has to be settled. I just don't want you aggravated by this shit. Don't worry about me. I can handle myself. I can even make some payment on what I owe so they leave me alone for a while. I mean, I'm no good to them dead. That doesn't means I expect to be killed or anything. I just don't want you to worry.

     Love,
     Bill

Chapter 38

Frankie and Johnny

Bill had never before run afoul of Frankie the Claw Colosimo and Johnny Two-Tone Torrio. Once he came close. Some years earlier, against his better judgment and explicit advice, he'd set up a meeting between Carmine Grasso, who had *connections,* and his brother-in-law, David Grossman. David was there as proxy for his friends Matt and Alexandra who were desperate to borrow money to open a Brazilian eatery called *Café Amazon.* Bill advised against it. Not because he thought the restaurant was a bad idea (it wasn't), but because he was a firm believer in Shit Happens and didn't want David to be collateral damage when Carmine's collection agents, Frankie and Johnny, came knocking at Matt's door regarding a debt that was sure to be past due. This particular story didn't have a happy ending (Matt and Alexandra lost the restaurant), but at least no one was badly hurt or worse, and Bill's own reputation as an honest two-bit gambler suffered no serious damage. That luck changed a few months later when Bill borrowed a substantial sum from Carmine and bet it all on a "guaranteed" return that was racing the next day at Belmont. Unfortunately, it seems the horse's warranty had expired before the race and Bill was unable to repay Carmine, which resulted in Frankie and Johnny being sent to look for Bill in his usual haunts on Upper Broadway. Because Bill was nowhere to be found, they paid a visit to his wife, who claimed not to know or care where the hell he was. Not finding Bill was an embarrassment for Frankie and Johnny and an insult to Carmine. Weeks passed and still there was no sign of Bill. Carmine's sources told him that Bill was no longer living in his wife's fancy hi-rise co-op in Riverdale. When a nicely worded warning to Bill's wife (left on her car windshield) did not result in Bill showing up with money in hand, Carmine sent Frankie and Johnny to find Bill for a little tête-à-tête.

Chapter 39

David and Ezra

Kidnapping David had been Jill's idea. Though she strongly believed his survival training might come in handy, she knew David would balk at the idea of spending three days and two nights alone with Ezra in the Wilderness. But she also knew that David was eager for new experiences to include in his novel, and that in the company and protection of Ezra he would open himself to new stimuli without too much interference from his usual fears and phobias.

David and Ezra had been hiking for about an hour and had reached a high ridge with an expansive view of the Wilderness's rough-cut charms: sharp gullies; canyons carved through layers of volcanic ash; frozen waves of ancient lava flow; cliffs, caves, granite outcrops; islands of dense ponderosa pine; receding hills spiked with conifers at the higher elevations.

"The Lord giveth, and the Lord taketh," said Ezra.

Not catching his drift, David remained silent.

"The Wilderness is blasted and blessed, rich in God's gifts but bereft of gold. Without the prospect of that which glitters, whites avoided this area. This helped keep the Yahi safe."

David nodded. "I love the irony," he said.

"The inscrutable hand of God," said Ezra.

For three days and two nights Ezra led David through the Wilderness. Ezra was firm and friendly in his instruction. He demonstrated ways to find drinking water, fish and forage, discern direction, build a shelter, start a fire, and more.

"The Yahi roam these parts?" asked David.

"They once did," said Ezra. "Eventually they became cave-dwellers. They couldn't risk being seen."

"Hadn't the bounties ended?"

"Many whites were still ruled by bloodlust: See an Indian, kill an Indian."

Steven Jay Griffel

"So, after all these years, the Yahi are alive but trapped?"

"Alive and adapted."

"How do they live in caves? Don't they need food and water?"

Ezra sat down on a low bench of black basalt that faced a wooded valley.

"When my great-grandfather, Ezra 1 as you call him, followed the route Ishi had drawn in the sand, he found less than a dozen Yahi living in a network of connected caves. They were mostly weak and sick. But my great-grandfather was able to communicate with them."

"He'd learned enough Yahi from published articles."

"Yes. And he had prepared himself with a practiced pantomime. He was very serious. He knew he was doing God's work."

"And they trusted him."

"He earned their trust. He introduced himself using the circle of black obsidian given to him by Ishi's mother."

"They trusted that?" David asked. "It might have been found or stolen."

"He was prepared for that. With his limited vocabulary and pantomime he played out his entire Ishi story for them. He described being a boy and working for surveyors who were following a stream they planned to dam ... and how he had been running ahead and saw Ishi standing in the rushing waters with a raised harpoon ... and how Ishi startled when he saw him and ran away and how the men tracked him the next day to an old bear's den on a high cliff. Then he told how he and the men entered the bear den and let in some light and found an old woman inside and how he gave her water and sang for her and how she pressed a circle of black glass into his palm."

"They believed the story?" David asked.

"They knew the story. It had been repeated many times among them."

"Oral history in the making."

"So it goes."

"Did your great-grandfather sing for the Yahi?"

"Yes, they asked him to and he did. And they seemed to recognize the song. They were very moved."

"Did he tell them the rest of the story?"

"He told them everything. He described how he had joined a church—a place where people prayed—and how it had burned down and how he came to realize that the only church he needed was the sky and mountains and woods."

"They understand that?"

"Yes. And then he told them as best he could how Ishi was found hungry and weak near a corral in Oroville and how he was brought by a great machine that rolled on wheels to a city called San Francisco and how—a few years later—he himself was able to visit this city and stand on a long line to watch Ishi demonstrate how he could string a bow."

"What was their response?"

"This part upset them. They seemed to feel that Ishi must have been forced to share his secrets."

"What happened?"

"My great-grandfather cleared that up quickly. He said that Ishi was a great man. Very intelligent and brave. And that he wanted to share information with the whites so they would believe he was the last of the Yahi."

"How'd that go over?"

"I believe there was a lot of wailing and crying. The thought of Ishi's sacrifice was very emotional—and inspirational."

"How did your great-grandfather handle it?"

"He was amazing. I wish I could have known him. It was different for the rest of us who followed him. He's the one who started it all. He's the one who met Ishi. He's the one who cared for Ishi's mother ... who comforted her ... who received her token. He's the one who first learned to speak Yahi and to develop a mime language."

"He's the one Ishi trusted."

"Exactly! That's the key thing. When my great-grandfather told the Yahi the rest of the story: how some years later Ishi led a few of his white friends on an expedition to Deer Creek Canyon ... and how Fate had arranged for my great-grandfather to be there ... and how he finally got to speak with Ishi privately and to show him his mother's black stone ... and then, the clincher! ... how Ishi led him inside a grove of manzanita bushes—where only God could see them—and how he drew in the sand the map route to the caves where the Yahi lived. That was it. The final link. With that, the Yahi believed my great-grandfather was special ... almost like an extension of Ishi himself."

"A kind of prophet," David noted.

"A kind of savior, too. My great-grandfather soon learned that the Yahi were prepared to follow Ishi's advice to stay hidden in the darkness for one hundred years after his death. That was when my great-grandfather understood his mission—his special calling. It would not be his joy to bring the Yahi to freedom. Or his son's joy or his grandson's. None of them would know fame or personal gratification—other than the joy that comes from self-sacrifice and the knowledge of doing God's work."

"Their job was to help care for the Yahi until the next Ezra was ready to take over."

"Exactly. But it's important to note that the Yahi are a proud and wonderful people. For thousands of years they didn't need anyone's help."

"But forced into caves—they needed help to survive."

"Yes."

"And Ishi foresaw all that," said David.

"Perhaps he had a vision. Perhaps God spoke to him."

"God speaks Yahi?"

"Don't get funny," said Ezra. "God's Word surpasseth language."

David was sorry he had joked.

"So, lo these past hundred years, what exactly did the Ezras do for the Yahi?" David asked.

"In some ways, as little as we could.... Don't laugh, I'm serious. My great-grandfather believed that helping the Yahi meant ensuring that their Stone Age customs and traditions survived. So, just like my fathers, I have always encouraged them to do all they can according to their ancient ways."

"Can they still live like that? Are they basically self-sufficient?"

"Not quite. They are limited to hunting and foraging and fishing at night, when it's much less likely that they will be seen. But it's also much more difficult for them to provide for themselves in this way, and that's why my fathers and I have helped them through the years."

"Doesn't that interfere with their ancient ways?"

"No," said Ezra. "We have never brought them modern tools or processed foods. I visit every other week or so, occasionally bringing some fresh fish or meat, some fruits and vegetables. Sometimes I bring a few blankets or some old clothing. Like my fathers, I don't have a set schedule. I don't want them to expect me on a certain day and worry if I don't arrive. I don't want them to be overly dependent on me. That would not help them."

"You and your fathers have been amazingly selfless and generous, but there must have been times when you wanted to do even more."

"I inherited a great deal of wisdom from my fathers, including the Ezra Golden Rule: *Let the Yahi sustain themselves. When they cannot, let God provide.*"

"Still, I imagine you have faced some tough calls."

Ezra paused to collect his thoughts.

"I've seen some terrible injuries and sickness when I knew a doctor might relieve pain or even save a life."

"You did nothing to help?"

"Letting God decide is not the same as doing nothing."

David paused to collect his thoughts.

"You ever watch a Yahi die before your eyes?"

"Yes. But I knew I shouldn't interfere."

"But God lets you bring gifts, like blankets and fish? Isn't that interfering?"

"It's a gray area. My fathers were men of God. I have followed them. Sometimes we do what we think God would allow."

David nodded.

"I think it's wonderful that you encourage the Yahi to maintain their ancient ways. But did it ever occur to your great-grandfather how increasingly difficult it will be to reintroduce the Yahi to the outside world after one hundred years of isolation?"

"I don't think so. He was still very young when he began his mission. He couldn't have known. But it has occurred to me, and I know it occurred to my father."

"It boggles my mind," said David. "I mean, Ishi staggers out of the mountains as a Stone Age Indian and a few days later he's on a railroad to San Francisco. I can't imagine what that was like. And now, after living in caves for the past hundred years, we're going to release an entire tribe of Stone Age Indians into the twenty-first century."

"I've been preparing them, especially in recent years, telling them things about the outside world. They know big cities exist. They know there are airplanes and giant ships. But they know all this in their way—not in clear detail."

"You never brought picture books or video?"

"No, but my great-grandfather began the tradition of bringing them photographs of Ishi."

"Which now hang in their Stone Age art gallery.

"Along with pictures of all my fathers and me."

"And Constant, too."

"That was a mistake, which I later made worse."

192

"What happened?"

"In the past few years I've grown somewhat close to one of the Yahi, a young man named Branch. He's about twenty-two: strong, handsome, and smart. The Yahi don't have a chief—they have a small group of elders who advise—but it's been clear for a while that they all look up to Branch. He's a hothead and something of a showoff, but he's their best hunter and a natural leader."

"You'll need his help when you lead the Yahi to freedom."

"Precisely. He's invaluable to me. Which is why I kick myself every day for the fiasco with Constant."

"What happened?" asked David.

Ezra drew a deep breath.

"I think I told you how I brought a few photos of Constant to the Yahi."

"Which they passed around and then hung in their gallery."

"Exactly. But what I didn't know was that the photos of Constant had made a particularly strong impression on Branch. One day he asked me if I had any more pictures of her. The question made me a little uncomfortable, so I pretended I didn't quite understand what he was saying. He seemed oblivious of my discomfort and asked if I could bring more pictures the next time I visited. I suppose I nodded, perhaps I even said okay, but then I blocked it out of my mind. The next time I visited, he pulled me aside right away and asked to see the pictures, and when I told him I'd forgot to bring them, he seemed very disappointed."

"What'd he say?"

"It wasn't what he said—he just seemed very agitated. He's a hot head.... I wasn't sure what he might do. And then it occurred to me: my cell phone. Normally, I don't take it with me when I go to the Wilderness, but that day I forgot to leave it behind."

"Let me guess: you have pictures of Constant on your cell phone."

"That's right."

"Perfect. I love it. What happened?"

"What happened is … I took my cell phone out of my pocket and tried to explain to Branch what it was."

"That could not have been easy."

"No. But I spoke simply and I didn't lie. I didn't say it was magic or anything like that. I told him it was a modern tool and it contained pictures of Constant and could be used to talk to people who were far away."

"Did he have any idea what the hell you were saying?"

"Branch is very smart—like Ishi smart. He makes quick connections and intuits things."

"Still, a Stone Age Indian and a cell phone."

"I'm never sure exactly how much he understands. But he seemed enthralled—with the cell phone and with Constant."

"What'd he say?"

"Not much. But he carefully watched how I handled the phone and when I let him hold it, he was already able to finger-swipe the photos to view them, one after another, backwards and forwards."

"Impressive."

"Indeed. But uncomfortable for me. He seemed unusually taken with Constant."

"You didn't show him sexy photos—did you?"

"No, of course not. But there were a few candid shots."

"How candid?"

"Photos of her walking in the woods. A few ballet poses."

"He might have found those particularly fetching."

"There was one he stared at for a long time. He wasn't at all self-conscious. And he didn't seem aware—or to care—how I might have felt. He just stared—with his fingers on the phone.

At one point he must have touched the screen in a way that expanded the picture—that surprised him!"

"Phone might have felt alive to him."

"Something like that. He almost dropped it."

"What was the picture?" asked David.

"A profile of Constant's face and upper torso," said Ezra.

"Sleeveless black T-shirt?"

"Yes."

"Braless?"

"I suppose."

"Her tattoo on full display?"

"Yes. The bloody claw marks.... He couldn't stop staring. And then he glared at me. I'm not sure what he was thinking."

"Any guess?"

"Don't really know. He didn't say ... wouldn't say. But I had the feeling that he resented me ... that he blamed me for her wound. Maybe he thought I had caused it ... or had failed to protect her."

"You talk it over?"

"No. I don't have that kind of relationship with him—or with any of the Yahi. My fathers always insisted that we keep a respectful distance. Anyway, we didn't discuss it."

"How did it end?"

"Not well. He wanted to keep the cell phone, but I wouldn't let him have it, for many reasons, which I didn't think I could explain, so I just shook my head No."

"He try to bargain?"

"Yes. He offered me a deer-handled knife that he'd made himself—beautifully carved, black obsidian blade. I think he was insulted when I wouldn't trade."

"Where does it stand?" asked David.

"Unfortunately, I think he's disappointed with me. Maybe even a little angry."

"And now he has Simon's phone. Bill told me."

"Oh, God, I know. When he bargained with Simon for it, he must have thought it had pictures of Constant."

"Does he know how to use it?"

"I showed him the basics.... I'm not sure he remembers."

"He might have received a call from Simon."

"I've thought of that," said Ezra.

"Simon might have called his own phone, thinking Branch might answer."

"It's possible."

"So, Branch might have heard Simon's voice coming from the cell phone."

"I suppose."

"What do you think Branch might have thought about that?"

"I don't know. I just don't know."

"Could he understand Simon?" David asked.

"I don't know. Maybe. Simon might know more Yahi than I do. And Branch knows some English.... But over the phone—without the help of pantomime—I have no idea if Branch could understand him."

"Or vice versa."

"That's right."

"But the fact that Branch—who is angry with you—has a cell phone and could, conceivably, be speaking with Simon ... raises some very interesting possibilities."

"I've thought of that," said Ezra. "Which is why we have to be prepared."

"That's why I'm here with you now, right?"

"Yes."

Chapter 40

Simon's Phone Call to Branch

A few weeks earlier, Simon and Morgan had been sitting in La Cantina, drinking beers. Simon had been talking about a wild Indian he'd met but had jumped back to his earlier description of the woman he'd led into the Wilderness for a onesie-twosie.

"Stupid blonde bitch. Even in a weak moon I could see she was too ugly to screw."

"What did you do?"

"I made like I had to piss and just kept walking. Let her find her own way home."

Morgan would have been horrified had he/she not been used to Simon's baseless boasting.

"Get back to the wild Indian. Who saw who first?" asked Morgan.

"I saw him before he saw me."

"What'd he look like?"

"He looked like a young Ishi: long wild hair, naked—except for the loincloth—but much younger—a strong young man. And he was holding a bow."

"Anything else?" asked Morgan.

"If he had a bow, he needed a quiver, right? Think before you ask stupid questions."

Morgan sighed.

"What was the quiver like?" asked Morgan.

"It was strapped across his back and filled with arrows."

"That's every quiver, you idiot. What was it made of?"

"It was the real deal," said Simon. "Not one of those pretty beaded things they sell at summer pow-wows. I think it was beaver. That's what it looked like. Beaver."

"How do you know what beaver looks like?"

They both burst out laughing.

"So, you just walk up to him and start talking?" Morgan asked. "You weren't scared?"

"Hell no. I know my way around."

"Shit. You got lost in the Bingo room: One room. One door. You got lost."

"I was drunk!"

"No excuse!"

"It was dark!"

They both burst out laughing.

"So, when you saw him, who spoke first?" asked Morgan.

"I did. I said hello."

"In English?"

"No, I said parley voo!"

They both laughed.

"He answered in English. But it didn't sound natural," said Simon.

"He had a Yahi accent?"

They both laughed.

"Actually, after I said hello—in English—I said: 'My name is Simon'—and I said it in Yahi."

"I'm impressed."

"You know, I'm part Yahi."

"I know: You're half Yahi, half Maidu, half Wintu—and full of shit."

They both laughed.

"Meanwhile, I got him talking, and he was talking Yahi—with some English thrown in. You know what that means."

"He's bilingual?"

"No, you moron. It means he's one of the surviving Yahi we've heard about. Don't you get it? I saw the living proof: Ishi was not the last of the Yahi—they're still around—and still living like it's the Stone Age."

"This is the thing you told Jill? The thing she wants to film?"

"Yes—and I'm not going to let that happen. Where the hell does she come off—coming here out of nowhere … And she's going to save the Yahi? She's going to grab the glory? She's going to get famous? Drunken bitch. I'll kill her first. Ezra too."

A minute of silence passed.

"Why don't you call the Indian who has your phone?" asked Morgan.

"His name is Branch. That's what he said."

"Why don't you call Branch? Here, you can use my phone."

Simon took Morgan's phone, found his own cell number, and pressed the green "Call" button.

"It's ringing…. 'Hello? Hello, Branch? Can you hear me? This is Simon.'"

Chapter 41

Marching Orders

Carmine had given his two henchmen a timetable:

"Two weeks. In two weeks you two geniuses are back here with all the money Bill owes or I want his head."

"Boss," said Frankie, "you don't really want his head, right?"

Carmine looked at his brawny nephew with the over-sized claw-hands: "What do you think?"

"I think I'll do what you want, Boss, but I'm thinking, bringing back a head is a messy business."

Carmine shook his head in wonder. "What do you think?" he asked Johnny, who stood at attention, his two-tone shoes buffed and shined.

"How much does Bill owe, Boss?"

Carmine smiled. "With accrued interest, late fees, and additional expenses: twenty-two grand, on the nose."

"Bottom line?" asked Johnny.

"Bottom line: He gives you eighteen grand in cash and you break his face. Then you go to his wife for the balance. She doesn't pay, break her face."

Continental Divide

According to Carmine's sources in Atlantic City and Vegas, Bill was working in a casino somewhere in northern California. Someone mentioned Sacramento. No one was sure.

Having checked a map in his glove compartment, Johnny (alpha thug and driver) decided that Route 80 West made the most sense: a relatively straight shot across the country—but a very long drive. To make it in four days Johnny knew he would have to let Frankie do some of the driving, but under no circumstance would he let him touch the radio. "Keep your goddamn claw off the music," Johnny warned.

THE ISHI AFFAIR

Three days later ... after two thousand miles of highway, Johnny pulled off the road at a scenic lookout to stretch his legs. It was August in the Colorado Rockies, but there were still plenty patches of snow. Twenty feet away was a big sign, mounted on a large base of fitted stones:

LOVELAND PASS
ELEVATION 11,990 FT.
CONTINENTAL DIVIDE
←PACIFIC   ATLANTIC→

"How does this sign divide the whole continent? The continent is huge," said Frankie.

"That's not what it means."

"What does it mean?"

"It means that all the streams and rivers, all the rain and snow on this side eventually flow into the Pacific Ocean. All the streams and rivers, and all the rain and snow on that side eventually flow into the Atlantic Ocean."

"How do you know all this?" asked Frankie.

"I know how to read."

"I can read."

"I read books. Books on science," said Johnny.

Frankie gave this some thought.

"Doesn't seem possible," said Frankie. "The ocean is far from here."

"It's a fact. It's science. It has to do with water and gravity."

"I don't believe it."

"Suit yourself—but it's true."

"I still don't believe it."

"Twenty bucks says I'm right," said Johnny.

"How you gonna prove it?"

"I'll show you the book."

"What book?"

"The almanac. Biggest book in the world. Contains every important scientific fact."

"You have an almanac?" asked Frankie.

"Everyone does. It's online. It's on the Internet."

Frankie didn't answer. He had to think this through.

Chapter 42

Sandy's Turn

As point-person on an outside, ad hoc consulting team, Sandy was helping a Fortune 200 conglomerate gather cash-flow data on their twenty-two multinational companies, each with factories, offices, and distribution centers on six continents. Her team was developing new software that would effectively maximize exchange rates among one hundred interacting currencies. If Sandy's team proved successful, they might save the supercorporation more than a hundred million dollars per year.

Sandy needed to be on her A-game, clearheaded and on high alert. She was angry that recent experiences had upset and distracted her: the threatening note left on her car windshield; anonymous text messages sent to her cell phone; black sedans surveilling her public movements ... or had she imagined these? Had she let the enemy get inside her head?

Sandy was a data-driven kind of gal. When she knew what she needed to know, she acted decisively. And when things didn't add up, or when she hadn't enough information, she rattled what variables she could and reassessed. Informed action was always the goal. Which is why (when she didn't know what to do about the thugs who were after Bill) she hired her own information collector: a private investigator named Phil Chambers who gave her the names and lowdown on Carmine, Frankie, and Johnny. She knew where they lived. She knew where they banked. She knew their criminal records. Mr. Chambers saved the worst for last:

"Frankie and Johnny left two days ago for California. They're looking for Bill. They want their money."

It was all Sandy could do to stifle an angry scream.

"How much does Bill owe?"

"Hard to say. It's not an official paper trail. For sure, he'll be asked to pay additional penalties and late fees, if you know what I mean."

"Give me a professional guestimate."

"I'd say he owes anywhere from fifteen to thirty grand."

Sandy was quiet, thinking.

"Do they know where he is?" asked Sandy.

"They know he flew to Sacramento. They know he's working at a casino."

"An Indian-owned casino."

"Don't say another word. Not on the phone."

Sandy was silent.

"There isn't much else I can tell you," said Chambers. "Is there anyone else there who can help him?"

"My brother is there too."

"Well, wherever they are, try to get them some advance warning. But don't call them on your regular cell phone. Don't text. I wouldn't even send an e-mail."

"How am I going to warn them?"

"And don't call the police. It's not a police matter—at least, not yet."

Sandy gasped.

"What should I do?"

"Tell you the truth, I don't know. But they're probably at least a day away from Sacramento. It's a big city. If they're going to track down every casino, large and small, not only in Sacramento but in the surrounding sticks, it could take them a week or more."

"Good to know."

"Also, I don't mean any disrespect but—"

"What? Just say it."

"They know your husband is shady enough to use a fake name. That's good. That will slow them down some more."

"Good work, Phil. Let me know if you learn anything else."

Greed

Sandy understood people—especially greedy people—and they all had this in common: they always wanted more. She knew if she paid Bill's debt it still might never be paid in full. But what could she do? More than once she considered washing her hands of the big galoot, but she still loved him—a realization that had come to her only recently, a result of her once-a-week therapy with Dr. Wechsler.

Though it pained her to think that bad men were coming Bill's way, she believed Bill should be a taught a lesson. She didn't think the bad men would kill him—he was no good to them dead—but if they beat him up a little—or even more than a little—it might improve his character and make him a more suitable companion moving forward.

What really frightened her—to the point of the shakes—was the thought that something might happen to her brother. If it did, it would be her fault. She was responsible for putting David in harm's way. She'd made it like she was doing him a favor, giving him a cushy job when he needed the money ... but she'd been selfishly calculating, preying upon his unemployment and the pressures she knew he faced from Allison. If David were hurt—or worse—she would never forgive herself.

Thoughts of David's death drove her to tears. She loved her older brother. And she loved his twin daughters—Lydia and Louise. And she loved Allison, her sister-in-law, who'd been in her life since they were both teenagers.

Untraceable

Sandy sat awhile, thinking of what she wanted to say to Allison. When she finished her glass of Zinfandel, she called her sister-in-law and told her all she knew.

"Oh my god! Oh my god! Oh my god!"

"I didn't want to worry you. I just thought you should know."

"Oh my god! What are you going to do?"

"I'm flying to Sacramento on Monday. I'll rent a car and drive to Los Molinos. I have the address of the Sierra Spa and Casino Hotel. I'm not at all sure what good I'll do, but I feel like I need to be there."

"Me too!"

"Allison, you have a job. You have a house. Stay home. I promise to call you every day."

Allison was quiet for several seconds. "Do you have a new phone number? Your name didn't come up on my screen."

"I bought a few burn phones to protect my privacy."

"What's a burn phone?"

"Cheap cell phone. Comes with a prepaid amount of service. Use it for a day or two, then toss it in the river—or burn it. It's untraceable."

"*Untraceable?* WHAT THE HELL ARE YOU TALK-ING ABOUT?"

"Allison, please, calm down."

"I am calm!"

"You're screaming."

"Of course I'm screaming. Screaming makes sense!"

"Look, I'm sorry I upset you. There's probably nothing for you to worry about."

A long pause.

"What time is your flight?" asked Allison.

"Why?"

"I'm going with you."

"But—"

"No argument. I'm going. We'll talk on the plane."

Sandy drew a deep breath. "Monday. JFK. Jet Blue. Meet me at 7:00 p.m. outside the terminal. I'll have your ticket."

After the call, Sandy smashed her phone until its circuit board and SIM card lay in pieces.

Chapter 43

Packing

Allison's Buddhist education effectively changed the way she prepared for travel. Deprivation and renunciation make for lighter packing. For sure, she was embarking on an eccentric trip: she had no idea how long she would be gone or the nature of her itinerary. Even so, rather than pack for every contingency, as she used to do, she limited herself to her bare essentials: a few long and short-sleeve shirts; two pair of shorts; two pair of long pants (one black linen, one blue denim); four pair of underwear (one sexy, just in case); one casual summer dress (which could be jazzed with a few accessories); two yoga outfits; one pair each of sandals, sneakers, shoes; a bamboo yoga mat; a drawing pad, and a single, fine-line, black Rapidograph pen. In a smaller suitcase she packed a one-pound bag of organic trail mix; an assortment of creams and lotions; insect repellent; and an unscented sun-screen spray (infused with aloe, cucumber, and algae to repair and hydrate skin).... Before she closed the suitcases, she looked about the bathroom and bedroom one more time to see if there were any other essential items she should bring.... On the far wall of her bedroom, above the bed she had shared with David for forty years, was a ketubah, the illustrated and calligraphed Jewish marriage contract she and David had signed under the loving eyes of their rabbi and parents, all long deceased. The ketubah was framed and protected under a shield of non-glare glass. Allison removed the ketubah from the wall and laid it face down on the bed. She then freed her marriage contract from its encasement, covered it in a long sheet of plastic wrap, and rolled it inside her bamboo yoga mat. She wasn't sure why she did this. If pressed, she might have said she wanted to be able to legally claim what was rightfully hers, if it came to that, for she intuited (correctly) that David's former teen sweetheart, with whom he had reconnected four years earlier, after not having seen her for forty years, was once again back in his life.

Unlike Allison, Sandy completed all her packing in just a few minutes. An experienced business traveler, she kept a packed suitcase at the ready. For this trip she added a can of mace and a seven-inch switchblade. In her carry-on, she planned to bring her computer tablet, wall-charging cord, car-charging cord, portable battery pack, burn phones, and an assortment of hi-protein energy bars.

An expected storm delayed their departure. Sandy and Allison had to wait two days—until Wednesday—before their jet could depart JFK at 9:00 p.m.

Chapter 44

Wiley's Bash

A warm, lovely night in Chico, California. Just a few blocks from the college, Wiley's *Chaps & Scraps* was in full groove: waiters—some striding, some sashaying—all hoisting heavy platters to crowded tables. David, a hungry non-vegan, blanched at the sight of spinach wraps, kale chips, and guacamole dip ... but was heartened by the plates of chicken wings, pulled pork, and barbecue ribs. The DJ music was jazzin', rockin', soulful. The surrounding walls displayed pin-ups of movie stars, sexy athletes, and muscled black dudes on gnarly Harleys.

"This place really is inclusive," said David.

"Oh, look, Wiley's coming over," said Jill.

Wiley led the way; Elliot behind him, in total eclipse. When Wiley arrived, he leaned right to hug Jill; at the same time, Elliot sprung upwards to hug David, a Jack-in-the-box surprise that caused David to leap backwards, banging into a waiter and toppling a glass of red wine.

Elliot was quick to smooth any embarrassment. "I have that effect on people. It's my shocking good looks."

"No. No. No," said David. "I just didn't see you." With that, he moved forward to offer a hearty handshake and then did the same with Wiley.

Elliot took a seat next to David, opposite Jill.

Wiley remained standing. "A few tables still need to be filled," he said. "Let me greet some more guests. I'll be back in a bit." Wiley floated through the crowd like a giant helium balloon, light and airy.

"So, how are you guys?" asked Elliot.

"Good," said Jill. "How about you?"

"Things are great. By the way, Kenneth and Gloria send their love."

"I was hoping to see them. They okay?" Jill asked.

"They're fine. They wanted to come, but they got tied up with something or other."

"They been busy?"

"Extremely. Last week they helped me run two production rehearsals for our film. Everything went great."

"What did you test?" asked Jill.

"We tested everything. We packed, transported, unpacked. We filmed, recorded ... checked light and sound."

"It's a wrap!"

Elliot smiled at David. "Not quite. We tested everything outdoors, but in relatively controlled conditions. We still have to test at night ... in the mountains ... and especially in caves ... We need to prepare for that special darkness and humidity."

"How many more rehearsals you think we need?" Jill asked.

"I think we're ready for our final rehearsal. We just need Ezra to lead us into the mountains to a suitable cave setting. And we should do it at night, just to make sure we can. By the way, is he coming tonight?"

"Sorry to disappoint," said Jill. "But this place isn't his comfort zone."

"Let me guess," said Elliot, "it's not the Scraps that give him problems."

Jill shrugged. "You had to figure. He's a religious guy. Different values. Different perspectives."

"Very different," said Elliot.

"But he really is a good man. He's very principled," said Jill.

"Can a good man be intolerant?" Elliot asked.

Jill put down her knife. "We're not having this conversation here. We have other things to deal with. And god only knows how all that will go."

David raised a forefinger. "For the record, I just spent three days alone with the guy in the Wilderness. We're very different ... but I'd trust him with my life."

The three friends tabled further serious discussion, focusing instead on their appetizers and another round of drinks. Wiley came back, but did not sit down.

"Sorry. Something came up. In any case, the band is about to start." With that, a heavy bass chord announced the band was ready to rock.

"C'mon, girl," said Wiley, reaching for Jill's hand. "Let's shake our booty."

Jill shook him off. "I need to get warmed up," she said, smiling coyly. "I need to be in the mood."

"Since when?" Wiley said, laughing.

Jill squealed. "You are in such trouble!" she said, laughing. "Go ahead, take care of your customers. We'll be out there soon. And you owe me a *slow* dance!"

Wiley bowed, took Jill's small hand in his giant mitt, and kissed it daintily. "I look forward to the pleasure, m'lady."

By the time the three friends had finished their freshened drinks, the band was cookin' and the dance floor was crowded.

"C'mon," said Jill, "let's have some fun." Elliot followed her lead, David trailing behind.

The three friends made an odd pas de trois. Jill danced as if she were alone and freewheeling. Elliot did his best to remain in front of her, displaying a few polished moves within a tight orbit. David pranced around them, thrusting and twirling a kind of disco Tourette. When the song ended, the dancers stopped and applauded. The next few beats suggested a slow dance—a pas de deux. Elliot and David looked at each other slyly. One of them would be odd man out. While each mulled who would cede and who would press, a thick-set, middle-aged man, his gray hair roughly cropped, bodied up to Jill for the next dance. Jill's defenses were down and she was taken by surprise. Before she could step back in protest, the man's burly arms encircled

Steven Jay Griffel

hers, clamping her in a body vise. So tightly was she clamped, her mouth was smothered against the man's chest. Only her eyes screamed terror.

When they saw her eyes, David and Elliot moved forward, but tentatively. A circle of seven men, all Indians, had formed a moving palisade around the couple. Elliot, then David, attempted to breach the circle, but their assaults were ineffectual. While they regrouped, rubbernecking dancers formed around the circle of Indians, who remained staunchly impassive. David and Elliot saw Jill's eyes filling with tears. The two were about to attack again, their intent redoubled, when two huge black men in motorcycle jackets and jackboots yanked apart the circle—and through the breach strode Wiley, a giant black colossus. When Simon saw Wiley, he pushed Jill aside and threw a flailing right cross, catching Wiley on his shoulder. The punch did not register, nor did the next one that struck Wiley high on his chest. Wiley moved forward, implacably. When he had closed in, he raised both his hands chest high, palms outward, and with a single, short, explosive thrust, sent Simon flying backwards, crashing to the dance floor.

Chapter 45

Breakfast with Bill

"Damn! Sorry I missed the fun," said Bill.

David finished buttering his toast. "It was actually pretty scary."

"Ever been in a bar fight?"

"I play a feisty game of tennis."

"You are one tough hombre."

David clinked his juice glass with Bill's.

"Jill was very upset. I've never seen her lose it like that."

"She'll be okay," said Bill. "She just wants to be better prepared. That's why she scheduled a practice shoot for tomorrow."

"Wait. What kind of shoot do you mean? I thought it was a film rehearsal."

Bill laughed. "Hardly. Pistols at twenty paces."

"We're not shooting at each other ... are we?"

Bill laughed again. "Unlikely. We go out to the desert.... Nothing around for miles.... We bring some old tin cans for targets."

"Who'll be there?" David asked.

"The usual suspects: You, me, Jill, Ezra, Constant—and Walther."

"Walter?"

"Walther. German-made gun."

"Oh, that Walther."

Shooting Practice

The group met the next day in the lobby at 7:00 a.m. David had balked at the early rise and shine, but Ezra explained that the desert sun was very strong—especially in August—and there'd be no shade to speak of. Better to get there early and avoid the mid-day beatdown. As soon as they were all gathered,

Ezra led the group to the parking lot. Jill, Bill, and David scrambled into the open back of the truck. Ezra got behind the wheel. Constant rode shotgun.

On the road, the sere landscape rolling by, David flashbacked to the summer of '70 (a year after he had disappointed Jill by not taking her to Woodstock): he was sitting in the back of a large pickup truck with a dozen other college students, racing the sunrise to a pine barren about ten miles from Chico, where the ancient Maidu once lived near a fast-flowing stream.... That was the summer he discovered Ishi. A year later, he met Allison.

Ezra used mostly backroads to arrive at a semi-arid basin, equidistant between the Cascade Mountains and the Sierra Nevada. They were effectively isolated, out of sight and earshot. Despite the heat, they all wore long-sleeved shirts, long pants, wide-brimmed hats, and hiking boots.

"Remember," said Ezra, "there are scorpions out here. Don't pull up any big rocks—or stick your hand down a gopher hole."

"Which is the worst kind of scorpion?" asked David.

"The ones with the pincers and stinger," said Ezra.

"And that would be—"

"That would be all of them. And they like bush shade, just like rattlers do, so don't sit your butts on the ground."

Ezra took two strides away from the group then turned about suddenly, effectively drawing everyone's attention. There was no more talk of flora and fauna; no survival tips; no Indian lore. Ezra was all business.

"Now, I really do not like guns. I never use them to hunt. I regard guns as a necessary evil ... a tool ... a means of protection, not aggression. But it appears we have ourselves a situation, so it's best that you are all prepared."

Jill and Bill were locked onto Ezra, but David found himself looking about, thrilled by the new environment: a surround of brown sands and thin grasses; small carpets of yellow asters; some clusters of sage and buckwheat in a variety of silvers and muted greens.

"Let's get to work," said Ezra. He led the group to a nearby dirt mound he'd built during an earlier training session. The mound was about three feet high, a little more than four feet wide, with a plateaued top about six inches deep. From a big canvas tote he withdrew a half-dozen tin cans (all washed clean, their labels removed) and arranged these along the top of the mound.

"Those cans don't stand a chance," said David. "They're sitting ducks."

No one laughed.

Ezra then led the group about twenty feet away and turned to face the mound. Everyone followed his lead. The sun was at their backs.

"Show me your guns ... pointed down."

Bill pulled a gun from his pocket. Jill withdrew two guns from her bag, handing one to David. It was the first live gun David had ever held.

"Now," said Ezra, "I don't expect anyone to be a sure-shot Annie Oakley, like Constant here, but I can teach you to be poised and careful. Remember rules one, two, and three: safety, safety, safety."

Everyone nodded.

"Because David hasn't had any training, I'm going to go through this as a beginner's lesson. Jill and Bill—probably a good refresher for the both of you, so please pay close attention. The guns are loaded with live ammo. So think of this as a real situation. There are consequences for careless mistakes."

Again, everyone nodded.

"Now, look at your gun, barrel pointed down. As you can see, it's relatively small, easily concealed, and fires a 9-millimeter bullet. That might not sound like much, but at twenty or thirty feet it will stop a man cold. Hit a vital, and he's likely dead."

Ezra waited for that bit of drama to sink in.

"Now, I have already adjusted the internal firing pin block, so the only thing preventing your gun from firing is the manual thumb safety. It's near the back of your gun. That's it, right there. You slide the safety up for engagement and down for disengagement. When the gun is live you'll see a little red light. When that light is on, your gun should always be pointed down—or at your target. Any questions?"

"How many bullets does it hold?" asked David.

"The magazine hold seven rounds. It's set up for right-handed users. If anyone here was left-handed, I would have to adjust it, by we're good to go. Later, I'll show you how to eject an empty magazine and insert a full one."

There were no further questions.

"Okay then, let's get started."

Ezra began by naming and pointing to the different parts of the pistol. He then demonstrated the proper shooting position, focusing on the arms, legs, feet, and shoulders.

"You can keep your knees bent or locked, but I think it's best to bend them a little—and lean forward slightly, like this. Never bend backwards. Keep your shoulders in front of your hips."

"Why?" asked David.

"Better balance," said Ezra. "Balance will help keep your body relaxed, which will help your aim. Balance will also help you recover from the gun's recoil. If the fired gun pushes you back, you have to adjust your balance and move your body position forward."

Ezra then demonstrated the proper grip and how to sight align.

"Last, but certainly not least, is pulling the trigger."

This piqued everyone's attention, the equivalent of saying *ready, aim* ...

"Follow this simple process: adopt the proper stance ... make sure you're balanced ... raise your arms ... lower them slowly … keep focused … breathe evenly … pressure the trigger … squeeze slowly… Bang!"

David's heart leaped.

"Let me show you what I mean. David, stand here and aim at the can on the far left."

David's heart was racing. When he was settled into his shooting posture, Ezra moved behind him, placing his left arm on David's left shoulder, his right trigger finger on top of David's. For a second, David was in the batter's box, his father behind him, adjusting his stance, lifting his elbow, cocking his bat. *Bend your knees, watch the ball, swing hard …*

"Focus," said Ezra. "Breathe evenly … Squeeeeeeze …"

Bang! The can blasted off the mound, shot through its tin heart.

Ezra stepped back and directed David to fire the next six bullets. After each shot he offered encouragement or correction. After David had emptied three magazines, Ezra instructed him to collect his spent round casings.

"Take care of the land, and it will take care of you," he said.

Chapter 46

Sacramento

Johnny explained to Frankie that California was the Far West but far from the Wild West. Frankie nodded, but he didn't get Johnny's point.

"Bottom line," said Johnny. "This state has very restrictive gun carry laws."

"What does the law say?"

"We can't carry guns."

"We could apply for a permit," said Frankie.

"No, we cannot. Think for a minute. No, let me rephrase that. Just listen.... One: It would take too long to process the permit. Two: We do not want to leave a paper trail. Three: We do not want to leave a digital footprint. We do not want any record of us being in this state. Capische?"

"We're not here."

"Very good."

"We're anywhere but here," said Frankie. "We're back in the Bronx. Maybe Jersey."

"Ok. No need to overthink this. We just want to keep a low profile. Remember that. We don't want to call any attention to ourselves."

"We're like ghosts."

"Exactly. We don't want anyone noticing us—and we don't want anyone seeing our guns. When we're driving, we'll hide them under the spare tire. At night, we'll hide them in our room."

"What if we need them?"

"We won't need them until we find Bill."

Chapter 47

Lunch in Los Molinos

After the practice shoot, Jill suggested they all go to lunch in Los Molinos.

"My treat. Let's go to the new place that opened near the post office."

Everyone agreed and happily scrambled back into the truck.

Ezra exited the roadless basin, drove a nameless back-road for several miles, and then accessed San Benito Avenue, headed south. When he turned left on Tehama Avenue and then right on Second Street, David recognized the neighborhood.

Continuing south on Second Street, Ezra drove past the restaurant towards East Gyle Road. Jill leaned close to David's ear: "Ezra probably wants to check in with Maxwell and Elena since we're so close."

Ezra slowed as he approached the house but drove right past when he saw Simon and seven Indians lazing on the porch, drinking beer, the windsocks and dreamcatchers swaying behind them.

The Indians recognized Ezra's truck. Three lifted their beer bottles in an ironic salute. Two sat unmoved. Two shook their up-yours finger. Simon, who saw Jill in the open cab, threw his bottle, which landed behind the truck, shattering with a faint pop.

Rather than turn around and face the Indians again, Ezra continued in a long loop around the neighborhood until he arrived back at the new restaurant, an American bistro with Indian pretensions named Shasta.

As soon as they were all seated, Jill spoke:

"That was a little scary. I hadn't seen Simon since the night at Wiley's. What about you," she said, looking at Bill. "Have you seen him? Has he been working in the casino?"

"I haven't seen him. I asked, but Morgan just shrugged."

"I'll call Maxwell this evening," said Ezra. "Maybe he heard something, but I doubt he'd say."

"Why?" asked Jill.

Ezra shook his head. "He's in a tough bind. He likes me. He respects me. We've built up a lot of trust over the years—"

"But?"

"I'm not Indian."

Jill looked Ezra dead in the eye:

"You were born and raised here. You know more about the Yahi than anyone alive.... For God's sake, you and your fathers kept them alive!"

"But I'm not Indian."

Jill drew a deep breath. "What about Elena? Maybe she heard something."

"I wouldn't do that to Maxwell."

"You wouldn't talk to her?"

"I wouldn't go behind Maxwell's back."

Constant nodded.

"What if they know something?" Jill said. "Something that could ruin our plans?"

Ezra leaned forward and put his arms on the table. His posture suggested conspiracy. Everyone moved closer to hear his softly spoken words:

"We have to be ready—sooner than we expected."

"Ready for what?"

"Ready to film."

"But we're not ready," said Jill. "Elliot hasn't run his cave rehearsal yet."

"It's not necessary," said Ezra.

Jill flashed anger. "Wait a second. This is still my show. I'm the director, not you ... with all due respect."

"I misspoke," Ezra said, softly but firmly. "Here's my thinking: Other than the Gallery, there's nothing about the cave that will add much to your film. The Yahi are the story, not the

220

cave. And their natural habitat—where you can really see them as God intended—is the Wilderness. You can film in the Yahi cave at any time. Next week, next month. Doesn't make much difference. The Yahi don't even have to be there."

Jill's look was a mix of shock and exasperation. "Where's this coming from? For months all you talked about was Ishi Ishi Ishi ... and Yahi Yahi Yahi ... and Caves Caves Caves. I know the whole damn story by heart."

"There's no need to curse."

Jill's eyes were flashing anger. "Oh, excuse me. I said a bad word. Meanwhile, for two months I've been preparing for a film whose main scenes would be shot in dark caves, and now you say: *Oh, never mind, we can shoot in broad daylight. Everything's cool.*"

"That's not what I meant. You didn't let me finish."

Jill reached for her coffee, but her hand was shaking. "Okay," she said, withdrawing her hand and willing herself to be calm. "Please finish. Tell me what has changed."

Ezra smiled and spoke in a very calm and friendly manner. "Everything I told you is true. The Yahi almost never leave their cave. Other than a chosen few who hunt, fish, or forage on moonless nights—the cave is their entire sphere of living. There is only one exception, and I've never mentioned it before, except to Constant, and that was just a few days ago."

"What's the big secret? Why did you never mention it?"

"I never mentioned it because I knew it would fascinate you. I knew you would press me to film it ... but that would have been impossible, unthinkable... until a few days ago."

"What changed?"

Over and Out

A few days earlier.

"Why don't you call the Indian who has your phone?" Morgan asked Simon.

"His name is Branch. That's what he said."

"Why don't you call Branch? Here, you can use my phone."

Simon took Morgan's phone, found his own cell number, and pressed the green "Call" button.

"It's ringing.... 'Hello? Hello, Branch? Can you hear me? This is Simon.'"

Branch held the ringing phone in his hand. Unable to read, he'd been hitting buttons at random, trying to find the pictures of Constant he'd seen on Ezra's phone. When Simon's phone suddenly vibrated and made ringing music, he hit a green button, just as he'd seen Ezra do.

"Hello? Hello, Branch? Can you hear me? This is Simon."

Branch was stunned to hear Simon's voice.

"Branch? This is Simon," Simon repeated.

And then the phone died.

Chapter 48

Canceled and Delayed

For two days, an early nor'easter lashed New York City with nearly hurricane-force winds, delaying all flights into and out of the metro area. Allison and Sandy remained housebound, brooding about their husbands.

In her heart, Allison felt the stretches of highway ... the endless plains ... the mile-high mountains that separated her from David. In her most positive moments she saw these geographical divides as physical thwarts to test her resolve, no more impeding than the predictable obstacles in a steeplechase. But in her low moments she wrestled with the idea that David may have wandered beyond her reach ... to a point of no return.

This made Allison wistful, not angry. She thought *beshert* had been a Divine sign; the ketubah, an inviolable agreement. But perhaps their union had an expiration date: perhaps it was in effect only as long as love lasted. Allison was unclear about her feelings towards David, and even less certain about his feelings for her. But if their marriage had any chance of surviving, Allison thought she must defend it with all her strength and passion.

Sandy, on the other hand, was more pragmatic and calculating. She loved Bill in her own way. Though she would not admit it (except to Dr. Wechsler), she loved his bad-boy guile and blue-collar outlook. Bill complemented her ... entertained her ... protected her. He was not irreplaceable, but she'd never met a suitable substitute. It was worth her while to keep him around, provided he could be reined in ... for the next rickety bridge he crossed might be a bridge too far.

As soon as the storm passed, the two women readied their plans to travel west.

Doorman's Phone Call to Carmine

Hello, Mr. Carmine?

Yes, who is this?

This is Sal Esposito. I'm the doorman at the Belvedere in River-dale.

That's very nice. What can I do you for?

Well, sir, thing is, two associates of yours, Frankie and Johnny, they spoke to me a couple weeks back and said if I had any news about a certain resident or her husband I should call them.

This resident have a husband named Bill?

That's the one.

[Carmine smiles]

What can you tell me, Sal?

I hope you don't mind me calling you. I've been calling Johnny, but he hasn't been answering his phone. I just thought, you know, you might like to know what I know.

What's that, Sal?

Earlier this evening, at six o'clock, I put the resident—you know, the woman we're talking about—in a cab going to JFK.

She say where she was going?

Not exactly.

What did she say?

She said she was headed west. She said she had a nine o'clock flight.

Anything else?

When I closed the door I heard her tell the driver: JFK. Jet Blue.

[Carmine smiles]

Thank you, Sal. I'll make sure Frankie and Johnny give you something for your help.

Thank you, Mr. Carmine.

Chapter 49

Passion Play

The group was still at lunch in Los Molinos. Ezra had just described Simon's voice on the dying cell phone, as told to him by Branch.

Jill put down her cheese-filled corn frittata, one of Shasta's specialties.

"Will wonders never cease?" she said.

"The Lord moves in mysterious ways," said Ezra. "I never saw this coming. But it changes everything."

"How do you figure?" Jill asked.

Ezra took his time before explaining.

"God brought Simon and Branch together in the Wilderness. I don't know why. But the cell phone ... Simon's voice hanging in the air ... You know what Branch said to me?"

"What?"

"He said Simon's voice coming from the cell phone was like God's voice coming from the burning bush."

"Oy!" said David.

"Worse yet," said Ezra, "Branch now sees himself as a cross between Moses and Jesus. I can't control him anymore. He's beyond my influence."

"Wait. I'm not following," said Jill. "Start with the Moses part."

"Okay. About six months ago, I reminded the Yahi that their 100-year exile was almost over. Soon they would be free again."

"How'd they respond?" asked Jill.

"Mixed bag. Some wept with happiness. Some wept in fear. Some are curious about the outside world. Some are used to their life in the Wilderness cave and don't want to change."

"Change is hard," Bill said.

"Not for Branch," said Ezra. "He actually seems enthused about rejoining the world. He asks me lots of questions and when I answer, he seems to pick up more English, which helps him to ask more questions. He's now the undisputed leader of the Yahi."

"Has it gone to his head?" David asked.

"That's a good question. I think it has gone to his head, but not necessarily in a bad way. He carries himself with more gravitas ... but he also seems more impetuous, as if some things are now his due."

"All this relate to the big secret you mentioned?" asked Jill.

"Yes. Time for me to explain."

Ezra swallowed the last of his coffee and signaled the waitress to refill his cup.

"My great-grandfather was determined to protect the Yahi. That was his mission, as he saw it. But he was also a Christian and believed with all his heart in the importance of saving souls. For him it was always a delicate balance: helping the Yahi preserve their traditions while informing them with core Christian belief. For the most part, he did this by telling them Bible stories, the basic and most dramatic ones: Noah, Abraham, Moses, David ... John, Jesus, Judas, Peter. He never pushed it. He was never heavy handed. But his efforts were tireless, continuous, always circling back to Ishi, emphasizing the great sacrifice he had made so the remaining Yahi might endure. Clearly, he wanted the Yahi to associate Ishi's sacrifice with Christ's."

"Good idea," said David. "Makes sense."

"Yes. And over the years he hit upon an idea to drive his point home, to make it dramatic and unforgettable. He invented a sort of Passion play in which the entire tribe would participate."

"What's a Passion play?" asked Bill.

"Good question," said Ezra. "Many Christian groups around the world, though mostly Catholic ones, celebrate Easter with a dramatization of Jesus's crucifixion and resurrection. It's a community event: part play, part parade, and can be very moving."

Jill was rapt by Ezra's explanation, the cinematic possibilities whirling in her head.

"As my great-grandfather conceived it, the Yahi Passion play would take place once every five years. Rather than on Christmas or Easter, it would be celebrated on August 29th and dramatize the day Ishi sacrificed himself to white civilization."

Jill was beaming. "I love it. I just love it. But ... how did your great-grandfather balance the risk? I mean, a community barnburner of a play ... isn't that noisy? Wouldn't that wake the neighbors? Wouldn't it put all the Yahi at risk of being discovered?"

With a series of nods Ezra indicated that such concerns had been considered.

"Yes, yes, yes. It was a risk ... but it was minimized by some cautions. The play was always performed silently and at night, without any illumination or music: no firelight to twinkle across a valley, no voices or drumbeat or flute notes to carry on the wind."

"Still," said Jill, "the whole tribe together ... after years of huddling in the cave. There must have been some chatter, a laugh, a sneeze, a baby crying ..."

Ezra laughed. "You're, right, of course. It's impossible to enforce complete silence on an entire tribe. But the Yahi always did their best to be careful. I think the shared danger gave them a sense of communal pride, which actually renewed their commitment and resolve."

"Oh my god!" said Jill, checking her cell phone. "August 29th is only a week away. Ezra, tell me the Yahi will be performing their Passion play."

"The Yahi will be performing their Passion play."

"Yes!"

"That's my big secret. And it will be their last one. My great-grandfather calculated the last performance should be on that day, celebrating the end of one hundred years of Yahi exile and their return to freedom."

"Oh my god, what a special occasion!" said Jill.

"And, to make it even more special," said Ezra, "it has been decided that this last performance will be held boldly in the bright of day—with music and song."

Jill gasped.

"Who decided that?" asked David.

"Branch did," said Ezra.

"By what authority?" asked David.

"Personal fiat," said Ezra. "Branch simply declared he would play the part of Ishi this year. For generations the honor was always bestowed on one of the tribe's elders—but Branch was having none of that. He's in charge now, and this play is, in his eyes, a kind of coronation."

"Anyone stand up to him?" Jill asked.

"No," said Ezra. "No one. He's now their indisputable leader. The Yahi see him—and he sees himself—as a kind of Moses, leading his people into a new land, after a long period of exile."

"I thought the Yahi saw you as a prophet, a kind of Moses," said David.

"They do ... or, they did. As their exile draws to an end, I think they now see me more as Facilitator than Deliverer. Branch has taken the lead as Moses."

"The man thinks big, give him credit for that," said David.

"Big balls," said Bill.

"Huge," said Ezra. "Branch sees himself as almost divine—part Moses and part Jesus—and he's playing it to the hilt."

"But," said Jill, "the Yahi, as a tribe, agreed to let us film them? That's still in place, right?"

"Absolutely," said Ezra. "The Yahi agreed to let us film all their various activities, including their Passion play. But it was Branch who decided it would take place in broad daylight."

"He wants to make sure everyone sees him," said Jill.

"He wants the event recorded for history," said David.

"Yes and yes," said Ezra. "And he made one more demand."

"What's that?" Jill asked.

"He wants Constant to play a part in the play. For nearly one hundred years it's always been played by a Yahi girl."

"What's the part?"

"I'd rather not say. But Branch is insistent."

All eyes turned to Constant.

"Are you okay with it?" Jill asked her.

Constant shrugged. "Not sure."

Jill's Phone Call to Elliot

Hi, Elliot you got my e-mail?

Sure did—and it threw me for a loop. You want to begin filming next week?

We have to. Timetable has changed. The Passion play is the Yahi coming-out party. We need to do our filming while the Yahi are still in the Wilderness as a reclusive tribe.

I understand.... But my volunteers aren't ready. They're all busy. No one's available.

No one?

No. Not even Kenneth and Gloria. They're vacationing in Laguna. They weren't expecting to shoot so soon.

What are we going to do?

[Elliot pauses to think]

Okay, here's what we can do. You and I will each have to work a camera. But we need at least two more people. Can you get Bill and David to help?

I'm sure I can.

Okay, good. If the four of us work together, handling all the cameras, mikes, and everything else, we can do it. It's a huge plus that we're filming outdoors in the daylight. That will save our asses.

I agree. We just need to film as many Yahi activities as we can.

We'll need to film quietly, informally—nothing stagey about it. We'll tailor our script around the final footage.

Exactly. But bring a couple extra cameras if you can, just in case we can get Ezra to help too. I want to capture the Passion play perfectly. This will be the pièce de résistance ... like the first native Ghost Dance ever filmed ... historic!

What about Constant? Can she help?

Not sure. She might be busy.

Chapter 50

Simon's Plan

Simon and his seven Indian friends journeyed four times into the Wilderness to see if they could find the living Yahi. One of the seven, a gardener and amateur cartographer, had made a map of the area where they suspected the Yahi might be hiding. He'd divided the map into eight sections and then systematically assigned each member of the group an area to explore. Each man also brought a pair of zoom binoculars.

It was a good plan, but it didn't work. No one found any evidence of the living Yahi, not even a distant sighting.

Simon was frustrated and becoming furious. He knew time was running out. He had eyes all over Los Molinos, especially at the hotel and casino, and knew that Jill and Ezra were getting ready to do their filming and freeing. *Damn it!* he thought. They would grab all the glory. He would have nothing!

At the end of the fourth exploration, tired and frustrated, Simon's group trudged back towards town. As a silly diversion, one of the Indians chased a young deer up and across a big brown hill, just off the beaten path. On the lee side of the hill, under the canopy shade of some giant oaks, he discovered Ezra's cabin.

Chapter 51

Carmine's Phone Call to Johnny

How you two geniuses doin'?

Not so great, Boss. We been visiting casinos and snooping around and showing Bill's picture—real subtle like—but no one knows him around here. He probably went north, Boss. There's a number of casinos north of here. It will just take some time. But we'll find him.

I want you to go to the Sacramento airport.

You flyin' us home, Boss?

Shut up and listen.

Sorry, Boss.

Go to the airport. The International one, not the county one.

Got it, Boss.

There are three car rental places there. Go to the one called Fleet. That's the higher-end one.

Got it, Boss.

Good. Go there around one a.m.

That's early, Boss.

Shut the hell up and listen.

Sorry, Boss.

Carmine then explained the rest of his plan: Johnny would mosey alone into the rental office—wearing a fake beard and a baseball cap—and do his best to avoid looking up at the security cameras. He would explain to the desk clerk that a family emergency had caused him to miss his sister's flight. Failing to meet his sister, she likely would have rented a car in the past hour or so. Unfortunately, he had left his cell phone home and had no way of reaching her. *Can you please tell me where my sister's car is now or where it has been? Her name is Sandra Manes. You must have a GPS log. Can you check? Please!* ... Carmine told Johnny that if he had to, he should peel off several C-notes, one at a time. He should sound real sincere—beg, if he had to. If that didn't work, he should add a couple more C-notes. If that didn't work, he should flash the gun in his waistband.

That's a good plan, Boss. We find the car. We follow the car. We find Bill.

New York–Sacramento

Neither Sandy nor Allison felt at all sleepy during the 6 hour, 25-minute flight. Sandy read two long articles in the in-flight magazine, one about Golden Gate Park and one about the prosperous wineries in Napa Valley. Allison alternated between looking out the window and rereading David's first published novel, *Forty Years Later*, on her plus-sized smartphone. David had written tenderly and pointedly about their marriage. He had also written about a woman named Jill Black, who Allison now suspected was with her husband in Los Molinos, and a major reason for him being there. She wondered how his new book was coming along, and whether Jill was included and whether she got top billing, once again.

Second Chances

The next day, shortly before noon, Elliot pulled into the parking lot of the Sierra Spa and Casino Hotel. Ezra was waiting by his truck. The two men had met once before and greeted each other warmly. Elliot popped open his trunk and Ezra helped him move three heavy boxes into the back of his pickup.

"Sorry," said Elliot, seeing Ezra choose the largest and heaviest of the boxes to lift.

"No problem," Ezra said. "These movie cameras?"

"Yup. And a small generator, batteries, wires and cables, and some other stuff."

"You excited?" asked Ezra.

"Yes. Nervous too."

Ezra nodded. "What's your biggest fear?"

Elliot stared. At that moment, he could not imagine a more pointed, personal question ... and yet it sounded—and felt—completely normal.

"Whoa, that's a tough one. Biggest fear ...?"

"Yeah, from the gut ... if you don't mind. I'd like to know."

"At the moment, I have two ... two basic fears."

"Okay."

Elliot drew a deep breath. "The first is about the film we're making. I really want it to be good. There's a lot riding on it. For me and Jill.... Has she told you about our history?"

"Little bit. Not much. I know you worked together on a Hollywood film."

"That's true. It was her directorial debut and my first job as an assistant producer ... and I really messed up. Because of me, the film was killed and the fallout knocked both Jill and me out of the industry. We're praying this film gets us back in the industry's good graces."

"I'm all about second chances."

"I know."

Ezra secured the boxes with some heavy-duty, nylon lashings.

"You said two basic fears. What's the other one?"

Elliot paused, suggesting that this second fear was even more difficult for him to discuss.

"I know all about the threats against us. And the guns.... I don't know what to say. Violence frightens me. I think it's against my religion."

"Your religion?"

"I'm a devout coward."

Ezra smiled, then patted his back. "Don't worry," he said.

"It will be okay?"

"Don't know. It will be what it will be."

Sierra Spa and Casino Hotel

The flight was on time and the two women had no problems reconnecting with their luggage. Sandy, who was familiar with the airport, led the way to the car rental pavilion, where a blue Camry was waiting for them. The two women had already agreed to spend the night in a local motel and drive the next morning to the Sierra Spa and Casino Hotel.

The next day, following a pleasant continental breakfast, Sandy and Allison headed north.

"According to the GPS, we have a choice of three routes," Sandy said. "They're all about 110 miles and less than two hours. One passes through Chico. That's where David went to school. Let's take that route."

"Fine," said Allison, who continued staring out the window.

Both women were nervous. Their husbands did not know they were coming. They knew this was chancy, but it had seemed like a good idea.

Driving north, the women avoided looking at each other, focusing instead on the passing landscape. Neither of them had ever been to the high desert country of Northern California where the hills were mostly yellow and dry, and the flats—at least those that were spring watered—spotted with alfalfa or covered with carpets of purple lupines and white poppies.

The women pushed on without a bathroom break. Neither mentioned the hotel accommodations until they saw a sign for Los Molinos. Sandy spoke first:

"Have you decided about the room situation?"

"I don't know. What are you doing?"

Sandy mulled the question. "I think I'm going to check into my own room. I don't want to put Bill on the spot. Right now I'm just worried about his safety. We'll work out the personal stuff later."

Allison felt differently. She had no reason to believe her husband was under any direct threat; even so, she did not want to surprise him—or herself. "Could I stay with you—until I figure things out?"

"Of course, whatever you like."

The women arrived at the Sierra Spa and Casino Hotel before eleven a.m. Ellie Hacklin was at the registration desk, as usual.

Sandy asked for a smoke-free room with two separate beds, far from the elevator and facing the back.

Ellie checked her computer for availability—even though she knew that all the rooms but seven were unoccupied.

"You prefer first floor or second floor?" Ellie asked.

"Whichever is most quiet," said Sandy. "Put us as far away from other residents as possible."

"Okay then. Room 152. How long will you be staying?"

Both women turned to look at each other.

"Not sure," said Sandy. "We'd like to play that by ear, if you don't mind."

"That's fine," said Ellie. "But I have to know before 11:00 a.m. tomorrow morning. Otherwise, I'll have to charge you for the room."

"No problem," said Sandy, producing her credit card. "We'll let you know in the morning when we come down for breakfast. There is breakfast, isn't there?"

"Of course. All meals are served in La Cantina—down that corridor to your right. Can't miss it…. Okay, one second … Here are your keys. Room 152, down the corridor to your left. Hope you enjoy your stay at the Sierra Spa and Casino Hotel."

Blue Camry

Seduced by the sight of the C-notes on the counter and the pistol in Johnny's waistband, the rent-a-car clerk displayed a very helpful attitude.

Johnny learned that Sandra Manes and a female companion had rented a blue Camry. For eight hours the car had been parked at the Red Ranch Motel (only three miles from the airport) and then had been driven north, passing Chico. According to the clerk, the car was now parked near the Sierra Spa and Casino Hotel in Los Molinos.

Chapter 52

Playing It Safe

Not since May 1914, when Ishi led an expedition of university anthropologists to Deer Creek Canyon, a former Yahi stomping ground, had a Stone Age Yahi been studied in his natural environs for the benefit of posterity. For two weeks that spring, fiftysomething Ishi, ostensibly the last of his tribe, sang Yahi songs, named dozens of plants, animals, and places, and demonstrated his range of hunting and fishing skills.

More than one hundred years later: Jill, Elliot, David, and Bill stood in the Ishi Wilderness, waiting outside the main entrance of a cave for the Stone Age Yahi to enter the twenty-first century.

Ezra and Constant (one holding an LED lamp, the other holding a movie camera) had already been inside for several hours, filming in the near dark, paying special attention to the Gallery and the community rooms where the Yahi lived and worked by firelight and candlelight.

Ezra had insisted that he and Constant do the indoor filming, citing the many tight turns and low ceilings, and the fact that the Yahi would feel overwhelmed by the sudden intrusion of so many strangers. Ezra's decision had also been informed by two other safety concerns. He knew well that the Yahi caves were actually sections of porous basalt lava tubes. For untold years, rain water had percolated downward through the porous basalt, compromising the integrity of the tunnels and migrating to the lower levels of the caves, where they collected into permanent water sources (a necessity for cave dwellers). Further, as a modern surveyor, Ezra was aware of the Beaver Creek and Cohasset Ridge faults that run basically parallel through the central and southwest sections of the Ishi Wilderness. Though officially active (there being evidence of surface movement in the past 1.6 million years), Ezra had never seen any significant land-slides or liquefaction in the area. Even so, he saw no reason to tempt Fate. With the Yahi freedom only two days away, he decided to play it safe and have Jill, Elliot, David, and Bill remain outside, along with the rest of their equipment. They would have plenty opportunity to film the Yahi in the light of day.

In the Light of Day

Forty-one Yahi would soon emerge from exiled darkness into bright freedom. Because the cave entrance was more of a narrow fissure-gap than a classic cave-mouth, they would emerge one at a time, except in those cases when an adult female held a baby or small child, or an adult required assistance.

Two static cameras, monitored by David and Bill, were positioned to record the emergence of each individual Yahi. Jill and Elliot, each holding a mobile camera, were prepared to follow chosen individuals to develop several ongoing storylines.

Before the first Yahi emerged, Jill turned to Ezra with a microphone in her hand. "Ezra, as I explained earlier, I'm going to count 3-2-1. On the count of 1, we begin recording. I'm going to make a statement and then ask you a question. Just answer as naturally as you can, from the heart. Here we go, 3 … 2 … 1…." Jill indicated the light was on and they were recording:

"Ezra Winship—thirty-nine years old, licensed surveyor, wilderness explorer, and man of God. You, your father, your grandfather, and your great-grandfather have shared one of the great secrets in American history. For the past one hundred years, ever since the death of Ishi—known to many as the Last of the Yahi Indians—your ancestors—and now you—have been the only persons in the world to know the truth: that Ishi was not the last of the Yahi—not the last Stone Age man of America. In fact, a whole tribe of Stone Age Americans—who have been secretly under your care for many years—are about to walk out of the cave we are facing and into the twenty-first century. What are your thoughts?"

The camera captured Ezra in his summer attire—denim shirt, khaki pants, low mountain boots, floppy brimmed hat—and then zoomed in for a close-up of his rugged face, intense with emotion. Several long seconds passed before Ezra spoke:

"I have given much of my life to this moment—as my fathers have before me. I thank them all—and I thank God—for the great privilege of allowing me to serve the Yahi and to help them preserve their Old Ways. In the coming days—and years—I pledge to do all I can to help them adapt to the new world—a world they know almost nothing about."

Two static cameras, directed at the cave entrance but set at different angles, began filming.

Branch emerged first. Whether this signified his elite status or whether he wanted to lead by example is not known. In any case, he looked tall and strong, every inch the leader. But he did not stand around posing. Along with Ezra and Constant, he greeted each of the Yahi that followed him, helping those who needed help acclimate to the sunshine and the idea of freedom.

The children appeared next. Up to about six years of age they were naked. A few seemed disoriented and timid, but most approached their freedom with the ferocious glee of kids let loose in a candy store.

Following the children, the Yahi women appeared. All were bare above the waist and wore skirts of shredded juniper bark, willow, or tulle. Most wore their long hair parted in the middle, each hank tied with a piece of rawhide and hanging in front of a naked shoulder. Some were smiling. A few looked frightened.

The men emerged next. They all were naked, save for a loin covering of buckskin or fur, tucked between their legs and secured by a waist belt. Each wore his long hair in a single bunch, hanging on his back.

Some of the adults, men and women, had their cheeks tattooed with two or three horizontal lines extending from the corners of their mouth. (As Ezra explained, the tattooing was not done with inks but by rubbing charcoal into skin cuts and then pricking the wound with bone awls or porcupine quills.) Nearly all the men and women wore earrings made of bone or wood. Many also displayed a nose-pin: a slender bird bone or twig inserted through a hole in the septum.

The last person to emerge was a young girl Ezra called "Holy." Around fifteen and obviously pregnant, Holy halted at the entrance, shielding her eyes against the strong glare. As soon as she sighted her parents she joined them ... but kept sneaking looks at Branch.

Bloodlines

By and large the Yahi did not look healthy. In addition to deficiencies of exercise and vitamin D, they'd been enfeebled by successive generations of inbreeding, resulting in some twisted torsos, a couple clubfeet, and one cleft palate. There might have been more examples of malformation, but their close blood relations had kept their infertility high and their birthrate low. The bright sunshine promised a healthier and happier future.

Steven Jay Griffel

Chapter 53

Women's Work

Together with Jill and Elliot, Ezra had planned which Yahi activities would be filmed during the two days leading up to the Passion play. Inasmuch as Ishi's hunting, fishing, archery, bow-making, and fire-making skills had already been recorded, it was decided to focus on other skills and customs, especially those usually performed by Yahi women:

In the quiet bend of a nearby stream a young woman pounds local soaproot, then tosses it into the water; a few minutes later, a couple fish float belly-up on the surface.

A grandmother drives a digging stick into moist soil, agitating angleworms from their subterranean stupor; she collects them, and later roasts them between hot rocks.

Two middle-aged women collect black acorns for bread, white acorns for soup.

Two other women demonstrate their basket-weaving, one favoring a coiling technique, the other preferring to twine.

One woman, fancying herself a feather expert, finds and fashions a variety of colorful feathers for adornment.

A sister spooks a nibbling jack rabbit … another sister catches it in a large net … another sister clubs it to death.

The mother guts the rabbit with a stone knife and roasts it in ashes; later, she skins the rabbit and mashes its whole body with a pestle stone before serving it to her daughters.

Jill and Elliot had hoped to film a birth and burial, but no Yahi was born and no Yahi died until after the Passion play.

Chapter 54

Simon Sees

The door to Ezra's cabin was closed but unlocked. Such was Simon's grudging respect for Ezra, he walked around the cabin twice before deciding the coast was clear. Even then, he posted a sentry atop the brown hill to warn of anyone's approach.

Simon poked his fingers into every corner of the cabin, admiring its manly, rough-hewn construction. But it was its homey touches—the quilted yellow blanket and finely filigreed plates—that made him envious of the man who had a woman who loved him.

Behind the cold iron stove Simon saw an impressive pile of stacked wood. Behind the wood, wrapped in a large square of oilcloth, he found Ezra's .50 caliber pistol. He unwrapped the pistol and measured its heft. It felt like a hand-held cannon. He was thinking about taking the gun when he turned towards the front door and saw the wall of open-mouthed animal traps. There was one, on the lower left, that looked familiar: an old trap whose mouth hung limp, its coil spring neutered. His father had given him that kill trap for his twelfth birthday. It was the only gift his father had ever given him.

Chapter 55

Under the Stars

Sandy and Allison waited all day and night to see their husbands. What they didn't know was that they were both lying under the stars in the Ishi Wilderness.

With only two days to film before the Passion play, Bill and David had remained on site rather than commute back and forth from the hotel and risk missing some once-in-a-lifetime film opportunity. They were both very tired. It had been a long and exhausting day and, by all accounts, a very positive one. Jill and Elliot had reviewed the first day's raw footage and pronounced it extraordinary.

Everyone was in a good mood, despite the looming threat from Simon and company. Even with that, Ezra's calm presence was reassuring. He insisted that they were in no danger and suggested that they all get a good night's rest. Everyone took his advice and soon were fast asleep. Ezra and Constant took turns keeping watch.

Husband Hunting

The next day, after breakfast in La Cantina (prepared and served by Morgan), Allison and Sandy sat in the lobby to discuss their husbands.

"Where the hell are they?"

"I don't know," said Sandy. "But no one's here. It's like a ghost town."

It was nearly true. The parking lot was almost empty. Other than Morgan's and Ellie's cars, both parked in the Staff Only section, there was only one car in the lot other than their own blue Camry—a hot little red convertible. Allison guessed it might belong to Jill Black, but she didn't want to think about it.

"C'mon," said Sandy. "We can't just sit here."

Allison followed Sandy across the lobby to the information desk.

"Excuse me," Sandy said to Ellie. "We're looking for two men."

"Good luck with that. Slim pickings around here."

"You don't understand. We're looking for our husbands."

Ellie shook her head. "On a good night there might be a few men in the casino, but they don't usually strike me as husband material."

Sandy took a deep breath. "Sorry, I wasn't clear. We're looking for *our* husbands. My husband is Bill Manes. Her husband is David Grossman. Do you know them?"

"Bill and David! Of course I know them. There aren't many of us here. We're like family."

"Wonderful," said Sandy. "Can you tell us where they are?"

"Sorry. No can do."

"Look, we just flew in from New York, and it's really important that we speak to them."

"I'm sure it is, but I don't know exactly where they are."

Sandy paused. "Do you know approximately where they are?"

"Yes."

"And where would that be?"

"The Ishi Wilderness."

Sandy took another deep breath. "Okay. How can we get there?"

"There's a trail right behind the hotel that leads straight there."

"How far by car?"

"You can't go there by car. It's not legal. It's a national park."

"How far is it to walk?"

"You'd never make it. Too far, too rugged."

"How did our husbands get there?"

"They went by truck."

Sandy wanted to scream. "Look, I'll give you two hundred dollars if you can get us there—and I don't care how."

Waiting in the Wings

Across the street, catty-corner from the hotel, was a shuttered grocery store. Frankie and Johnny had been parked in its driveway for eleven hours. From there they had a clear view of the hotel parking lot and the blue Camry parked in the middle, all by its lonesome.

"We haven't seen Bill or the women," said Frankie.

"I know," said Johnny.

Fifteen minutes passed in silence.

"How long we gonna sit here?" asked Frankie.

"Until we see Bill," said Johnny.

"What if he isn't here?"

"Then we wait for the women to leave—and we follow them."

"How long you think it'll be?"

"I have no idea."

Chapter 56

Act Two

The previous evening, a few of the Yahi had returned to the cave to sleep, but by late morning they all had re-emerged, without any fanfare. Following a large communal breakfast, Jill and Elliot took their time filming a half-dozen more Stone Age customs and then began filming interviews. Working with Branch, Ezra had chosen more than a dozen Yahi (male and female, young and old) who were naturally engaging and who had something special to share. Branch assisted with the phrasing of the questions and the translation of the responses.

Unfortunately, a fierce argument arose about interviewing the Yahi who were significantly malformed. Jill and Elliot insisted that they be filmed as a matter of historic record. Ezra and Branch argued against the idea, saying it would dishonor the Yahi and would make people think poorly of them. Jill believed that Branch and Ezra regarded the twisted bones and clefts as stigma against the quality of their leadership. She assured them both that the afflicted Yahi would be portrayed as biological anomalies, which would eventually disappear over the next few generations. She gave Branch and Ezra her personal assurance that the film would address the issue with the greatest sensitivity and include some expert interview or voice-over that explained the situation.

When the Yahi interviews were completed, everyone turned their attention to preparing for the next day's Passion play. This would be the climax of the film. Following the play, the Yahi would celebrate the official end of their one-hundred year exile. On the following day Ezra would set in action his plans to re-introduce the Yahi to the world, beginning with coverage from local media. He knew life would never be the same for the Yahi, but he was okay with that. He had fulfilled his mission and they had survived. The rest was in God's hands.

Simon's Minions

Simon had given up on the idea of becoming famous for freeing the Yahi. His inability to find the Yahi had stymied his plan. His only option now was to ruin whatever coming-out party Ezra had planned for the Stone Age tribe.

But even that idea was on hold. At the moment, Simon had big problems: His not-so-magnificent seven would not be at full strength until the next day (one man had to work an extra shift; one had to take his wife to the dentist; one had to stay home while a new sump pump was installed).

Simon did not think he could create enough havoc with only four men.

He knew his window of opportunity was closing.

He knew he would have only one more chance.

Ellie's Text Message to Constant

Bill & David's wives are at the hotel.
Surprise visit.
They say it's an emergency.
I know you're in the Wilderness making a film.
Can you pick them up and bring them wherever you all are?

Constant's Quandary

Constant wasn't sure what to do. Doing the right thing wasn't always as clear to her as it seemed to be for Ezra. For example: When she wondered aloud why Bill wasn't living with his wife or why David wore a wedding ring, Ezra cautioned her not to judge too harshly. And when she asked Ezra why Branch treated Holy so dismissively, he encouraged her to be more tolerant of the ways of others. And when Branch started paying too much attention to her when he should have been taking care of Holy ... and when Ezra supported Branch's request that she play a role in the Passion play that should have gone to a Yahi girl, she began to ask herself: *What about me? Who is honoring me?*

Constant and Ezra had an understanding. What she didn't have was an engagement ring or even a firm promise of one. When she read Ellie's text about Bill's wife and David's wife, she imagined a pair of disrespected women who deserved better. Constant sent a text message to Ellie:

Tell them to sit tight.
Their husbands are here.
We're all fine.
We should be home in less than 48 hours.

And then, without further ado, she set out for the cabin to be alone with her thoughts.

Wait and See

Frankie and Johnny kept their eyes on the blue Camry in the parking lot and on the hotel's main entrance.

Suddenly, two middle-aged women exited the main entrance and walked towards their rented car. The shorter woman led the way, walking briskly, as if hurrying to a business meeting. The other woman, taller, followed behind, looking more nervous.

"That's her," said Johnny. "The first one. That's Bill's wife."

Frankie nodded. "Who's the other woman?"

"Don't know. Just watch. And keep quiet."

The shorter woman opened the driver's side door and removed a folded map that had been left on the seat. She then closed the door and laid the opened map on the hood of the car.

Out There

Sandy pointed to different parts of the map and read the label names: "Cascade Range ... Mount Shasta ... Sierra Nevada ... Mount Lassen ... Ishi Wilderness."

Allison repeated each name silently.

"David told me about these places," she said. "I looked them up on the Internet. I want to see them all ... with David."

"I know," Sandy said, staring at the map, unable to meet Allison's eyes.

The women remained awhile in the parking lot, admiring the manzanita bushes, the foothills, and the mountains beyond. Eventually they returned to the hotel.

Frankie and Johnny stayed in the car. Every couple hours they took turns walking to a nearby diner to buy something to eat or to use the bathroom.

Chapter 57

Simon's Brainstorm

The next morning, Simon returned to Ezra's cabin with his seven-man force at full strength.

He had a plan, of sorts. Knowing there were big doings out there in the Wilderness, and assuming that the cabin was a sort of staging area, it occurred to Simon that Ezra or Constant, or both together, would likely stop by ... and when they did, he would follow them all the way to the Yahi ... and once there ... Well, Simon's plan didn't go that far. But he figured if he and the boys kept thinking, they'd probably come up with some good ideas.

Sentry Sighting

Simon's seven friends were unruly guests. If Simon hadn't quieted them with his pointed gun they might have pissed the yellow quilt or smashed the blue-filigreed plates. Even with the pointed gun, there might have been a melee of destruction if the sentry atop the brown hill hadn't burst through the door.

"Someone's coming!"

War cries! Whooping yells! Shouts for a showdown! But Simon's voice of reason prevailed.

"C'mon, we need to move fast. We'll hide in the oak grove out back. We can watch the cabin from there. And clean this place up. Leave no sign we were here."

Neglected Love

Constant had made the trip from the Yahi cave to Ezra's cabin in just under two hours. While walking, her mind had been occupied with roiled thoughts of Ezra. She remembered how she'd met him on a Wilderness expedition and fallen in love.... She remembered how surprisingly shy he'd been about their intimacies.... She remembered the first time he'd brought her to his cabin: rugged and primitive it was, but she'd loved the two of them alone in the Wilderness, like Adam and Eve, like they were inventing the world together, like humanity depended on their sane choices…. Most of all she remembered the day he told her the story about the living Yahi. Having grown up in Northern California, she knew the outline of Ishi's story, but listening to Ezra was a behind-the-scenes tour, a privileged eavesdropping on history. And when he described his fathers' sacrifices to help the Yahi—and his own sworn duty—she loved him beyond all measure. But this past year had been a trial for them both. Ezra was preoccupied with fulfilling Ishi's prophecy and with bringing his duty to a close. Constant felt neglected at times … but how could she complain when Ezra was saving a people and making history? Still, a little more personal attention, even if it did not include an engagement ring, would have satisfied her. These were her thoughts as she hiked to the cabin. And when she arrived, flipping a simple block lever and pushing the door open, she saw the many feminine garnishes that complemented the cabin's rustic grace. She lay down on the bed's soft quilt, her head on the plump pillows, and rested awhile with a contented heart.

Trailing Constant

An hour later, hidden in a dark recess of the oak grove, Simon and his men watched Constant leave the cabin. He was certain she would lead them to the Yahi hideout.

"We'll follow," he whispered. "Give her a five-minute lead. Pauley, you go first. Art, wait five minutes then you go. Then Red. Then Mickey. Wes, Ted, Willard, you follow. I'll bring up the rear. Put your cell phones on mute. If anyone gets lost, send a text to the man you're following—but no talking. Voices carry. Pauley, when Constant gets where she's going, find a place where we can watch without being seen. When we all catch up, we'll figure out our next move. We'll show them bastards."

Simon surprised himself. It was the first time he had ever demonstrated any thoughtful leadership. After a lifetime of feeling damned and disrespected, it felt fiercely exhilarating.

By Heart

Constant knew the trail by heart: every twist, every switchback, every step from ravine to ridgeline ... from the shadows of canyon ramparts ... through valleys and arroyos ... past pools and streams ... past pillars and cliffs ... to the porous lava caves of the Yahi.

Simon's men followed behind.

Chapter 58

Penny for Your Thoughts?

After filming the last interview, everyone enjoyed a respite except Ezra, who was busy reviewing plans for the next day's Passion play. (The route had already been rehearsed with Jill and Elliot, who had decided where all the static cameras and microphones would be positioned. Only she and Elliot would handle the mobile cameras.)

Having finished writing in his notebook, David got to his feet and walked away from the group along a scruffy minor path. Jill followed him, waiting until they were both quite alone before calling his name.

"David!"

David knew her voice. More, he had half expected her to follow him. He knew—and he knew that she knew—that their relationship needed to be discussed.

"Where you going?" Jill asked.

"Don't know," said David.

For both, question and answer seemed perfectly apt. No other words seemed immediately necessary.

The path widened and they walked side-by-side in silence. After a couple minutes, Jill asked: "Penny for your thoughts?"

David felt he had nothing to say that Jill didn't already know. Still, forty years of marriage had taught him a thing or two about women, and he knew he needed to utter the words that were hanging in the air.

"I'm glad we reconnected ... yet again."

"Why?" she said, a twinkle in her eye.

"You want me to spell it out?" he asked, smiling.

"Yes. I want to hear you say it."

David paused. "I think we both got what we wanted."

Jill paused. "What did I get?"

"The same thing I did."

"And that would be—?"

David paused again. "We explored our shared past ... we deepened our present affections-"

"And?"

"We both recharged ourselves for our futures."

Jill paused. "Our separate futures," she said.

David nodded. "All futures are separate. Some people happen to live together."

Jill was silent awhile. "You've grown cynical over the years."

David shook his head. "I don't think so. To me, *cynical* means bitter. I'm not bitter. In fact, I'm quite happy and grateful."

"For what exactly?"

"I'm happy for my health. I'm happy to be a published novelist. I'm happy to be working on a new novel. I'm happy to have family and friends."

"Me included?"

"Near the top of my list. I mean it. You're one of the main reasons I'm happy. If I didn't reconnect with you, I'm just another guy looking at life in his rearview mirror. Without you, I don't write *Forty Years Later*. Without you, I don't write *The Ishi Affair*. Without you, I'm just a guy with regrets. You've made a huge difference in my life."

Jill started to cry. "I love you, David."

"I love you too."

The two friends hugged for a long time.

"I'm glad you took me to Woodstock," Jill said, wiping away her tears. "Even if it took you forty years."

David laughed.

"And I'm glad you came out here," Jill continued. "I know you have a wife and family. I shouldn't have asked you ... but I'm glad I did. I think I knew all along I couldn't keep you.... But without you, I don't think I would have made it. Because you came, I'm going to have another film. I know it's a small film … but it will be important … and it will get noticed. It will open some doors and put me back in the conversation. I owe all that to you."

"That's not true. You did that yourself. You were driven."

"Like, crazy driven?"

David laughed. "A little…. Maybe more than a little."

Jill laughed too.

"But that's what you needed," he said. "That craziness is what drove you."

"Yeah, I was driven," Jill said. "But out of control. You helped me focus…. You came when I asked. I can't ask for more. Thank you, David."

Elliot's Thoughts

Things are going well, really well. If the film is successful … if we can get some great reviews … some public buzz … some film festivals … hello second chance … hello Hollywood…. Nice to be back….

Ezra's Thoughts

I should have married Constant by now. I have not done right by her. I haven't honored her. When the Yahi are free, I will ask Constant to marry me. We'll get married in the Wilderness. The mountain will be our altar. The sky will be our canopy…. And we will have children. More than one, if it pleases God…. Who knows, perhaps God will see that my work is done and send me a daughter … Eliza. I have always liked that name.

Chapter 59

Rehearsal

Though all the Yahi would participate in the Passion play, there were only two roles (the part of Ishi, and the part of the girl who washes his feet) that had to be rehearsed. Branch was ready to rehearse his role, but Constant was nowhere to be found. She hadn't said a word to anyone about the text message she'd received from Ellie. She'd simply left camp, trekked back to the cabin, collected her thoughts, and then commenced her return trip through the Wilderness.

Ezra assumed her absence was temporary, a fit of pique to express her displeasure of having been strong-armed into playing the part of the young Yahi water girl. He was confident she would return in plenty of time.... But it was getting late. Less than an hour to go—and still no sight of Constant. He wasn't particularly worried. He was confident in her sense of duty and knew she could take care of herself. Still, she might have met with a snake or scorpion, or some hungry feral beast. With each passing minute, his worry increased.

Branch and Holy

Branch pretended not to be bothered by Constant's absence. Truth be told, he'd long suspected she would not fulfill her role, which is why he'd tried many times to speak with Simon, using the cell phone he'd received in a trade for his quiver. But the cell phone made no more lights or sounds. The dead thing was no more useful than a stupid rock, and Branch was never able to use Simon as leverage against Ezra, to show that he had other contacts in the outside world, including some who were Indian.

As young as he was, Branch was politically astute. He knew he must always appear determined and intrepid. So, rather than sulk about the absent Constant, he made a show of seeking out Holy, as if she'd always been his preference for the role of ceremonial bather.

Branch's attentions made Holy's parents proud. They hoped for a happy future for their daughter and for their unborn grandchild, imagining a baby boy who would grow up to be a Yahi leader.

Chapter 60

Via Dolorosa

Ezra 1 conceived the Yahi Passion play as a way of enjoining Christian belief and Yahi tradition. Inspired by Jesus's Via Dolorosa, he imagined Ishi's sacrificial journey from Deer Creek to Oroville. To symbolize that experience he designed a one-mile course, beginning at the main entrance of the Yahi cave and ending by the shore of a small, clear-water lake, which he named Little Galilee.

According to tradition, the Ishi march begins under the noonday sun: God's fierce eye demands penance before grace.

Arduous Trek

Constant moved swiftly through the challenging terrain of the Wilderness. Her ballet training and exercise regimen had prepared her well for the arduous trek. As usual, she kept a quick pace but took precautions. She rested where the shade was cool. She wore a hat and sunscreen. She kept properly hydrated.

Her trackers, however, were ill-prepared. Though Simon and his Indian friends had some familiarity with the local terrain and some vestigial protections against its rough treatment, they were far removed from their grandfathers' daily communion with the great outdoors and struggled to keep up.

Only Pauley had brought a water canteen. The others had brought only small water bottles, which they soon depleted. They sweated and gasped. Their sweat turned quickly to caked salt, which hindered efficient perspiration. Because cell phone service was sketchy and could not be trusted, the men were fearful of falling behind and getting lost. No one rested for more than a minute. Each man struggled to keep the man ahead of him in view. Their breathing was labored, their bones ached, and each man considered giving up.

View from the Ridge

Constant arrived while Ezra was still helping the Yahi organize the order of the procession. Though she had initially felt strong about her decision to leave the camp unnoticed, she now felt nervous that she had left a hole in the Passion play. Instead of inserting herself into her designated place, she remained atop a ridge that faced the main Yahi cave entrance, less than thirty yards away. From there she thought she might assess the situation. She was worried she might have ruined Ezra's plans. She prayed to God to make it right.

Ezra saw her before she saw him. He was able to use hand signals to catch her attention and to indicate that he would come to her.

With what seemed like only a few bounding strides, Ezra climbed the ridge and faced her. After a quick embrace he whispered that Holy had been given her role and that all was well. He did not let on that he'd been worried about her. But Constant felt his relief. She smiled and pressed his hand. Her eyes were teary. Ezra said that David and Bill were about a mile away, near Little Galilee, ready to film the ceremony there. Now that she was no longer in the Passion play, he suggested that she follow the ridge to the lake, where it was considerably lower, barely a rise, and hunker down during the ceremony to avoid being seen in the film. After the ceremony, everyone but Branch would immediately return to the camp outside the Yahi cave. This would be a relatively quiet time, a period of prayer and reflection. When Branch finally rejoined his people, there would be a celebration. At that point, Ezra said, Constant could join him and they would rejoice together.

Chapter 61

Penance

Branch was young and evolving, learning about himself each passing day. Because there were so many old and new Branches to account for, he did not readily share his feelings, not even with Ezra or Holy.

Unknown to anyone else, Branch had been fasting for several weeks, taking only small sips of water, bits of jerked meat, and a few manzanita berries. The thinner he grew, the closer he felt to Ishi. He did this for himself and for his people. He thought if he felt Ishi's passion more nearly and dearly it would make him a better man and a better leader. He did not seek praise. It was enough, he thought, that his ancestors could see his thinning body and strengthening spirit.

Branch performed one other selfless task in the weeks leading up to the Passion play. In his free time, and with fading strength, he secretly built a four-by-five-foot tumbrel from local woods and stone. It was his wish that any Yahi too old or infirm to walk the mile route could be wheeled to the lake and then back again. Minutes before the procession was to begin, he showed the tumbrel to Ezra and asked if he would convey the weak Yahi who wanted to travel but couldn't. With deep emotion, Ezra accepted.

August 29

The Passion play was a special holiday, a day filled with lamentation and joy, memorializing Ishi's great sacrifice and celebrating the Yahi's enduring spirit.

Yahi men marked their grief by close-cropping their hair and nicking their scalp. The Yahi also showed their joy. Men and women painted red and white stripes across their chest and wore circlets of twisted grass on their upper arms. Headbands and belts were decorated with tufts of feathers, quills, and woodpecker scalps. Men wore necklaces of bear claws. Women wore bracelets of perforated acorns.

The procession was led by three elder males in bear robes. They chanted prayers and songs, one of which was the "Dancing Song of Dead People." Their voices were like a choral drone, powerful, but with little modulation.

Behind them walked Branch. His hair had been singed impressively close to his scalp. Above his loincloth, his ribs and sinews were emphatic. His gaze was focused. For the moment, Branch was Ishi.

Behind Branch came the rhythm section: males clattering split-sticks; females shaking acorn-filled gourds and cocoon rattles.

Behind the musicians marched three elder females, each with long, flowing gray hair, decorated with tufts of feathers. Each of the ancient women held a long reed whistle, which they blew in unison: a high, piping sound.

At the rear of the procession stood Holy. This was a break with tradition. For one hundred years a young virgin had performed the ceremonial lavation of Ishi's feet, a baptism of sorts. But when Branch had chosen Constant for the role, no Yahi had dared gripe too loudly. In Constant's absence, the Yahi were happy to have one of their own fill this role, even if she were not a virgin. In fact, they all agreed that the obvious sign of Holy's fertility suggested a happier Yahi future than any young girl's innocence might suggest.

Twenty feet behind Holy, Ezra pushed the crude tumbrel, heavy with five old Yahi enfeebled by age or crippled with disease. With each step, Ezra's hands grew raw from the rough wood, his knees and shins bloodied from the continual barking. With each painful step, Ezra thanked Branch and God for the opportunity to serve.

THE ISHI AFFAIR

Late Arrivals

By the time Pauley arrived, the procession was halfway to the lake. By the time Simon had caught up, Ezra had transported the last of the Yahi to the shore of Little Galilee. Simon and his men followed Ezra to the lake. At that point they all were dry-mouthed and exhausted. The only thing on their minds was to drink from the fast-flowing stream that fed the lake and rest awhile on the cool grasses along the shore. But they waited. Because they couldn't risk revealing themselves, they remained at some distance, parched and dusty, hidden by a cluster of oak. From there they watched the scene.

Little Galilee

All the living Yahi were gathered at the shore of Little Galilee. Jill and Elliot covered all the filming angles with a pair of mobile movie cameras. David and Bill manned the stationary cameras.

Hidden behind some oaks, Simon and his men watched with intense curiosity. Hunkered behind a low ridge, Constant had her own point of view.

To begin this part of the Passion play, the three old Yahi men removed their bear robes and stood to the side like three wise and silent burghers. The three old women, their long gray tresses fluttering in the breeze, piped a delicate tune on their long reed whistles.

Branch passed between these elder witnesses to stand by the edge of the shore, then turned about so he could be seen by all. He looked deeply serious. The former brash boy and fearless hunter was now a modest young man of stern character.

Holy approached him slowly. She was barefoot (as were all the Yahi) but unadorned, except for a single pink primrose in her hair. In her arms (and resting lightly on her distended belly) was a beautiful example of Yahi basketry: a vessel about fourteen inches wide, twined with willow roots and displaying a deer-rib and arrow-point design that suggested strength, fortitude, and robust health. The vessel was light but not empty. Inside was a gopher pelt: soft gray fur on one side, smooth shiny skin on the other.

Holy stopped a few feet from Branch and laid the basket on a patch of rocky ground by the shore. When she stood up, her eyes met Branch's and he smiled, and all the Yahi who saw the smile felt their hearts warmed.

Save for his deerskin loincloth, Branch was as he was born, unmarked with any paint or ornament. His fasting dramatized his ribs and sinews. He was pared down to his core. Holy removed the gopher pelt from the basket and laid it on the ground. Then she waded into the lake until the water reached her calves and filled the basket halfway. She then turned and walked back to the shore. Very slowly, she poured water on Branch's left foot, and then on his right. She then laid the basket to the side and reached for the gopher pelt. With its soft gray fur she dried Branch's feet.

At this point Ezra stepped forward. His palms were bleeding, as were his shins and knees, but he was unmindful of any pain. Draped on his left arm was a worn but clean dark suit. In his right hand he held a pair of old leather shoes by their laces. In his back pocket he carried a banana (a fruit unknown to Ishi in 1911). He presented the suit to Branch. Slowly and carefully Branch slipped the pants over his loincloth. Then he slipped his arms into the jacket. He then took the shoes from Ezra and eased them onto his feet. When he was done, he shuffled his torso and stamped his feet to settle the fitting. Holy then approached him again, removing the pink primrose from her hair and attaching it to his lapel, near his heart. Then Ezra approached one last time, taking the banana out of his pocket and presenting it to Branch, who made as if he did not know what to do with it. Ezra mimed that the banana was for eating. Branch then placed the banana in his mouth (not the denuded fruit, but with its thick skin intact) and took a small bite. Ezra smiled, took back the rest of the banana, and patted Branch's shoulder.

Simon watched the events with growing fury. In his eyes, Ezra had created a humiliating pageant to malign Ishi's reputation and to diminish the Yahi. He must be punished! Jill, Bill, Elliot, David ... they must all be punished!

The ceremony nearly over, Holy turned and walked away, followed by the silent procession of the three old men, the musicians, and the three old women. Now following a slightly uphill course, Ezra put his shoulder to the tumbrel one last time.

When all the Yahi were gone, Branch began the first of five solitary walks around the lake (one for each year Ishi had spent away from his people). After the completion of his first circuit, Bill and David disassembled their cameras and tripods and carried them back to the camp. Constant rose from behind the low ridge, where she'd been hunkered, and followed them.

Return of Ishi's Spirit

Following his fifth and final walk around the lake, Branch rested awhile by the shore, in the shade of a large oak. He was all alone and there were many things on his mind.

In the weeks leading up to the Passion play he'd spent much time in the Gallery, studying the newspaper and magazine photographs of Ishi. He knew it was a great honor to represent Ishi, but he also knew there was a huge difference between playing a role in a ceremony and actually leading his people out of isolation and into the modern world. He gave this issue much thought.

When he was ready, Branch removed his suit and shoes—the outward signs of his civilized life—and laid them on the shore of Little Galilee. Wearing only a deerskin loincloth, he marched slowly back to the Yahi camp, followed by Simon and his men.

All the Yahi awaited his return. This was the last part of the Passion play: the return of Ishi's spirit to his people.

Chapter 62

Cast Party

With help from Ezra and Constant, a modest feast had been prepared. Two deer had been arrow-shot while standing by a salt lick in the moonlight. Several cottontail rabbits had been clubbed and roasted. A variety of birds had been caught with basketry traps, along with a few waterfowl. Four rainbow trout had been netted and three large salmon speared. Hundreds of acorns had been gathered to make soup and bread.

As a nod to the past (when the Yahi danced in a large dwelling lodge around a central stanchion), a stalwart yew pole had been inserted into a hole in the ground outside the Yahi cave. Branch stood beside the pole, striking it rhythmically with a split-stick rattle while singing a guttural, barking song with his eyes closed. All the Yahi, young and old, danced around. They twirled, they hopped, they leaped for joy and gratitude, knowing they owed their lives to the sacrifice of Ishi … knowing they would soon be led out of darkness and into freedom.

Simon and his men were transfixed. Never before had any of them felt such deep kinship with their native past. This was their history they were watching; this was their living culture—and their future too, if they could remember these old ways and preserve them.

As the dancers danced, the air was alive with primordial smells: deer meat sizzling, rabbits roasting, fish searing … and what with the rhythmic rattling and Branch's singing, Ezra and Constant felt drawn into the circle of Yahi dancers, soon followed by Jill and Elliot, then Bill and David.

Simon stood, shocked by the sudden intrusion of foreigners. It was an outrage, like watching six cancerous cells invade someone he loved. Hard for Simon to imagine a more terrible sight, but then four of the six cells metastasized, each attaching itself to a healthy Yahi cell: David danced with a bare-breasted Yahi woman his own age; Bill danced with one of the longhaired female elders; Jill danced with a burly Yahi man, and Elliot danced with a Yahi boy. With each intermingling, Simon felt a piece of himself destroyed. He did not think it could get worse, but then Branch stopped singing and took Constant by the hand ... and when Ezra approached Holy, gently petting her stomach before leading her in a dance around the yew pole, Simon squeezed his hands with all his mighty rage. The .50 caliber pistol he'd been holding (stolen from Ezra's cabin) exploded like a cannon shot. The reverberating echo ... the loud ricochet ... the wail of the wounded ... made it seem like several shots had been fired.

Chapter 63

Under Fire

Despite his bleeding left arm, Bill tried to calm Jill and shield her from danger. Meanwhile, Ezra sprang into action, quickly locating Constant and Elliot and guiding them to the far side of a rocky outcrop where they had all stored their bedding and gear. While Ezra guided, the Yahi ran helter skelter towards the cave. Holy helped mothers with their babies and children. Branch helped carry the crippled and confused. When all the Yahi were safely inside, Branch and Holy joined them.

As a reaction to the shot, David had clapped his ears and crouched. Seeing people run in different directions, he felt disoriented and paralyzed.

Beyond the rocky outcrop, Ezra saw that David was still out in the open, about thirty yards away. He grabbed one of his own Desert Eagle pistols from his rucksack and went back into the fray, scooting from boulder to boulder. Meanwhile, David had crawled behind a large bush whose spindly branches offered no protection against bullets but prevented Ezra from seeing him. Unable to locate David, Ezra had no choice but to retreat across the open space, leaving David behind, alone and vulnerable.

Shot for Shot

Bill peered over a rocky escarpment to discover the position of the shooter. As it happened, Simon (still stunned from inadvertently firing the gun) was standing tall and appeared to be wielding a weapon. Wounded, and in no mood to take any more shit, Bill fired a shot in Simon's direction. It missed. But it shocked Simon into action.

"All right, boys, give 'em hell!" he said, returning fire with another blast of Ezra's gun.

The seven other Indians looked at each other. They had not planned or even imagined a gun battle. Pauley had brought a large canteen and a pair of binoculars, but no gun. Mickey did not own a gun, and Willard had sold his to pay for his new sump pump. The other men brought loaded weapons but no clear forethought of violence.

Bill fired another shot, which zinged off a rock only several feet away from Simon.

"C'mon!" screamed Simon. "Shoot!"

The five Indians with guns fired away. Their shots were unaimed or badly aimed, and the bullets went in all directions—as did their ricochets—giving the impression of an even larger force. After each fired round, Simon's men ducked for cover. Lucky for them, they had taken position in what looked like a big bagel of a rock formation—about four feet high and three feet thick—which provided excellent protection and a panoramic view of the situation.

Ezra's predicament was much more precarious. He'd planned to lead his group into the caves if they were attacked. But the timing and angle of the attack had been surprisingly (if unintentionally) effective, cutting Ezra's group off from the caves and leaving it in a position that was exposed on two sides.

Ezra knew he had to change his group's defensive posture. The status quo was indefensible. Though he hadn't yet decided his next move, he asked everyone who had a gun to ready their weapon and ammo.

"Bill, can you still shoot?"

Bill nodded. "It's not bad," he said, indicating his bloody left sleeve.

Always prepared, Ezra quickly cleaned the wound with gauze and applied a tourniquet.

Meanwhile, Constant and Jill each drew a gun from their rucksacks and checked their ammo. Elliot shook his head, indicating he was useless in a gunfight.

Suddenly, Jill pictured David, alone and terrified. "David!" she howled from the depths of her soul.

The shooting stopped. It seemed everyone was listening for David's response.

David was huddled behind a bush, shivering with fright, fearful of giving away his position. With no response from David, all eyes turned to Ezra.

Ezra studied the open territory between his own position and the Indian shooters', noting several boulders and several clumps of bushes. He assumed David was hidden behind one of them. If he knew which one, he might be able to create a diversion and quickly extract him to safety. But without knowing how many guns were trained on the area, and without knowing David's exact position, he could not justify an attempt. It would likely be a suicide mission ... and he was responsible for the others in his group—and for the Yahi too, if it came to that.

"David!" came another blood-curdling cry.

This time there was a response—a volley of bullets tore through the air, several finding their way into Ezra's camp.

Oh God God God, thought Jill. *Please protect David. Don't let him die. Even if he's not mine, please let him live!*

Oh God God God, thought Elliot. *Please protect me! Don't let me die.*

Constant, Ezra, Bill, and Jill returned fire. When they ducked for cover, the Indians let loose a couple ferocious volleys. Bullets crisscrossed the entire area, ripping into trees and bushes.

While David remained crouched and shivering, a dozen Yahi men emerged from their cave with their bows and arrows. A few shook spears.

"No!" screamed Ezra. "Get back inside!"

Just then Branch joined his men, moving to the front.

"No!" screamed Ezra. "Get back!"

Ezra desperately needed a better defensive position. He also needed to protect the Yahi and to watch over David.

Another volley of bullets buzzed through his camp, one ripping through Constant's duffel bag.

Ezra assessed the situation: Simon and his group might move closer. They might split up and attack from two sides. For his part, he might have to secure the cave.... His defenses were vulnerable and spread thin. It did not look good.

Jill saw the look of worry on Ezra's face and had an idea. She grabbed her cellphone. The battery was fully charged but the reception was very weak.

"Where are we?" she asked Ezra. She explained her idea.

Ezra took out his military-grade compass and checked their exact GPS coordinates, accurate to within three feet.

Jill knew she had a much better chance of sending a text message than completing a call. But unless she got a return message, she would not know if her text was received.

Jill's Text Message to Wylie

SOS! Big emergency—life or death.
Use GPS.
Bring friends! HURRY!
N 38° 6' 48.235"
W 121° 29' 36.912"

Jill's Passing Thoughts

He isn't answering! Maybe he's working in the restaurant. Maybe the music is loud and he doesn't hear his phone. Maybe he's loving his friend Ralph. Maybe he's shopping or swimming.... Wylie, please answer!

The GBBB

Wylie was hosting a big party at Chaps & Scraps. The California chapter of the Gay Black Bikers Brigade had just finished its monthly luncheon. They were rowdy and fraternal and ready to hit the road.

Wylie was saying goodbye to his guests when he received the text message. He was simultaneously shaken and resolved. He quickly explained the situation, which rallied his guests.

"Gentlemen, start your engines."

Chapter 64

Rode the Brave Thirty

A cavalry of sorts: thirty men on motorized steeds ... large and lovable men who had known hate because of the character of their love and the color of their skin. Fewer than twenty minutes they rode on Route 99 ... and then, following Wylie's lead, they roared east through the quiet streets of Los Molinos, passing the Post Office and High School, until they reached the Sierra Spa and Casino Hotel. Then, still following Wylie's lead, they roared across the parking lot and picked up the Lassen Trail.

Foxhole Pledges

Bill (to the absent Sandy): "I'm sorry I messed up. If I get out of this, I promise to make it right. I swear to God."

David (to the absent Allison): "Allie-pie, can you hear me? I love you, baby. I'm so sorry for all my nonsense. I love you and the girls."

Jill/Elliot: "Oh God, Elliot, I'm so sorry I brought you here." "I knew the dangers and I agreed." "But what if we don't live to see our film?"

Ezra/Constant: "You have always been by my side, strong and patient. When this is over, I want to marry you and raise a family." [Constant, who'd been reloading her gun, touched Ezra's hand, leaned forward, and kissed him.]

Branch/Holy: [translated from the Yahi]: "Our child must live. If the terrible happens, run to the light. You know the way. Do not wait for your parents. Do not wait for me. Just run. I will find you." "I know the way," said Holy.

The Other Woman

Thirty men on a mission of mercy, each man and his motorized steed weighing half a ton. Thirty thousand pounds of men and steel roaring down a rocky, rutted trail.

For a half hour, sporadic shooting continued outside the Yahi cave. One of Simon's men lost a smartphone: a bullet through the heart of its touchscreen. Jill was hit above the right eye by a tiny fragment of stone. Constant approached her to lend assistance. "Let me help," she said.

Jill shook her head no. In recent weeks she felt that Constant had grown judgmental, silently scorning her for being David's other woman.

"Please," said Constant, gently pulling Jill's hands away from her wound.

While Jill looked away, Constant stared at the wound and wondered what David thought when he stared at Jill's face.

"It's just a scratch," said Constant. "But it's dirty … or something might be lodged there."

Constant reached into her personal first-aid kit and brought forth a tweezer. "Hold still," she said, deftly extracting a stone splinter from Jill's forehead. She then cleaned the tiny wound with a tissue, disinfected it, and applied a Band-Aid. For several minutes their faces were so close, she imagined David kissing her.

"He has a wife," Constant said, looking away.

"I know," Jill said, her voice breaking.

Quiet on Both Fronts

For five minutes there was a lull in the shooting. Meanwhile, the shooters in both camps were getting skittish, imagining that their opponents were readying an assault.

Simon, with more options, acted before anyone else could.

The High Ground

One by one, Simon's men left their boulder-protected positions, moving way right of the cave, beyond the sightlines of enemy fire.

[Thousands of years ago, lava flowed downhill from a local volcanic vent and filled an open channel. Eventually, lava crust formed a roof while most of the molten lava flowed through, creating a lava tube cave, which branched in several directions, forming a large dendritic network. Some of the cave sections were large enough to house a tribal photo gallery. Some were so narrow a child could not crawl through. Over time, some of the branches and sections had collapsed.]

To the right of the main cave entrance, one large branch of former roof had collapsed, creating a low-grade ramp that lead to the top of the Yahi cave. Simon and his men saw the top of the cave as a defensible high ground from which they could shoot at their enemies. One by one, they skulked up the ramp, taking positions behind whatever natural blinds—boulder, bush, stump—they could find. And then they opened fire.

Distant Thunder

Simon's men poured down bullets like insults … like hatreds … like a hundred requited hurts. Some of the bullets bounced harmlessly off the rocky escarpment, but most zipped through Ezra's camp. Constant was grazed on her right shoulder, adding a fifth stripe to her tiger claw tattoo. Elliot was dropped by a shot to his gluteus maximus, and Bill just missed having his throat smashed.

Bullets rained down like a meteor shower. Against such a withering barrage it was almost impossible to return fire. The situation seemed hopelessly dire when a distant rumbling, like a tropical thunder, was heard beyond the hills to the west. Simon checked the cast of the sky. It was blue and cloudless … and yet the thunder grew in intensity, shaking the air, rumbling the ground…. And then, in the mid-distance, there appeared a roaring dark cloud, like a sandstorm, like a stampede.

The Crash of Cultures

A motorized cavalry, single file and sinuous, appearing to stretch for a mile, was approaching fast. Simon and his men looked about for an escape route. They saw that on the opposite side of the cave there was another ramp (the result of another tubular collapse) and fled toward that last resort.

The last of Simon's men was halfway down the far ramp when Wylie—leading the charge—hurtled up the opposite ramp, followed by the rest of his motorized brigade.

Thirty thousand pounds of rumbling weight placed an unbearable pressure on the porous crown of the cave. Inside, the Yahi heard a terrifying roar as small tremors coalesced into a giant, seismic-like shake, driving them into the deeper darkness. One by one, all the pictures in the Gallery fell to the earthen floor. Stalactites crashed. Rifts and fractures rippled through the cave network. The Yahi fled in a half-dozen different directions, trying to outrun the collapsing terror. Most ran simply to outpace death, but a few ran towards the light.

Chapter 65

Justice Served

The ensuing media coverage inspired a national sensation:

Stone Age Tribe Discovered—and Murdered!
New Film Records Live Ancient History
Ancient Cave Dwellers Killed by Gays!

It took weeks to sort out the mayhem. It took the better part of a year for the Bureau of Indian Affairs to complete its report to Congress. Several civil suits and criminal cases took even longer to resolve. In the end, justice was served, more or less:

Simon Lescault and his seven cohorts were convicted of attempted murder, aggravated assault, conspiracy to kill, and an assortment of hate crimes. Maxwell and Elena Cross were witnesses for the prosecution. Their testimony was crucial in convincing the jury of the defendants' motivation and intent.

Wylie and the GBBB were convicted of attempted assault with a deadly weapon and reckless endangerment. As a result of their "mercy mission" defense, they were given suspended sentences. Wylie's friend Ralph visited him every day while he was in jail and on trial. A year later, Wylie married Ralph and together they manage Chaps & Scraps.

Frankie and Johnny

Responding to the tragedy, federal investigators set up a field office in the parking lot of the Sierra Spa and Casino Hotel. Frankie and Johnny had no idea what was going on but figured it was time to vamoose. In the dead of night they slipped out of Los Molinos and drove back to NYC, making the return trip in just four days. Though Carmine was furious they had not recouped any of the money Bill owed, he was secretly glad they had avoided contact with the Feds, which would have likely shined an unfavorable light on his own activities—something to be avoided at all costs.

Jill and Elliot

Following the tragedy, government authorities confiscated all the unedited film as state's evidence. After the trial, the government refused to return the more than sixty hours of raw footage because Jill and Elliot had never received permission to film on federal lands. Jill and Elliot filed suit, hoping to regain control of their creative property and resume their careers. Decisions pending, Jill returned to Santa Monica; Elliot to the University of California, Davis.

Debt Paid

Following the tragedy, Bill and Sandy were reunited at Ampla Health in Los Molinos. After Bill was patched up and released—and after his interrogations with local police and federal agents—he followed Sandy back to New York, but she wasn't quite ready to forgive and forget. She said she needed time and space to think it over. Bill agreed but was desperate for a place to stay. One night he took Jill's advice and slept in a bat-themed vampire's crypt in the city. After a fitful sleep, he called Sandy the next morning: "I know I said I'd go to Hell and back for you—but I didn't mean it literally!" Sandy laughed when he told her the story, but said she still needed more time.

Later that same day she called Phil Chambers, the private investigator. She said she wanted evidence against Frankie and Johnny that could potentially be used against Carmine. Chambers flew to Chico and then drove to Los Molinos. After a quick lunch in a local diner, he drove to the Sierra Spa and Casino Hotel. Ellie Hacklin, the front desk clerk, talked his ear off for fifteen minutes before putting him in touch with her manager, who led him to a back room where the security tapes were stored.

Chambers cued the tapes to the day before the terrible tragedy and soon found what he was looking for: visual confirmation that Frankie and Johnny had been staked out across the street, catty-corner from the hotel, hours before the Yahi massacre.

Sandy called Carmine that evening on his home phone, when she assumed he'd be eating dinner with his family. Wasting little time, she told him who she was and politely asked about his wife Mary and their two young sons, Anthony and Thomas. Without pause, she told him she had hotel security tapes that placed his two henchman at the site of an ongoing federal investigation, which would make them both *persons of interest*. Without giving him a chance to respond, she simply said that her husband's debt was to be considered repaid, effective immediately. Further, she said that if he or any of his associates ever approached her or her husband again, the FBI would receive the tapes and other damaging information by immediate electronic transfer. Carmine choked on his veal picatta. The next day he told Frankie and Johnny that Bill's stupid bitch had paid his debt—and they were never to say another word to him. "Capisce?"

Chapter 66

Love on a Short Leash

Sandy used a list of debits and credits to evaluate whether to take Bill back into her life. To Bill's credit, he was good looking and could be damn amusing. He satisfied certain needs. He was a good companion but not a competitor. He did the shopping and the cooking. He did the laundry. He drove when they went out at night. He always made her feel safe. On the debit side, he did not fit the profile of a corporate consultant's spouse. Worse, he had become increasingly involved with lowlife gamblers and mobsters; eventually, dangerous thugs had come to her door to collect Bill's debt. [*This is the last straw,* Sandy had said to herself, handing Bill his walking papers. *Let him see the errors of his ways. Let him get straightened out. When he's contrite and controllable, I might take him back.*]

Two weeks after returning to New York, Sandy invited Bill to meet her in a local diner to discuss the situation.

As soon as Bill sat down, Sandy looked him in the eye:

"What am I going to do with you?"

"I'd like to come back."

Sandy shook her head.

"I can't go through this shit anymore. I'm too old. I deserve better."

"You're right," said Bill. "Not the old part. But you do deserve better."

Sandy started to cry.

"Thing is," said Bill, "so do I."

"What do you mean?" Sandy asked, wiping her eyes.

"I mean, I'm tired of my own bullshit. Horses ... poker ... it's all bullshit. There's other things I want to do."

"Like what?"

"Home projects."

"Such as?"

"Our bedroom closet. Those louver doors don't fit right anymore. We need sliding doors, with mirrors."

"Anything else?"

"Yeah. The hallway is gloomy. Makes a bad first impression. I've seen some snazzy track lighting that would be great."

Over the next half hour Bill continued to make his case, suggesting (among other things) new window treatments and a desire to go hiking with her on weekends.

"Let me think about it," Sandy said.

Two days later, Sandy called Bill:

"You can come home—but you're on a short leash."

Bill smiled.

"Better to be close to you, mon amour."

Chapter 67

Forgiveness Workshop

Following the Yahi tragedy, Allison found David in the hotel lobby, sitting alone in the middle of a large, over-stuffed sofa, looking like a little boy.

Though David had handled his police interview with aplomb, he was unnerved by Allison's sudden and unexpected appearance. [In all the hurly-burly, Constant had forgot to tell him that his wife had arrived.]

Allison sat on the sofa, close beside him. "How are you?" she asked softly.

"I'm okay. How are you?"

"Mostly fine."

Silence. David assumed she knew about Jill. He didn't know if he should plead the Fifth, offer explanation, or beg for mercy.

"I'm sorry if I surprised you," said Allison. "That wasn't my purpose. Sandy's had a hard time. That's why we're here."

"What happened?"

Allison told him about the bad guys who were looking for Bill.

"As soon as Sandy knew they were getting close, she decided to come out here. She thought you might also be in danger. That's when I decided to come. She didn't want me to, but I insisted. I was worried."

David nodded. "I'm okay. I didn't know about the guys looking for Bill. We haven't seen them."

"I hope you never do," said Allison.

Silence.

"How are the girls?" David asked, changing the subject.

"They're fine. They want to know when you're coming home."

David winced. He felt shamefully exposed. "Sooner than I expected. I thought I would get paid to babysit Bill a while longer ... but this amazing Yahi story just came to a shocking end."

Allison nodded. "I met a woman named Constant and she told me about it. It's one of the most amazing stories I've ever heard."

"I'm writing a novel about it."

"I want to be the first to read it."

David smiled, grateful.

"One of my reasons for coming here was to visit Chico," he said. "I thought I might be inspired to finish the book I started writing when I was boy.... But I never expected this."

"You can't predict life," said Allison.

"No, you can't," said David.

Pause.

"David—"

"Yes?"

"Do you love her?"

David hesitated.

"Who?"

"You know who."

David drew a deep breath, preparing himself to come clean.

"No," he said, without naming her. "I feel like I owe her a lot. Without her friendship I would not have written *Forty Years Later*. And I wouldn't be here, writing my second novel."

"But it's more than a friendship, isn't it?"

David shook his head. "I don't love her, if that's what you mean. I never have."

Allison looked into his eyes. "Are you coming home?"

"Of course. Home is home," he said, a little too glibly.

"What about me?" she asked. "Do you love me?"

David was awash with warm sensations ... and a few that were barbed and irritating. Their forty-year marriage was an

283

imperfect partnership. He couldn't say it was forever. But he did love her.

"I do."

Peace World

Soon after arriving home, husband and wife resumed their basic routines. David worked on his new novel every morning and played tennis every afternoon, weather permitting. Allison went to work every weekday morning, continuing her extended freelance assignment. In the evenings they often watched TV together. David seemed copasetic with the arrangement, but Allison was unsatisfied and said so. She craved a marriage that was honest and more passionately committed. David concurred, but there was little heat in his words. He wrote with heat, but he no longer loved with heat. Allison said something must change. She couldn't live with things as they were. She gave David a choice: He must either agree to join her in weekly couple's therapy or accompany her to Peace World for another four-day marriage workshop.

"What kind of workshop?" he asked.

"The Positivity of Love and Forgiveness. I'll show you the brochure."

The day they were to leave for Peace World, David received an e-mail from Jill. He hadn't heard from her for several months. Though he was sorely tempted, he didn't read it. The e-mail would still be there when he returned.

Chapter 68

Last of the Yahi, Redux

Two days after the cave collapse, a fine detritus still filled the air. Along with the police and investigators, Ezra wore a protective mask as he explored the collapsed channels.

According to his personal records, there'd been 41 Yahi at the time of the Passion play. With each discovered body, Ezra crossed a name off his list. By the time the entire cave network had been explored, Ezra had crossed off 39 names. He told the authorities that all the Yahi had died.

Ezra's guilt was enormous. Day and night his fathers' baleful eyes excoriated him. Only his Heavenly Father gave him hope, and this by way of a dream: There were two Yahi, man and woman, but soon three … and they flourished … and they multiplied … and they were happy.

Following the trial, the government stripped Ezra of his assistant park ranger status and took possession of his cabin—but agreed to drop all formal charges. (There are laws against caring for Stone Age Indians without proper authorization; further, the Yahi had been natural-born U.S. citizens and their existence should have been reported.)

Even without his cabin and assistant park ranger status, Ezra's professional career thrived. The Yahi massacre was a huge national story and the media spotlight drove many people to the hotel to seek out Ezra's expert tutelage. With so many clients, Ezra was able to leave the hotel and buy a local parcel of oak-shaded land, on which he built a very solid and pretty home with the help of his wife Constant. A year later Constant gave birth to a daughter, whom they named Eliza.

On Eliza's thirteenth birthday her father brought her into the Wilderness and left her there for five days. He and Constant were confident that her training and God's loving Eye would keep her safe. When Eliza found her way home (hungry, tired, but exuberant), the family celebrated. After the meal, Ezra took Eliza outdoors and asked her to walk with him. About a mile away, in the shade of a large manzanita grove, he gave his daughter the circle of black obsidian that Ishi's mother had given to his great-grandfather and told her the full story of Ishi and the part that he and his fathers had played. He then told her about Branch and Holy and their child, who would be about fifteen by then. In the days and years that followed, he taught Eliza all he knew about the Yahi, just in case she one day went looking for them.

The End

Acknowledgments

I reviewed hundreds of resources during the course of my research. These were particularly helpful:

Tools of the Old and New Stone Age by Jacques Bordaz (photographs by Lee Boltin)

Indians of Lassen National Park and Vicinity by Paul E. Schulz

Ishi's Brain by Orin Starn

Discovery of Ishi, the Last of His Tribe – YouTube Video

Ishi Discovery Site – YouTube Video

ABOUT THE AUTHOR

Steven Jay Griffel is the bestselling author of *Forty Years Later*, *The Deadline*, *Grand View*, and *Grossman's Castle*. He lives in New York with his wife Barbara.